taint

Also by S.L. Jennings

Fear of Falling
Dark Light
The Dark Prince
Nicolai
Light Shadows

Coming Soon

Tryst

taint

A Sexual Education Novel

S.L. JENNINGS

wm

WILLIAM MORROW
An Imprint of HarperCollinsPublishers

TAINT. Copyright © 2015 by S.L. Jennings. All rights reserved. Printed in the United States of America. No part of this book may be used or reproduced in any manner whatsoever without written permission except in the case of brief quotations embodied in critical articles and reviews. For information address HarperCollins Publishers, 195 Broadway, New York, NY 10007.

HarperCollins books may be purchased for educational, business, or sales promotional use. For information please e-mail the Special Markets Department at SPsales@harpercollins.com.

FIRST EDITION

Designed by Diahann Sturge

Library of Congress Cataloging-in-Publication Data has been applied for.

ISBN 978-0-06-238971-8

15 16 17 18 19   OV/RRD   10 9 8 7 6 5 4 3 2 1

taint

TAINT

v. **taint·ed, taint·ing, taints**
1. To corrupt morally.
2. to sully or tarnish (a person's name, reputation, etc.).

n.
1. a defect or flaw.
2. An infecting touch, influence, or tinge.

Don't try to defile the English language.
I can think of a few other things I'd rather dirty up.
—JUSTICE DRAKE

Introduction

*D*ay One is always fucking exasperating.

The tears. The glassy-eyed looks of confusion as they try to piece together where their vapid relationships went wrong. The stupid, incessant questions about how I could possibly live up to my word and earn every cent of the small fortunes their husbands have paid to send them here.

Sit there and shut up, honey. One of us is a professional. Now, if I need help making a fucking sandwich or getting a wine stain out of a linen tablecloth, I'll ask for your opinion. Otherwise, shut those powder-pink lips and look pretty.

That's all they're good for—looking pretty. Shopping. Primping. Taking care of disgusting, snotty-nosed spawn.

Stepford wives. Trophies. High-class, well-bred prostitutes.

They seem perfect in every way. Beautiful, intelligent, graceful. The perfect accessory for the man who has it all.

Except for one thing.

They're as dull as lukewarm dishwater once you get them on their perfectly postured backs.

As they say, looks can be deceiving. Sexy does not equate to good sex. More often than not, this theory holds true. If it didn't, I wouldn't be in business. And let me tell you, business is good. Very good.

I take a sip of water as I scan the varied expressions of shock and horror that typically follow my usual first-day speech. This class is larger than the last, but I'm not surprised. It's the end of the summer—a season when wearing less clothing than is socially acceptable. Husbands' eyes have strayed, and so have their dicks. And in an effort to save their picture-fucking-perfect marriages, some have commissioned to me, in hopes that by some miracle, I can make their husbands look at them like they see more than a well-groomed melee of coiffed hair, veneers, and filler. Others weren't as lucky to be in the know, having been sent here by their loving benefactors like summer camp castaways. They actually thought they were coming to a spa. Silly, clueless girls.

A slender hand goes up, and I nod toward the young, waif-thin brunette who's shaking like a leaf in her floral Prada frock. It's ugly as shit, and makes her look like a middle-aged bag lady. She reminds me of one of those half-twit wives from *Mad Men*. Not the hot secretary—the one that just sat her ass at home, eating bonbons in front of her black-and-white television set while her husband screwed everything that moved.

"So . . . what exactly do you do? Are you, like, a teacher or something?" she asks, just above a whisper.

"More like a consultant. You all share a very serious issue and I hope to . . . guide you toward some techniques that may improve your situation."

"What situation?"

Holy fuck. Testing, testing. Is this thing on, or has Botox already begun to corrode her brain cells?

I smile tightly through the aggravation. Patience is key in my profession. Most days, I feel more like an overworked, underpaid day-care provider than a . . . *lifestyle* . . . coach. Same, same.

"I thought I explained the situation, Mrs."—I squint at the file in front of me, matching her face to the name— "Cosgrove."

Lorinda Cosgrove. As in Cos-Mart, the place where you can go shopping for honey buns, cheap lingerie, and a nine-millimeter at 3 A.M. while wearing cutoff booty shorts and Crocs. No lie, there are websites dedicated to these train wrecks. Google that shit.

"Yes, I am aware of your assessment, as crude as it is. However, what do you expect to achieve?"

I shake my head marginally. There's one in every class. One that doesn't want to accept the ugly truth staring her in the face. Even though she's read the manual, signed the contracts, and undergone all the necessary briefings before arriving, she still can't grasp her reality—flashing bright, neon arrows toward her dried-up vagina. Good thing I have no qualms about reminding her.

"You suck at sex," I deadpan, my expression blank. Audible gasps escape from almost every collagen-plumped lip, yet I continue to drive my point home. "You don't satisfy your husband sexually, which is why he wants to cheat on you, if he hasn't already. You may be a fantastic wife, mother, homemaker, *whatever,* but you are a lousy lover. And that trumps all."

Lorinda clutches her chest with a shaky, manicured hand. The woman sitting next to her, a heavier-set, forty-something housewife—whose husband's midlife crisis, and his love of barely legal debutantes, have turned their marriage into a media circus—steadies her with a motherly squeeze on the shoulder. Aw, how sweet.

"And that goes for all of you," I say, casting my glance around the room. "You're here because you know you're about to lose the one thing you've worked your pretty little asses off for—your man. You love the lifestyle you live, and instead of licking your wounds and moving on, you'd rather fix your broken marriage. And I'm here to help you."

"But how?"

A slow, sardonic smile unfurls across my face. "I'm going to teach you how to fuck your husband."

More gasps. More pearl clutching. Even a few shrieks of *My word!*

"But that's not . . ." Lorinda screeches above the flurry of discontent. "Not proper. Not dignified."

And there it is.

It's the reason why her husband, Lane Cosgrove, likes to bend his pretty blond secretary over his desk and fuck her senseless while she calls him "Daddy." He has a thing for anal—giving and taking it. His secretary keeps a strap-on in the locked file cabinet beside her desk for Thursday nights. Lane always works late on Thursdays, leaving Lorinda to her usual book-club meeting, women's Bible study, wine tasting, etc., etc. Nothing Lane does on Thursdays is "proper." Letting his secretary probe him with a ten-inch dildo while his mouth is stuffed with her panties to muffle his cries is anything but dignified. And he knows it. That's why Lorinda can't satisfy his needs. And letting your very rich and powerful husband leave home sexually unsatisfied is like giving him a loaded gun. Sooner or later, he's going to pop off a few rounds.

On cue, my head of concierge services, Diane, enters, followed by several members of my staff. Time to move this little welcoming party right along before any more tears are shed.

"Ladies, if you think that you do not need this program and have ended up here by some mistake, please feel free to leave. Our drivers are prepared to take you straight to the airport, and you will be given a full refund. We just ask that you honor the nondisclosure agreements you and your spouses have signed."

No one makes a move to stand, so I continue. "If you would like to stay and learn how to improve your sex lives and, ultimately, your relationships, our staff will show you to your rooms. You will find that they are fully equipped with en suite facilities and amenities, plus we have a twenty-four-hour chef and staff at your disposal. The property also houses a state-of-the-art fitness center, spa, and salon for all your personal needs. Comfort is key here. Welcome to Oasis, ladies. We want you to consider this your home for the next six weeks of instruction."

Eleven sets of eyes stare back at me, waiting for the first command. No one wants to be the first to jump out of her seat, arms flailing as she screams, *Pick me! Pick me! Teach me, I want to learn!* They all want this; they all want to know the secrets of marital bliss. And they know everything I've said is true.

Each and every one of these women knows that someone else is fucking their husband because she herself doesn't know how to do it herself.

And deep down, I feel for them. Hell, I even sympathize with them. They made it their life's goal to meet and marry someone who would catapult them from their mediocre backgrounds and send them flying to the comforts of wealth and luxury.

It's a regular *Pretty Woman* syndrome. They go from lying on their backs for lavish gifts or some inconsequential promise of commitment in the form of a cheap, dime-store diamond ring, to more jewels than they even have limbs to wear them on. But what these ladies fail to realize is that whatever they had to do to nab their Richard Gere, they have to do that—and more—to keep him.

The staff ushers the women up to their private rooms, leaving me alone in the great room just as the Arizona sun begins to set, slowly sliding down the azure sky. It morphs into a life-size canvas of ombré oranges, pinks, blues, and purples, the breathtaking view not sullied by towering buildings or jigsaw highways. Oasis is tucked far away from civilization, away from paparazzi, designer bullshit, and reality television.

This is my favorite part of the day—when gravity pulls that scorching, desert sun above, coaxing it into the outstretched, jagged arms of mountains and cacti. Even the most tortured souls seek comfort and solitude.

I make my way across the courtyard toward the guesthouse. I own all the property, but I don't sleep in the main house. There's a level of privacy and professionalism that I must uphold, and being locked in a secluded mansion with eleven women can be . . . difficult. My business is sex. I instruct sex. I live and breathe sex. And I need it, just like their duplicitous husbands.

So thanks to my don't-shit-where-you-eat policy, I endure six, sexless weeks during instruction, only sating my sexual appetite between the four courses I host per year. Even then, I'm discreet. Being any other way just isn't profitable in my line of work.

After letting the shower rinse away the day's aggravation, I dress and head to the dining room for dinner. The ladies trickle in one by one, quietly taking seats around the grand table. They're all still here. Eleven women desperate to reconnect with the men they hope to be tied to until death. The men who promised to move heaven and earth in exchange for their promise of commitment. The men who have broken their vows in order to sate sexual deviancies and feed their egos.

The women are silent as we're served the first course. Hardly anyone touches the starter of foie gras, elaborately dressed with poached apple in a fig reduction. Not even the scrape of silver against china echoes through the vast space.

I chew slowly, surveying the eleven, perfectly poised women from the head of the table. All are determined to avoid eye contact as they pretend to nibble their appetizers and numb their nerves with wine.

"So . . ." I start, drawing their reluctant eyes. "When was the last time any of you masturbated?"

A symphony of coughs and gasps coaxes my mouth into a satisfied grin. This group should be fun.

"Excuse me?" one sneers, after downing her red wine. A server moves to grace her with a refill of velvety courage, knowing she'll need it.

"Did I stutter? Or do you not know what it means to masturbate?"

"What? I know what"—she cringes, flustered, and shakes her head in embarrassment.—" . . . *masturbating* is. Why do you feel the need to ask such crude, inappropriate questions?"

I examine the striking redhead still glaring at me, her cherry lips tight with irritation. Her too large, almost animated eyes narrow in abhorrence, burning right through me with unspoken judgment. Even with her face twisted into a scowl, she's stunning. Not overly done up or glamorous. She's old Hollywood beautiful, yet there's something fresh and simple about her.

I frown, because that type of beauty is too much for this place. Yet it's not enough for the world that she lives in.

Allison Elliot-Carr. Daughter of Richard Elliot, owner and CEO of one of the largest investment banks in the world. Her husband, Evan Carr, is a trust-fund baby from an influential, political family, and Allison's father's golden boy. He's also a pretty boy, a philandering bastard with no qualms about fucking anything in Manolos from Miami to Manhattan. Of course, that tidbit of information is not publicized. It's my job to know these things. To get inside their heads. To expose their darkest secrets and make them confront them with unrelenting honesty.

Allison purses her lips and shakes her head, her mouth curling into a sardonic smile. "You like this, don't you? Humiliating us? Making us feel flawed and defective? As if *we* are the cause of our less-than-perfect marriages? We're responsible for the way the tabloids rip us to shreds? You don't know me. You don't know any of us. Yet you think you can help us? Please. I call that bullshit."

I set down my silverware and dab my mouth with a linen napkin before giving her a knowing smirk. "Bullshit?"

"Yeah, complete bullshit. I mean, who the hell do you think you are?"

A smile slowly spreads my lips. I imagine licking my chops as a lion would before devouring a graceful, delicate gazelle. "I am Justice Drake," I state smugly without apology. It's a promise and an omen, gift-wrapped in two little words.

"Well, *Justice Drake* . . . you, my friend, are a bullshit artist. You know nothing about our situations. There's no magic, cure-all remedy for our marriages. But you wouldn't know that because you don't know a damn thing about us. You're not a part of our world. Hell, you probably do your research on Page Six or TMZ." With a wave of Thoroughbred arrogance, she settles back into her chair and sips her red wine, her blue, doe eyes trained on my impassive features.

Mimicking her actions, I ease back into my own seat and steeple my fingers under my chin, elbows propped on the arms of the high-backed chair. A beat passes as my gaze delves into hers, unearthing traces of pain, embarrassment, and anger—feelings she's been taught to hide in the face of the public. Still, no amount of MAC or Maybelline can mask the undeniable hell etched into her ivory skin.

"Allison Elliot-Carr, wife of Evan Winston Carr and daughter to Richard and Melinda Elliot. Graduated from Columbia with a degree in business and finance in 2009, though your true passion is philanthropy, and you spend your free time working with various charities and nonprofits. You pledged Kappa Delta Nu sophomore year, where you met Evan, a senior, legacy member, and president of your brother fraternity. You were exclusive to Evan throughout college, and during Christmas of 2008, he proposed in front of both your families at your parents' winter estate in Aspen. You were wed the following summer in New York City and honeymooned in the Caribbean. You hate spiders and scary movies, and think sweater vests should be outlawed. You can't function without Starbucks, have a borderline unhealthy addiction to *Friends* reruns, and you eat ice cream daily. Mint chocolate chip is your current drug of choice, I believe. And according to the tabloids, your husband is sleeping with your best friend, and charming the panties off half of the Upper East Side. Plus you two haven't fucked in months. But that's just a little something I didn't pick up from Page Six." I lift an amused brow and lean forward, taking in her horrified expression. "Shall I go on?"

The deafening silence swells and becomes uncomfortably dense, painfully pressing into my temples and crushing my skull, serving as punishment for my questionable conscience's failure to intervene. Allison's eyes mist with tears, transforming into an endless blue ocean of hurt. I don't care. I shouldn't care.

"Well," she croaks, her mouth dry and her wineglass empty. "Congratulations, asshole. You know how to navigate Wikipedia." And as graceful as the elegant gazelle she was bred to be, she slides her chair back and stands, head held high, and glides out of the room.

I go back to enjoying my meal while the rest of the table stares vacantly at the space that once briefly housed Allison's retreating back. One down, only ten more to go. She isn't the first, and she won't be the last.

"Make her stay," a meek voice barely whispers. Lorinda. The prim and proper housewife who's more concerned with being dignified than where her husband puts his dick.

"Why should I?"

"Because she needs you. We all need you." Several heads nod in agreement around the table. "Maybe her more than anyone else."

More nods. Even a few cosigning murmurs.

I exhale a resigning breath, knowing exactly what I'm about to do, though it goes against every principle I've learned to live by for the past six years.

Never get emotionally vested in a client.

Never pressure or persuade them; it has to be their choice.

And never, ever *apologize for my unconventional technique, as cruel or brash as it may seem.*

The door to Allison's suite is slightly ajar, but I knock anyway, letting it creak open to reveal her petite frame. "What do you want?" she snaps, refusing to look up from the suitcase she's furiously stuffing with clothes.

I step inside, not bothering to wait for an invitation, and close the door. "Going somewhere?"

"Home. This was a mistake."

"That's funny. I never pegged you for a quitter."

"Really?" she asks sardonically, casting an angry glare through thick, wet lashes. "Because you know everything about me, right? You know my entire life story. Height, weight, Social Security number . . . hell, do you have my gynecologist on speed dial?"

"Don't be absurd." I smirk with a wave of my hand. "You know there's no way in hell I could ever learn a woman's true weight."

Allison raises her gaze from her Louis Vuitton luggage and shakes her head, dismissing me and my dry attempt at humor. But before she can turn away, the tiniest hint of a smile reveals itself at the corner of her mouth.

I move closer, close enough to smell the Chanel dabbed behind her ears. "Mrs. Carr, it is my job to make your business my business. In order to best serve my clients, full disclosure is key. There is no room for dirty little secrets here. We've all got them, and trust me, yours pale in comparison to most. And believe it or not, no one in that dining room is here to judge your situation. They're all too worried about their own reasons for being here.

"With that said, I apologize if you felt my brand of honesty was too potent for you. It was callous of me. Still, that's no reason to throw in the towel. Not when we've hardly scratched the surface."

She barks out a forced laugh and looks away toward the window. A sea of glittering stars dot the blackened sky, lighting a path toward a full moon. The paleness of night floods the room, bathing her fair complexion in the glow of diamonds and sorrow.

"You said I was exclusive," she says just above a whisper, her voice distant yet melodic enough to echo in my head.

"Excuse me?"

She turns to me, eyes painted in angst. "You said *I* was

exclusive to him in college. Not *we*. As if I was faithful while
he was not."

She isn't angry, or surprised, or even embarrassed. She's
stuck somewhere between jaded and indifferent. In perpet-
ual limbo, writhing in the space between being hurt beyond
words and too fed up to give a fuck anymore.

She needs to give a fuck. I need her to give a fuck if I'm
going to help her save her marriage.

"I'm aware, Mrs. Carr. And so are you."

Allison smiles the kind of smile that's meant to be a grimace. The kind contorted by deep-seated hurt and shame.
"You think I'm stupid, don't you? That since I knew what
kind of man he was from the start, yet married him anyway,
I deserve this?"

"It's not my job to think that, Mrs. Carr."

"Right." She smirks. "Just your job to point out what
we're doing wrong in the bedroom." I open my mouth to
object but she raises a palm to stop me. "I get it, you know.
We all signed up for this. We all knew what we were getting
into. That doesn't make it any less humiliating."

I look at her—*really* look at her—and my head swirls with
inner turmoil. Of course, she's beautiful—they all are—but
Allison is absolutely flawless. She wears very little makeup,
and her face is unmarred by the telltale signs of plastic surgery or injections. Tiny, tan freckles dot her slender nose,
giving her an almost innocent, youthful appeal. The fact that
she hasn't tried to hide or surgically remove a little piece
of herself that society would deem a blemish, intrigues me.

Shit, it makes her kind of badass. Such a small act of rebellion, yet such a monumental *fuck you* to a world that celebrates narcissism and bullshit images.

Allison's fiery halo of red hair falls to her shoulders in deep waves. It's full and healthy, but not overly styled with product and extensions. It's . . . her. Simple. Classic. Perfection.

"What are you looking at?" she asks, her voice laced with a mixture of annoyance and amusement.

"You." The word is out of my mouth before a lie can even begin to stifle the truth. Shit.

"Why?" Less annoyance, more amusement.

"You have freckles."

She twists her mouth to one side and raises a cynical brow. "That I do. Would you like to count my moles? I may be able to scrounge up some scars for you too."

"No, I don't mean it like that. It's just . . . you didn't get laser surgery or bleach them. You don't even try to hide them."

"Look, I know that I'm less than perfect, but you don't have to be an ass—"

Just as she turns away from me, her face flushed with anger, I clutch her elbow. Our heated gazes collide before sliding down to her arm, where my hand is grasping her soft, ivory skin. I pull away before the act is misconstrued as inappropriate as my traitorous thoughts.

"I like it."

Can't. Stop. The. Word. Vomit.

I'm a lot of things—crass, stubborn, brutally honest, egotistical—but one thing I am not, is careless. I know my boundaries, and I never cross them. In a business where lines can be easily blurred, those boundaries are outlined in black Sharpie, traced in gasoline, then set the fuck on fire, ensuring that no one even gets close enough to inhale the fumes of temptation.

Yet here I am, touching, tempting, testing the limits. Begging to get burned by an angel with a halo of fire.

"My apologies, Mrs. Carr." I straighten, my defiant hands balled into tight fists at my sides. "I assure you—"

"You like it?"

I meet her eyes, which are as big and bright as the moon, casting an ethereal glow across her face. This close, much closer than most people would deem innocent, I see they're not quite blue, as I'd initially thought. Flecks of green and gold illuminate the irises, and I find myself getting lost in the liquid depths, wondering what secrets lie beneath. What past pain is hidden behind those long, auburn-hued lashes.

Yes, I like it. Much more than a narcissistic asshole like me should.

Liking these women isn't what made me the man I am today. It isn't what built my solid reputation. I'm not known for my bleeding heart of gold or sugarcoated tongue. What I am known for is results. And that's all Allison—or anyone else, for that matter—will get from me, and not a damn thing more.

I'm facing the entrance to her suite by the time I realize I've abandoned her, leaving her mouth agape and her question unanswered. I imagine those blue-green eyes narrowed in confusion at my erratic behavior, but force myself not to look. There's nothing to see there that I haven't seen already. Just another poor, little, rich girl.

"Class is in session at ten A.M. Don't be late." My gaze stays fixed on the dark, cherrywood door. I am dying to break free. The walls are closing in, suffocating me, demanding I turn around and face my cowardice. That I confront my weakness, currently bubbling up like bile as I pass the threshold of her suite—away from those enigmatic eyes and the temptation to play connect the dots with those freckles, in hopes of uncovering more of her beautifully blemished skin.

Day-fucking-One. I'm so screwed.

Attraction

"Unless he's completely desperate or under the influence, a man can't—and won't—fuck what doesn't get him hard."

Fewer gasps this time, but every perfectly powdered face is beet red with embarrassment, causing my mouth to slide into a sardonic smirk.

Truth be told, I love this shit. I love ruffling their meticulously groomed feathers. Their obvious discomfort entertains me. Seeing the rosy hue of coyness bleed through their blush is like a balm to my little, sadistic soul.

"And in that case," I continue, "you don't want him anyway. What you do want is for him to be salivating at the soles of your Jimmy Choos. And let's face it, ladies . . . that's not happening. Why do you think that is?"

Crickets. Fucking crickets.

"Anyone? Come on, ladies. I can't help you unless you want to be helped. So unless you all have picture-perfect marriages, and husbands that blow your backs out on a regular, I should see some hands."

This time I'm rewarded with an almost simultaneous intake of eleven breaths. They're all still here. All willing to bare their souls and dirty laundry, in an attempt to rekindle the doused flame between their thighs.

You see, women are liars.

Yeah, I said it. L-I-A-R-S.

They want intimacy just as badly as men do. But to them, intimacy is more than just the physical act of sex. They want to be cherished, yet want a man who will get down and dirty. They want tenderness, but crave to be banged like a two-dollar hooker. They want a man that'll go all night but still have the energy to kiss and cuddle and talk about his feelings afterward.

Listen up, ladies. We're fucking tired! You try going jackrabbit-style, throw in some Cirque du Soleil moves, and see if you can keep your eyelids peeled. Us passing out after sex is a compliment—a testament to how good it was. And quite frankly, if your dude can hop out of the sack and go to work or run a marathon, then he still has energy left for sex. He's just done having sex with *you*.

Much to my surprise, a hand goes up, pulling my attention. Of course, fate would have a sick sense of humor.

"You're saying our husbands aren't attracted to us anymore," Allison states flatly.

As much as I want to dispute her answer and curse that pathetic excuse for a man known as Evan Carr, my game face is
fastened tightly in place. Still, I look down at my notes, not
trusting my restraint wholeheartedly. *Business, Drake,* I tell
myself. *Business before bullshit.*

"Correct, Mrs. Carr."

"Ally," she retorts, causing me nearly to choke on my words.

"Excuse me?"

"Call me Ally. Just call me Ally. No one's called me Allison since St. Mary's Prep. And if you call me Mrs. Carr
again, I may have to sue for slander. *Mrs.* Carr is my *lovely,
gracious* mother-in-law," she replies with a hint of snark.

Finally, someone who speaks my language.

It's no secret that Mrs. Elaine Carr is a raging bitch in
designer heels. Since her stint on *The Real Housewives of
NYC* a few years back, she's been known as the Wicked
Witch of the Upper East Side. When the show caught
backlash after one of her Pinot-fueled tirades involving a
gay server and derogatory slurs, she wasn't invited for the
following season. She was furious, of course, and threat-
ened to sue the network. Not that she needed the money.
It was the humiliation of being thrown out on her little,
augmented ass.

Lucky for her sake, Allison refused to be taped, yet Evan
turned out to be as much of a camera whore as his mother.
As much as he enjoys screwing housewives, *being* a housewife seemed even more enticing to him.

"Well," I say, clearing my throat. "Where were we? Attraction, ladies. It's a powerful thing. It's what nabs them, captivates them, and keeps them coming back for more. And it goes far beyond physical attributes. Plain and simple, you have to be what they want. You have to offer what they desire. You see, men are simple creatures. We want what we want. And if you aren't what we want, we find something—or someone—we do."

"That's disgusting," murmurs a voice toward the back of the room. I look up, immediately recognizing the platinum-blond hair and disgruntled face of Lacey Rose, wife of legendary rocker Skylar Rose, who is also forty years her senior. They met and married when Lacey was only sixteen, which quickly sparked a media storm surrounding the child bride's intentions and the musician's penchant for adolescent poon. That was ten years ago, and now that Lacey has blossomed into a woman and birthed two children, Skylar's been trolling Forever 21 and mall food courts for another young flower to pollinate.

Does this shit sound wrong to anybody else?

"Disgusting, but true, Mrs. Rose," I reply with a nod.

"So, what . . . we're getting makeovers? We're supposed to change who we are just so they'll be attracted to us?"

"Not necessarily. Think of yourselves as perfectly wrapped presents. All of you spend thousands on your appearance, so there's not much we need to work on there. We just want to present the package in a different way. Not change what you have, just exploit it. Let me show you. Mrs. Rose?"

I leave my place behind the lectern and go to stand in

front of her with an outstretched hand. Reluctantly, she places hers in mine and stands, letting me lead her to the front of the room.

"What are you going to do to me?" she asks, her eyes darting around the room nervously as I move behind her.

"Relax, Mrs. Rose. As you all have read in the documents you've signed, I will never physically harm or violate you. In some instances, though, I will have to touch you. Guide you. If at any time you feel uncomfortable, simply say stop. That's all. Now . . . may I touch you, Mrs. Rose?"

Her shoulders rise and fall with her labored breaths as she anticipates the feel of my hands on her. This is the tricky part. I know what I do to these women. I know what they see, what they feel from me. They're used to powerful men—they're attracted to them—and that fact alone draws them to me. Add in the denim-blue eyes and six-foot two-inch dominating physique, and I'm reduced to high-priced man candy for the next six weeks. That's why I keep things very professional. My tone is always clipped and straight to the point. While I try to be cordial, I'm never overly friendly. So, while they may be attracted to the physical, I'm too much of an asshole to warrant unwelcomed advances from lonely housewives.

"Yes," she breathes. I can almost visualize her eyelids fluttering closed.

As I tower over her from behind, the callused pads of my fingertips lightly graze the sides of her arms, raking over her skin in a harsh whisper. She shivers under my touch, her breath coming out in quick pants while the rest of the women stop breathing altogether, their mouths agape in lustful envy.

I move in closer, letting my front mold into her back. She shudders for just a second before melting into the hard contours of my chest with a sigh. "You have amazing arms, Lacey," I say just above a whisper, my lips only a breath away from her ear. "Toned, tan, smooth. Your shoulders are sexy. Has anyone ever told you that? Imagine hands massaging them—gently at first—kneading away the day's tension. Then a little more pressure. Harder. Then harder still. Feels good, doesn't it? Imagine lips trailing kisses across them before moving up to your neck. A tongue snakes out to taste you . . . so sweet . . . so soft . . ."

Just as an anxious noise escapes her throat, I take a step back, causing Lacey to fall backward into my arms, channeling her inner Scarlett O'Hara. Before she gets too comfortable, I set her on her feet, making it known that I'm nobody's Rhett Butler.

Her face flushed with embarrassment and arousal, Lacey quickly staggers to her seat as ten women pelt her with questioning stares.

"Now," I bellow with a loud clap of my hands, capturing their attention. "That was the art of attraction—working with what you've got. Playing up your strengths and being confident in your sexuality. Any more volunteers?"

Eleven hands shoot to the sky. No, wait . . . make that fourteen. A few ladies are double-fisting.

AFTER A DAY of stroking fragile egos and another awkward dinner during which I painfully watch most of the diners push food around their plates pretending to eat, I nearly sprint to the main kitchen for a cold beer and to check in with my staff.

"What's up, J.D.? How're the Erotic Eleven treating ya?" greets the Oasis sous chef, Riku. The kid is an anomaly. Half Japanese and half Brazilian, he's used to getting mauled by horny housewives enamored of his jet-black hair, broad build, copper-colored skin, and fine, Asian features. When I asked him how his parents managed to merge their cultures, he replied, "Everyone's fluent in the language of love."

Yeah, right.

Still, he's a good guy, if not slightly green when it comes to matters of the heart. If someone like me had friends, Riku would be one. But, alas, I *am* someone like me.

I grab two cold ones out of the fridge and pop them open before handing one to Riku, which he gladly accepts.

Everyone here knows that, while I may sign their paychecks, I am as far from a boss as possible. There is no "Mr. Drake" here. No formal reprimands or hoops to jump through. The rules are simple: if you want to work with me, great. Do your job. If not, fine by me—everyone is replaceable. With the pay, benefits, and mutual respect among all employees, whether you're a dishwasher or head chef, I am rarely dealt the task of hiring or firing.

"Erotic Eleven? Hmm . . . not much different from the last group. What'd you call them? The Sizzling Seven?"

Riku laughs before tipping back his beer, then looks down at the label. "Krombacher, eh? Where'd you get this one?"

"Germany."

"That where you spend your summers? Corrupting a bevy of beauties in Berlin?"

"One of the places." I shrug. "Kinda just wandered through Europe. Stopped in Amsterdam, Brussels, Prague— even made it down to Spain."

Riku shakes his head, his mouth curled into a smirk. "You make it sound like you were backpacking and sleeping in hostels or some shit. Be real, man. You did it up play- boy style like you always do. Probably found your very own Heidi Klum out there."

"Nah. Never that."

Riku is half right. I did roam Europe in style, driving up the coast to Monaco, staying at luxurious resorts and indulging in the most amazing cuisine. I also indulged in my fair share of hot, European pussy. But, hey, I was on vacation.

"Sure, sure," he remarks, not the least bit fazed by my aloofness. He already knows that privacy is a big deal to me and that I rarely disclose any personal information. "Just toss one my way if you ever find your hands too full to juggle all those Vicky Secret angels you like to keep stashed away."

One swimsuit model. *One.* And suddenly I'm Hugh Hefner with a fresh Viagra refill.

I finish my beer in silence, listening to him ramble on about the insanely frustrating demands of our guests.

"No butter. No gluten. No dairy. No fat, no calories, no flavor. What the hell do these chicks want to eat? Air?"

"If you could put it on a plate and garnish it with parsley, it'd be a hit."

"Fuck that," Riku remarks with a shake of his head. "I want a woman that eats. Someone I can cook for and feed while she's curled up next to me in bed. Ain't shit I can do with a bag of bones. I mean, have you seen most of them? Shit, if they turn to the side, they fucking disappear. I'll take tits and ass over Skeletor any damn day."

I nod, feeling the double-edged sword of his words. Of course, these women want to eat. They crave rich foods and sugary desserts just like anyone else. They detest having to spend every waking moment obsessing over every pound and calorie. But when you live in a society that praises skinny and shames anything that doesn't fit that extra-extra-small mold, you make sacrifices. And that's exactly what they've done. They've sacrificed their happiness, their peace of mind, and in many cases, their health. And in the end, it's not even about food or body image. It's just another notch in the good ol' fucked-up, modern America belt.

I drain my beer before crossing the courtyard to my home. It's warmer than usual, and under the dark cloak of night, I decide to take a swim to clear my head. After stripping off my suit and tie and changing into something more liberating, I dive into the turquoise water, letting the coolness drown the heat building deep in my gut.

This time feels different. I've been in this business for years, yet I feel oddly unprepared. It's only the end of Day Two, and I'm already on edge, temptation closing in on the edges of my rationale. At this rate, I won't last.

Okay, I lied before. Not *lie*-lie. Just didn't tell the whole truth. When I said I endure six, sexless weeks during instruction, what I *meant* to say was that I *try* to endure six, sexless weeks. Sure, I'm nearly always successful, but I must admit, there are slipups. That's why I always keep a girl on standby. Very few outsiders know where the property is located, and the few who do know are given that information under special conditions. No strings, no expectations, just someone to scratch that proverbial itch so I can concentrate on the task at hand.

I swim the length of the pool, feeling my muscles flex and pull, igniting an entirely different burn in my thighs, calves, and biceps. I push off the edge of the pool once more, causing my body to slice through the water forcefully. Damn, it hurts good. I want to keep going—keep pushing—until I'm too exhausted to think about what I really crave. I want to feel this burn of exertion until it eclipses the fire currently licking up my spine.

Most think I'm some kinda health freak. They see me doing laps, running, banging out push-ups like they're going out of style. But in reality, what I do is necessary. It's the only way I can avoid what I really want. Without that release, I'd combust from the inside out. Either that or jerk my shit until it falls off. *No bueno.*

"Wow, no wonder there's no decent junk food in this place. The owner is Ryan Lochte."

I spin around to take in a pair of pale legs draped in floral silk to just below the knee. My curious gaze trails up those stems to the bend of soft hips that taper into a narrow waist before flowing into the bottom curves of full, pert breasts.

A grand says she not wearing a bra. Two says her nipples are practically winking at me under that maliciously thin sheath of silk.

Saliva collects in my mouth like a hungry lion and I swallow, forcing myself to look away before I allow myself to know the answer for certain.

I don't need to see the rest. I already know. I can nearly smell her perfume in the whisper of wind that's followed her to me. Hell, I can almost imagine the smirk that undoubtedly rests on those delicate lips.

"Seriously, what's a girl gotta do to get some real ice cream around here?"

From the corner of my eye, I see Allison bend down to sit at the edge of the pool and tentatively dip her toes into the water. I turn to watch, amazed at the sight of the fragile gazelle at the watering hole. She visibly shivers, and those large, animated eyes smile with amused wonder.

I clear my throat, praying that when I finally grow the balls to open my mouth, actual words and sounds will come out.

"Perhaps the kitchen would be the best place to direct your request, Mrs. Carr."

Too absorbed with every other (forbidden) part of her, I

don't even notice the spoon and small dish of ice cream in her hands.

"Yeah, but it's some nonfat, soymilk crap that tastes like baby poop," she replies, wrinkling that freckled nose.

I allow myself to take a few steps toward her. I've earned them. I've been a good boy . . . sorta. "And you know what baby poop tastes like?" I ask, cocking a cynical brow.

"Well, I don't know, obviously. But based on how it smells, I would say this ice cream is pretty darn close." She sets the dish down beside her after giving it one last, shaming grimace. "So what are you doing out here? I'd think you'd be exhausted from that very . . . *hands-on* lesson today. Very enlightening, Mr. Drake."

"Well, we try our best, Mrs. Carr," I respond with a blank face, though my voice is teeming with amusement.

Allison rolls her eyes and shakes her head, her auburn hair brushing her bare shoulders. "I told you—do *not* call me Mrs. Carr. I have no interest in eating my young or nursing them until they're old enough to pay taxes." She brings her feet to the surface of the water and watches as she wiggles her toes. "So . . . is that how it's going to be all the time?"

"What do you mean?" I take a few steps closer, a frown pinching my forehead.

"I mean, will you always be so intense with us?" Before I can brace myself, her gaze locks on to mine, piercing straight through my impassive facade. "Will you . . . touch us like that? Say those things to us?"

"All physical contact is specifically outlined in the contracts, Mrs. Ca—excuse me, Allison. Now, if at any time you feel uncomfortable with the physicality or feel as though I'm being too demonstrative, say the word, and it stops. Understand? Are you saying I make you uncomfortable, Allison?"

I don't even notice how close we are now, as if the ebb and flow of our chlorinated sea has somehow pushed us together. Only inches of water, breath, and clothing separate us, yet I know any space we share will feel too intimate.

I know what I need to do. It's what's right, what's responsible.

I need to tell her to leave.

I need to send this woman back to her cheating, piece-of-shit husband and let her work out her issues like the rest of America—with therapy, pills, and the occasional bad decision. But most importantly, I need let her do it without my help. Because, right now, all I can think about is helping myself.

"No," she says suddenly, as if those bright eyes have infiltrated my mind. "You don't. And, remember, it's Ally."

She pulls her feet from the water and stands, collecting her now-melted nonfat-soy-milk-baby-poop ice cream. Before she turns to walk away, she smiles at me, not at all put off by my icy approach as I had hoped she'd be.

Note to self: Be more of an asshole.

And get real ice cream.

Temptation

Today on the *Hollywood Reporter,* playboy billionaire Evan Carr caught with another woman while wife vacations solo at a spa?

Sources close to the couple say the pair had been having problems for months, amid outrageous cheating rumors. Claims have even been made that wife Allison Elliot-Carr has not been at a spa retreat, but rather in rehab after a mental break. With her unavailable for comment, and whereabouts unconfirmed, *Hollywood Reporter* reached out to Evan Carr, who did not deny, or confirm, rumors of infidelity.

I click off the television and scratch the short layer of hair on my chin, my jaw tight with irritation. Fuck. This is ex–

actly why all outside communication is forbidden during instruction: shit like this worms its way into the ladies' heads, sucking out whatever tiny glimmer of hope they have left and sending them running back home.

Of course, they'd have reason to, since 95 percent of these stories have some truth to them. Where there's smoke, there's fire, and the Carr marriage has been a blazing inferno of lies and deceit since before Allison even said "I do."

I should know.

With a huff, I make my way toward the main house, just as the women are finishing up breakfast and morning yoga. One by one, they trickle into the great room, silently taking their seats. A few of them glance up at me through long, false lashes. Others knead their hands in their laps, their cheeks red and warm with memories of my hands touching them, coaxing their inner deviant to come out and play. Yet I don't notice it. I don't see their longing stares. I just keep watching, waiting, until she walks in.

Once I see her filing in with the rest of the ladies, something hot and heavy collects in my gut. It's torture. It's relief. It's goddamn confusing. I'm too edgy, too anxious, and there's fuck-all I can do about it now. Impulse takes over, and I'm striding toward her just as she takes her seat.

"Stand up," I command. I don't ask. I never ask for what I want.

"Excuse me?" Allison asks, with a frown wrinkling her forehead. I want to reach out and smooth those tiny creases, but I don't. I'm not a total narcissist.

"Stand up, Ally." I extend my hand to her, which she studies cautiously before taking. Her palm is warm and soft . . . everything I imagined *her* to be. Simultaneously smoothing her dress down her backside, she stands, closing the small space between us.

I hold her hand a beat longer than I should, before pulling it back. "Turn around. Let me see you."

"Wha . . . ? Um, I don't understand what you—"

My hands are on her shoulders, my boldness catching her off guard and causing her to gasp. I guide her, turning her body a hundred and eighty degrees. "This. This is what determines whether or not a man fucks you, ladies. The packaging. The allure. The temptation." I turn her back toward me, letting those questioning, blue-green eyes bore into mine unabashedly. I can't turn away. I can't even fucking blink. I talk to her like she's the only one in the room, yet I make sure my voice carries to the other eager ears. "Men are visual creatures. They need to be enticed. Excited. And while A-line dresses and ballet flats may be sensible, they're not sexy."

"This is Alexander McQueen!" she scoffs.

"It's ugly as day-old sin. Fuck the labels."

Her eyes grow wide at first, her cheeks pink with embarrassment. Then my words sink in, and pain creeps onto that porcelain canvas of sandy-brown freckles. I don't want to hurt her, but shit, the truth hurts. Life hurts. Hell, it hurts like a motherfucker.

Before she can protest, I'm touching her hair, pulling out

the silver pins that secure it in a practical bun. Flames cascade down her back, spilling into her face and kissing her shoulders. I coil an auburn lock around my finger and inch my face closer to hers so only she can hear the words I shouldn't say. These words that threaten to eat away at the once-steel fortress of my logic.

"I think you're sexy as fuck, Ally," I whisper, my breath tempting the skin right below her ear. "You just don't know it yet."

Just as swiftly, my touch abandons her, and I'm hurriedly making my way to the lectern, away from her. Away from the temptation to rake my fingers through that fiery mane before fisting the hair at the nape of her neck—pulling her head back so she has no choice but to see me. But is that what I really want? For her to see who I really am? Or do I continue to spoon-feed her, and everyone else, the illusion that will provoke their own inner temptress?

I clear my throat, fidgeting with the lapel of my linen suit jacket. Allison is still standing, still looking at me with eyes wide and mouth agape. What I said was necessary. I had to tell her. Who knows what spin the tabloids will put on her absence from the public eye?

Yes, yes, all part of my teaching methods.

I'm full of shit.

A hand goes up, saving me from the turmoil of my fucked-up inner monologue. "Yes?"

The sound of my voice prompts Allison to take her seat, and I force my eyes to Maryanne Carrington, the portly, middle-aged woman from Day One who has proved to be the mother of the group. Probably because her husband likes to fuck girls young enough to be their daughter. "It's evident that I'm no longer a spring chicken," she says in her endearing southern drawl. "I'm not a size two, and gravity has taken its toll. There's only so much nippin' and tuckin' I can do without looking like a circus clown. How can I be tempting? What can I do to make my husband find me sexy again?"

"Mrs. Carrington, forgive me, but do you have tits?"

"Wh-what?" she stammers, clutching her chest with phantom palpitations.

"Tits? You have them, right?"

"Well . . . yes. Of course." Her cheeks heat with crimson, and she lets out a nervous chuckle.

"And ass?"

"Why . . . yes."

"Then you can be sexy. You *are* sexy. You just need to believe it enough to make your husband see it too." I scan the top of every coiffed head, speaking to no one yet needing everyone to hear me. "It's not about being the skinniest, or having the biggest breasts, or the best ass. We don't give a fuck about pumping your lips full of collagen or threading extensions in your hair. We just want you. We men are simple creatures, ladies. Give us something that makes our mouths water. Strut around in that frilly lingerie and heels while you dust the furniture, pretending to be totally oblivious to our stares. Bend over to pick something up with the top buttons of your blouse undone so we get a peek of that cleavage. Wear your hair down so we can imagine the feel of it between our fingers, pulling it while you cry with passion."

Almost as if the movement were rehearsed, my eyes meet Allison's lively gaze. She thinks these words are for her. She probably thinks she's somewhat special. But what she doesn't see is the real reason I am so drawn to her . . . so tempted to taint her perfectly poised facade.

I pity her.

She believes that I'm an outsider, a mere spectator to her world, yet she herself suffers the same fate. This life of glitz, glamour, and garishness is not for her. She and I are cut from the same cloth—misfits among millionaires.

She may have the money and the status, but she's faking it. She can't even be honest with herself, and that is why, as much as she intrigues me, she disgusts me just as much.

At least that's what I tell myself.

I finish the class, shoulders tight with agitation, counting down the minutes, the seconds, until I can escape to the one place where I can be free. I'm already stripping off the restraints of Calvin Klein by the time I hit the front door. But I don't change into my swim trunks or running shorts like I've done almost every evening. I head straight to the shower, setting the water to scalding temperatures even though it's warm outside, the dry desert heat sucking the life out of my parched skin. The water burns, but I don't register the pain. A different kind of heat consumes me right now, my body aching to extinguish the flame.

I take my cock into my slick, wet hand and squeeze, relieving some of the pressure. I feel it throb against my palm, urging me to put it out of its misery. Eyelids heavy and muscles taut, I stroke it slowly, grunting out a curse. That's all I should give myself for being such a careless fucker, but I need this. I need to rid myself of this longing. I'm no better than those cheating bastards—I *am* those cheating bastards—but at least my alternatives don't hurt anybody. Stroking my dick doesn't make Page Six. E! News won't show clips of me coming in the palm of my hand.

I grit my teeth as I tug my shit, chanting the fire out of me with deep groans. Eyes tight, I come so hard that my knees buckle, hot seed spilling into my hand before dribbling down the drain. Under the scorching spray of water, I stand panting, bracing myself against the marble-tiled wall. Even with my skin flush and pink from the water, I feel cold. I feel empty. I feel . . . alone.

Hours pass before I resurface, towel draped over my shoulder and dressed for my nightly swim. It's quiet tonight. Still. Not even a breeze to keep me company under the canopy of sparkling, luminescent stars.

I swim until exhaustion greets me and my lungs burn. My muscles ache and quiver until they feel like jelly. Yet I prolong my torture, pushing my body past its limits. Past pain, and pleasure, and feeling, altogether.

She doesn't come tonight.

Maybe she pities me too.

Adoration

"here's one thing that a man wants you to stroke more than his cock: his ego. Throw in the money and power, and you've got a Hulk-size ego that needs to be fed around the clock."

I step around the lectern, a devious smirk playing on my lips. I'm better today. My head isn't clouded with bullshit thoughts that I shouldn't be thinking. My balls don't ache every time my gaze touches her. And, after killing myself with running and swimming, my body is just sore enough to be a physical reminder of why I shouldn't give two shits about her, or her perfectly flawed face, or the waterfall of silken red that's draped down her back.

It's not for me. None of it is.

Allison didn't come here because she wants Justice Drake

to fuck her. She came because she wants Evan Carr, her spineless fraud of a husband, to fuck her. She wants him to want her. She wants him to love her. She wouldn't be here if she didn't.

"Feed the beast, ladies, and it'll come to you every time it's hungry. Make your man feel like he's the biggest, baddest motherfucker on earth, inside and outside of the bedroom, and he'll adore you."

Lacey raises her hand and speaks up. "So what if he's not? What if he's an old, wrinkly has-been that can only last five minutes before blowing his load?"

A few ladies giggle, but my expression remains stony. "Lie."

"Lie?"

"Lie your ass off. Tell him how big he is, how full he makes you feel. Tell him it almost hurts when he's inside of you. Tell him that it feels so good that you wanna die. Who's ever faked an orgasm?"

Every head nods, and murmurs resound around the room, altogether less surprised and disgusted by my brashness. After a few days of instruction, my words have nearly lost their shock value. Still, every so often, I have to shake the women up to keep them from getting comfortable. Because being in love, being locked down in the endless, spiraling purgatory known as marriage, is about as uncomfortable as it gets.

"Good. Then you can fake everything else. Shower your man with adoration, and you leave no room for another woman to take your place. Men are like children. They constantly need positive reinforcement. And if they don't get that, they settle for negative reinforcement."

"You mean, they cheat?" Lacey interjects, her ice-blue eyes narrowed into slits. She purses her doctor-enhanced lips, making them look like two giant wads of bubble gum.

"Correct. Not because the woman is more beautiful or younger, but because she makes him feel like fucking Superman. Invincible. All-powerful. They want to believe the fantasy."

Lacey stands so that every eye is drawn to her, and places a hand on her narrow hip. "So if it has nothing to do with age or beauty, why are they fooling around with these Pop-Tarts fresh outta high school?"

A few ladies murmur in agreement. Maryanne Carrington even throws in an approving *mmm-hmm*.

"Honestly? Intelligence. Those girls are easily impressed, thus easy to bed. A bottle of champagne, a limo, and it's pretty much a done deal. They don't want someone they have to work to seduce. That's what they have you for."

"So they want an easy lay?"

"Precisely." I nod.

"But that doesn't make sense," Lacey insists, shaking her head in disbelief. "We're their wives. Of course they could come to us for sex whenever they want!"

"Really?" I move from behind my lectern and stride over to where she stands flustered and unconvinced. I invade her space, stepping in closer than what would be deemed comfortable. But that's exactly what I need from her: I need her uncomfortable enough to be honest. I need her to see where her fault lies so she has no reason to distrust me. I need her to need me.

I graze her jaw with the tips of my fingers, stroking the skin from her chin to her ear. She moves into my touch, soaking up my warmth as if she is cold and starving. And in so many ways, she is. Starving for attention, affection. Cold from being left alone and unloved.

These are feelings I understand. Feelings that I've exploited to make myself a very rich man.

"Lacey," I breathe, low and raspy. "You see him for what he is. You see past the money and the cars and the adoring fans. You see him bare and naked. And that scares him. So instead of facing his cowardice, he fucks little dumb twits to make him feel like more of a man. But you don't want that, do you?"

I watch the movements of her slender neck as she swallows before answering. "No. No, of course not."

"So you know what you have to do, don't you? You have to be his little dumb twit. You have to be his whore, his groupie. You have to make him feel like he's on top of the world when he's with you."

"So you want her to dumb herself down?"

I look up, and my hand instantly drops to my side, releasing Lacey from my spell. Allison stands, eyes narrowed and lips pursed. Even with aggravation clearly etched in her face, an uninvited sensation snakes up my thighs at the sight of her. I grind my teeth, biting down the unbidden feelings.

"In certain ways, yes," I answer, stepping away from Lacey. I almost feel ashamed, as if I shouldn't be touching this other woman. "The wife drives the ship. She is the puppet master. But in order to maintain a happy home, you must let the man believe that he calls the shots."

"Is it not enough that we bear their name and let them dictate our future?" Allison scoffs. "Now we have to pretend to be idiots just so our husbands don't feel intimidated?"

I want to tell her how right she is to feel indignant, but that would be a total contradiction of what I know and believe. "More or less."

"That's bullshit. You and I both know it. Tell me, *Justice Drake,* do dumb girls turn you on? Do you like giggling schoolgirls hanging on to your every word? Does stupidity get you hot?" She's challenging me, hoping to make me eat my own words. I stare back at her, unshaken and totally in control.

Well . . . almost. Minus the tightness in the front of my slacks.

Without breaking eye contact, I step back to stand behind the lectern to hide my semi-erection. "No, Allison. Stupidity does not get me hot. But as you pointed out last week, I'm not a part of your world. I'm an outsider, remember?"

I stab her with a mocking glare, daring her to refute my claim, yet hating the way she's somehow made me feel the need to prove myself. Who the hell is she to me? She's a client—another stiff, lonely housewife. A Prada-clad paycheck—nothing more, nothing less.

Allison doesn't answer me. Just remains standing, silently smoldering, those animated eyes flickering with disdain. I take pleasure in her reaction, craving more. I want to keep pushing until she finally pushes back.

I lean forward and rest my elbows on the podium, my eyes trained like a sniper, ready for the kill. "And, *Mrs.* Carr, why do you even care what turns me on? Shouldn't you be more concerned with what turns on *Mr.* Carr?"

I watch as the pink in her cheeks bleeds to crimson, and her eyes turn dark. "I—I don't. I wasn't saying—"

"Oh? So you don't care what turns him on?"

"You're an asshole," Allison spews. Then she turns rigidly and stalks out of the room.

Mission accomplished.

THE DESERT SKY glows in twilight, bringing with it a cool, relieving breeze. I sit out on the verandah, sipping a beer while listening to the muffled chatter from inside the main house. I look up and close my eyes, blocking it out. That's what I do with most of the world. Reality is just white noise.

"What the hell is your deal?"

I look up to find Allison hovering over me, angry stars twinkling in her pale eyes.

"Excuse me?" I ask with a cocked brow and an amused grin.

"Your deal. Your problem. The reason you act like someone pissed in your Cheerios."

I sit up and motion for Allison to take the seat beside me,

though she doesn't flinch. "I understand the sentiment, Mrs. Carr—"

"Ally, dammit. Ally."

"Excuse me, Ally. I understand the sentiment, although I'm not sure what you're referring to."

Completely unmovable, Ally stares daggers from those cerulean eyes—so still I'm not even sure she's breathing. "So that's your angle," she finally says. "I get it. You think this crap is funny, don't you? We're all just entertainment to you—your very own live reality television. You don't care about helping us; you just want to hurt us more than we've already been hurt."

I'm on my feet in the next breath, stealing the cool breeze that whips through her scarlet hair. "Don't ever question my motives, Allison. And don't ever fucking think I would hurt you. Ever."

Her eyes grow wide at my proximity and my heated declaration, but she doesn't move. She shares this space, this moment, with me. "Fine. But don't you ever think I could be here for any other reason than to fix my marriage."

This would be the perfect opportunity for her to storm away, fire trailing behind her in a blaze of glory. The proverbial period on her fervent statement. But she stays, matching my earnest glare, hers just as obscure as mine.

Maybe I'm not the only one being dishonest here. In fact, I know I'm not.

I take my seat on the lounger and pick up my beer. This time she sits in the chair beside me. The act is an unspoken truce. We'll lay our swords down for now.

"I know you're not the dick you want people to believe you are," she says after a long beat passes. I open the cooler beside me and retrieve another beer, handing it to her. She smiles her thanks, and I nod.

"What makes you think I want people to believe I'm a dick?"

She shrugs, taking a swig of beer. "I don't know. Easier that way, I guess. You reject people before they have a chance to reject you."

"Humph," I snort. "I wasn't aware you had an interest in psychology. Seems as if I've missed something in my research."

Ally shakes her head before leaning back on her lounger. "Nothing to do with psychology. Everything to do with experience."

We sit for several minutes in companionable silence, enjoying the late-summer breeze. The stars shine brighter tonight, revealing shapes and patterns on that giant midnight-blue canvas. Even the moon appears bigger, closer than ever before.

"So tell me, Ally. What did bring you here?"

She turns her head toward me and offers a pained grin. "I thought you knew all about me."

My eyes remain trained on the sky, but I see her. I've seen her since the day she strolled into my home and into my life, a halo of fire and eyes birthed from the stars. "I do. But I want to hear you say it."

I hear her swallow and then the hushed rustle of fabric as she fidgets with a loose string on her dress. "I thought . . . I thought if I was what he wanted . . . I thought if I could be—"

"But you are." I don't know why I interrupt. But just the thought of her believing that she is anything less than perfect has my hand tightly locked around my beer bottle. I catch myself and put it down before it shatters in my grip. "I mean . . . you *are* what he wants. He married you, didn't he?"

"Yeah." She shrugs. "But of course that doesn't hold the same connotation as I once thought it did."

"Once?"

She doesn't answer, but I hear her sigh. Then without rhyme or reason, I reach over and grab the bottle out of her hands, placing it next to mine. "Come on," I say, climbing to my feet.

"Huh?"

I hold my hand out, waiting expectantly for her to take it. And why wouldn't she? *Strange man under the influence of alcohol telling her to follow him without explanation, late at night? Sounds legit.*

Yet, with those crystalline eyes trained on my earnest expression, slowly she places her hand in mine. She's trusting me without question, though I've done nothing to earn such a gift. But like the selfish bastard I am, I take it, pulling her to her feet. My fingers impulsively lace with hers, causing a contradictory mix of alarm and comfort to surge in my veins. I look down at our locked hands as we both pull away.

"Follow me." I frown, leading her toward the much

smaller guesthouse. I'm breaking another one of my rules: Never bring a housewife into my home.

"I don't think I should be here," Ally says, yet she steps inside, taking in my living quarters. I know what she sees: bare, white walls, no photographs, no personal touches. Nothing to show who I really am. "How long have you lived here?"

"About eight years," I reply, watching her as she tries to school her reaction.

"Oh. It's so . . . clean." She flashes me a sympathetic smile before looking at the floor.

I frown. I know what she really means: cold and sterile. And the fact that she feels the need to feel sorry for me, as if I am beneath her, irritates the shit out of me. Here I thought she and I shared common ground—that we were both misunderstood souls in this world of the fake and phony—when, in reality, she is one of *them*. She has been all along. And how fucking stupid of me to have thought otherwise.

I'm about to tell her to take those sad eyes and get the fuck out, when she suddenly looks up at me, a genuinely warm smile on her lips. "Don't tell anyone," she says with a chuckle. "But I'm kind of a slob. Seriously. Cleaning is not my strong point. Is housekeeping part of the syllabus? Because I think I could learn a thing or two from you."

I release my aggravation in a relieving breath and turn toward the kitchen to hide my own smile. Shit. Why the hell am I grinning like the damn Cheshire cat? And why do I find her confession so goddamn charming? Like the fact that she's messy makes her sorta . . . *real*?

Without a word, I go to the freezer and set a carton on the marble counter. Allison looks at the container, then looks up at me, and for a moment I swear I see tears swimming in her eyes before she quickly blinks them away, shielding her face with a curtain of crimson.

"You bought me ice cream?" she whispers with a strained ·voice.

I shrug though she can't see me, still refusing to meet my gaze. "You weren't happy with the selection in the kitchen so . . ." I shrug again.

Finally, she lifts her head to look at me, her face so full of light that it's almost blinding. "Thank you."

Her grateful smile and the weight of those two words hit me like a two-ton semi, bringing me back to reality. "Well, we try to provide you all with the niceties of home. That includes non-baby-poop-tasting ice cream." I turn to grab a bowl and a spoon before opening the carton and scooping out silken ribbons of cream and chunks of dark chocolate.

"Oh. Well, still . . . thank you," she replies, buying my bullshit excuse. Because that's exactly what it is: bullshit. What I could've and *should've* done was leave the ice cream in the kitchen and let the staff serve it to her when she was craving frozen, sugary goodness. But no . . . I had to go and complicate shit and bring it back to my house, giving me the opportunity to satisfy her need, as superficial as it might be.

She'd need me. And not for sex or relationship advice to apply to her marriage. For fucking ice cream.

I slide her the bowl and wait for her to take a spoonful. She looks up at me with the same expectant expression.

"Well?" I ask, tapping a finger.

A frown puckers her forehead and she wriggles her nose, bringing those freckles to life. "What? You're not going to have any?"

I shake my head. "For you."

Ally takes a seat and scoops out the first spoonful, placing it on her tongue. Her eyelids flutter closed in ecstasy, and a downright orgasmic sound rumbles from her chest. "Oh my God."

"Good?" I'm smiling, but only because she can't see me, wrapped up as she is in a creamy cocoon of mint and chocolate.

"Amazing," she replies through another mouthful. She finally opens her eyes, and a deep blush paints her cheeks as if she's just remembered my presence. "Thanks for this. Sure you don't want any?"

"All yours."

Ally takes another bite and puts her spoon down, propping an elbow on the counter and placing her chin in her hand. "If you could only eat one flavor of ice cream for the rest of your life, would you pick Rocky Road or mint chocolate chip?"

"Excuse me?" I sit on the stool across from hers, brows raised in question.

"Just humor me. Rocky Road or mint chocolate chip?" She smiles amusingly and digs back into her ice cream.

I'm not sure what to make of this girl. First she's calling me an asshole, and now she's asking me about ice-cream flavors? I frown in confusion.

"Please?" she says just above a whisper. "I haven't had a regular conversation about something other than shoes or handbags, or who our husbands could be sleeping with, in days. I just need to . . . forget. Just for a little while."

I nod and let out a breath, my chest suddenly full of some foreign, unnamed emotion. Sympathy? Yes. But something else too. And it has nothing to do with pitying her.

"Well, being that I've never had mint chocolate chip, and I vaguely remember trying Rocky Road as a child, I'd have to go with that flavor," I reply with a shrug.

Ally's eyes grow wide with playful shock. "You've never had mint chocolate chip ice cream?"

I shake my head. "Nope."

"Then you haven't lived!" She scoops out a small bite and offers it to me, the spoon a mere inch from my lips. "Go ahead; try it."

Okay, I've got two choices. Door Number One: I refuse to play along with her little game and kick her out of my house, offending her and demolishing any ounce of trust she has for me. Or Door Number Two: I let her innocently spoon-feed me ice cream and force myself to see the act for what it is—a chaste, nonerotic gesture between two adults.

Yeah, right.

I lean forward so that the cold tip of the spoon just grazes my bottom lip. Ally slowly eases it forward, causing me to open wider for her, my tongue reflexively jutting out to taste the first sweet drops of cream. I wrap my lips around the mound of chocolaty mint and suck it off the spoon, letting out my own sounds of pleasure.

"Good, right?" Ally beams, nodding her head.

"Hell yeah," I half-groan against my better judgment. But it's too late. Allison Elliot-Carr has weakened my defenses with just a spoonful of Häagen-Dazs.

"I told you! Ice cream is the answer for everything. It's the ultimate cure-all."

I chuckle as she feeds me another bite, and I devour it hungrily. "You might be onto something there, Ally."

"I could totally spend the rest of my life eating only this and nothing else." She places another helping onto her tongue from the same spoon I just made sweet, passionate love to. "I still can't believe you never tried it."

I shrug, instantly feeling like an idiot because I've shrugged at least half a dozen times tonight. But there's just something about Ally that leaves me . . . uncertain. Maybe a little flabbergasted. She's unlike any client I've ever worked with and the total opposite of any woman I've ever found myself attracted to. But there's something about her—something so genuine and unexpected—that makes me almost enamored with her. Maybe she's the riddle that I can't figure out. Or maybe she's just so damn perfectly imperfect that it's endearing. But whatever it is, it's got me. Fucked up as it sounds, it's got me.

That's why it doesn't surprise me when I find myself saying, "There was a lot of stuff I didn't get to have growing up. And as I got older, I just learned to go without."

Ally drops the spoon and looks at me through those too-large eyes, compassion pouring from turquoise pools. "I'm sorry," she whispers.

I wave her off and shake my head. "Don't be."

"Really. I'm sorry. I shouldn't have assumed that you were . . . you know . . ."

And it all comes back to me.

The very reason why I keep everyone at a safe distance. The assumptions, the sympathy. This shit right here. Right now Ally thinks she knows me. Hell, she probably thinks she's better than me. And as much as her bleeding heart may not want to, she pities me.

How stupid of me to think that I could be seen as more than just a charity case. I'm just the hired help, available to be bought and sold like a glorified servant.

"Are you done?" I ask tersely, nodding at the half-empty bowl.

"Wha . . . ? Um, I didn't mean it if I—"

I snatch the bowl from in front of her and throw it into the sink. The jarring sounds of clattering porcelain and metal echo throughout the room. I look up at Allison just as she flinches, her ruby lips fixed into a grimace.

"It's late, Mrs. Carr. I think you should retire to your room for the evening."

Without argument, she turns and quickly makes her way toward the door, fire trailing behind her like a sad, shooting star. She pauses marginally at the doorframe, but doesn't look back, her flame becoming just a distant blur of red as her whispered "I'm sorry" carries in the balmy summer breeze.

Seduction

*O*ver the past week, I've taught you how to exploit your best assets. Showed you how to make your man crave you emotionally, just as much as he does physically. I've even taught you how to stroke his fragile ego. That was the first phase of our program, and if you feel that it's left you teetering at the limits of your sexual tolerance, I suggest you leave now. Now it's time to kick things up a notch."

I walk up to one of the housewives in the first row, not really seeing her at all, and help her to her feet. I don't even look at her face as my hands find the pins in her tightly wound updo, quickly releasing a cascade of wavy, golden-blond locks. Next, my fingers trace the shell of her ears, down her jaw, until they rest on the string of pearls that is kissing her collarbone.

"Does this make you uncomfortable?" I say, close enough that my lips graze her ear.

"No," she squeaks. She's lying. Fucking lying is all these women have seemed to master. Fine. Time to call her bluff. A devious smirk on my lips, my fingers find the top buttons of her blouse. Her green eyes widen as I pop the top one, revealing more of her smooth skin.

"How about now? Does this make you uncomfortable?"

"No," she replies, matching my raspy tone. Her eyes slide shut, and she releases a whine from her slender throat.

"What's your name?" I ask, undoing the second button. She gasps as her blouse falls open, revealing the top of her cleavage.

"Shayla. Shayla Adkins," she relays, panting. Of course, I already knew that. *Shayla Dawn Adkins,* married to George Adkins Jr., heir to the founders of a popular weight-loss program that most of these women swear by. George, affectionately known as Georgie, also happens to be gay. And while she's here with me, he's gone off for an extended vacation with his best friend/personal trainer, Arturo. Needless to say, there is nothing I can teach Shayla that will make her what her husband desires unless she makes a trip to Thailand and starts calling herself Sherman. And the sad part is, she's completely clueless about her husband's proclivities. She believes the bullshit he feeds her about being too stressed out at work to make love to her. She's even proud of the dedication that leads him to spend countless hours "training" at the gym. Poor girl is as naive as a baby lamb in a den of wolves.

"Shayla." I step in so close that our bodies meet, her heat melding with mine. She sucks in a breath. "Shayla, do you want me to stop?"

"No."

"Good."

Silence falls around us, and not even the sounds of heated breaths or the distant clattering of dishes from the kitchen can be heard. Just the muted rustling of fabric slipping over another ivory button fills the space, coupled with Shayla's shallow panting.

My index finger falls on the front clasp of Shayla's white lace bra, and she stops breathing altogether. I rake my fingers over the delicate fabric, toying with her, making her ache for what comes next. She lifts her head and gazes at me through long lashes, begging with those green eyes. How long has it been since a man touched her? How long has it been since she felt desired?

"Seduction," I breathe, and I feel her shiver under my touch. I pull open her blouse just a bit more, exposing her chaste lingerie. A hiss slips through her teeth as I splay a hand on her bare chest. "It lies in the sway of your hips when you walk. The light, breathy tone of your voice. The way your hair whispers across smooth skin. The way you're looking up at me through your eyelashes right now, eyes hooded and smoldering." I barely caress the shell of her bra and she quivers, drawing her bottom lip into her mouth. "Seduction, Shayla. I'm going to teach you how to seduce me, just as I have seduced you."

In the next breath, I'm a foot away from her, yet my eyes are still locked on her angelic white lace bra. "Your bra is . . . cute. Practical. But it's not seductive."

I look around the room, addressing all of the ladies. "And I can bet money that each of you is wearing similar undergarments. Which is why you all have an assignment. In order to be seductive, you need to be confident. And that's something that can't be taught. It needs to come from within. So for today's exercise, we're going to do something a little different. You'll all go back to your rooms and change into something a bit more . . . seductive. You'll find that your suite has been stocked with lingerie from Agent Provocateur, and not a stitch of it is considered sensible or practical. I want sexy, ladies. I want suburban slut. Housewife meets whore. Sell it. Make me believe it. Own it."

"You want us to strut around in lingerie?" asks the matronly Maryanne Carrington, pulling her cardigan closed.

"Not right away. But today, you will strut around in front of me. By the end of the course, you'll be comfortable enough to walk around practically naked on Rodeo Drive while drinking a latte."

Horrified murmurs resound around the room, yet only one voice has the nerve to speak up. "Don't you think that's a little uncalled for? We came here to improve our marriages and our sex lives. Not to abandon our morals and become your personal strippers."

Numbly, I turn my gaze on Allison's rigid expression, the light in her eyes dimmed by her annoyance. It's the first time I've let myself look at her since last week. Since the day I kicked her out of my home with fallen stars drowning in her eyes.

"Like I said before, Mrs. Carr, if you find my teachings too risqué for you—if you think you don't need this course—you can leave."

Ally narrows her eyes into slits yet doesn't say a word, choosing to wring her hands instead. I lift a brow, challenging her to storm out of this house and my life for good, restoring the carefree, I-don't-give-a-fuck attitude that has sustained me for almost thirty years. My indifference has always been my safety net. And now . . . now I'm fighting just to hold on to it.

You reject people before they have a chance to reject you.

My head snaps to Allison as if she had just murmured the words herself. I know it's just my conscience messing with me. My Jiminy Cricket has a sick, twisted sense of humor.

"So . . . how is this supposed to work?" Shayla asks, her face still flushed and top buttons still undone.

"Starting in about half an hour, someone from my staff will come to retrieve you one by one, then lead you to a secluded room. From there, we will have a private session of sorts. I want to gauge both your strengths and weaknesses so I can determine the best way to personally work with you. So . . . ladies, if you will . . ." I extend my hand toward the hallway the leads to the staircase. The staff is already lined up, waiting to assist the women in any way they can. Once the last reluctant face disappears from sight, I make a beeline for the kitchen.

"A LITTLE EARLY for a brew, eh, J.D.? Let me guess: Lingerie Day."

I nod at Riku before tipping back my beer, nearly draining it in just a few gulps. I open the fridge and grab two more, handing him one. A little midmorning beer never hurt anyone. Hey, it's five o'clock somewhere in the world.

Riku pops the top of his beer and takes a swig. "Wait a minute. Don't you usually do that around Week Three?"

I take another big gulp. Holy hell. I'll soon be half drunk if I don't get some food in me. "Yeah. But these girls . . . they need to be shocked. They're too comfortable. I need to push a bit and see if they actually push back."

Riku shrugs. "You're the boss. But don't be surprised if one of those chicks gets a little fire in them and pushes you right on your ass."

I turn toward the fridge and immerse myself in a hunt for snacks to hide my expression. If Riku only knew how right he was.

Someone did push back. And now it's become physically impossible to get back up, dust my shit off, and walk away.

I pop a few grapes into my mouth to keep from speaking the bitter truth. Then I drain my beer and prepare to give these women what their husband's hard-earned money is paying for.

"BRING IN THE next one."

I wipe my brow with a handkerchief and take a calming breath. So far, five ladies have been brought to me, all shaking like leaves on their six-inch hooker heels. But they came. No matter how reluctant they may have been, they came willingly.

Minutes pass before I hear the telltale sounds of stilettos on hardwood. The sounds grow louder, echoing in my head, mimicking those of a ticking time bomb. I know this portion of the program is inevitable and I've been through it hundreds of times. I'm almost immune to the sight of scanty lace stretched over round, full breasts. I've seen more than my fair share of thong-clad asses. And every pussy looks good when it's kissed and caressed by buttery-soft silk.

Still, none of my experiences could have prepared me for the vision that stands in the doorway in the next instant.

Allison steps into the room just far enough for Diane to close the door behind her. She flinches, though she's trying like hell to remain cool and indifferent to being half naked in front of me. I stay seated, choosing to remain in my safe zone. Standing would only make the urge to rip that goddamn cocktease of a satin robe off her shoulders that much stronger.

"So?" she asks, raising a brow.

"So."

"So . . . I'm here. Now what?"

I stroke the dust of hair on my chin, contemplating my next move.

She's just like everyone else. She's nothing special. Just a pay-check.

I chant this mantra in my head over and over again until it becomes real. Or at least believable.

You're full of shit. She's more than that, and you know it. And you hate it.

"Take off your robe," I say brusquely, trying to silence the voices in my head.

Allison hesitates, still straddling the imaginary fence between the doorway and the actual room space. She pulls the robe around her tighter, the drawn satin revealing the curve of her hips. My mouth waters.

"I can't help you if you won't let me, Ally." My voice is softer than it should be. Probably softer than she deserves. "Take off your robe . . . *please.*"

She doesn't fight, though I know she wants to. Instead, she takes a breath and clenches her eyes shut. Then slowly, almost painstakingly, her grip loosens on the pinched fabric. Light brown freckles adorn the top of her chest and shoulders. The contrast between those tiny sprinkles and her milky-white skin, and between her skin and that scarlet hair frosting her shoulders, reminds me of a red velvet cupcake. I lick my chops lazily, the urge to feast on her sweetness growing stronger and hotter.

When the robe slips over the bodice of her corset, my head and limbs become disjointed, and all sense of control begins to slip away. I can feel my legs aching to stand, and my hands burning to touch her. To trace the mosaic of cinnamon freckles blessed with the privilege of living on her creamy skin.

Allison looks down as the satin uncovers more of the lace cinching her breasts and waist as if she's seeing it for the very first time. Eyes wide with wonder, it's as if she's experiencing the same effort of restraint I'm struggling to maintain, and is surprised by her own willpower.

The robe drops to the floor, unsheathing the embodiment of heaven in heels. Her lace bustier and panties are winter white, adorned with rose-pink detailing around the cups of her pert breasts. White stocking are hooked by a matching garter belt over long, toned legs.

She's an angel. My angel with a halo of fire.

Against the bare walls and sparse furnishings, she looks out of place. A woman like her should be surrounded by beauty, immersed in all things soft and gentle.

Not cast into the darkness of tainted desire.

Our gazes find each other, and our mouths part, yet no words are said. There aren't any. Just indefinable friction filling this space, the electricity so thick that even the surface of her skin seems to glow. She's luminous

"Walk to me," I command.

Allison takes a few shaky steps toward me before I halt her advance by raising my palm. "Stop."

Hurt and confusion flash across her face. "What?"

"Don't just stalk over here like you're walking the green mile. Exaggerate the sway of your hips; sashay to me. See how the heels elongate your legs and sculpt your calves? Give me time to appreciate that, okay? Now try again."

She rolls her eyes before a steely determination settles in them. Head held high, she slowly takes a step forward, and something hot descends into my gut, leaving a scorching trail of lust down my spine. Another sinful step, those teal eyes locked on me like a seductive sniper, and the heat twists and radiates into my lap. A third step with those round luscious hips playing peekaboo from under the frilly lace of her panties, and I feel like my pants will burst into flames, causing me to jump to my feet and swiftly stride toward her.

I know Allison can read the desperation and urgency in my hungry eyes. I know she notices how my hand shakes as I reach out to tuck a lock of her strawberry mane behind her ear. Yet no witty remark or snarky joke escapes her. Instead, she sucks her bottom lip into her mouth and gently rakes her top teeth over it. Without even thinking, I slowly run my thumb along her mouth, coaxing out that tormenting lip. Ally releases it, and with it still glossy and glistening, my thumb trails her mouth once more.

There is nothing between us now but air, opportunity, and forgotten obligations. I don't care about it any of it. With one hand gripping her back and the other tracing her lips, all the rules and boundaries just fall away.

To hell with the consequences.

I close my eyes, because touching her and seeing her is just too much to bear. "What the fuck are you doing to me?" I whisper. I don't expect her to answer, or even hear me, for that matter. But I want her to. I *need* her to.

The angel tumbles down to earth and lands in my own personal realm of lust, hedonism, and shame. With eyes the color of the ocean and her halo of fire burning as bright as the desert sun, she speaks to me. And while she is raw and sullied, tainted by this beautiful hell, her words breathe life into the darkest, loneliest parts of me.

"Exactly what you taught me."

Reality rushes in, throttling me into an icy-cold pool of awareness.

I'm touching another man's wife.

I almost kissed another man's wife.

I want to fuck another man's wife.

Thinking it—letting it linger on the edges of your conscience—is one thing. But admitting it? Knowing that shit for a fact, so much so that it damn near hurts not to be near her? To anticipate every glance and sigh as if they drive my very existence?

This is madness.

I step away from her and keep stepping away until I am at the door. And even as I watch as pain dims the light in her eyes, I know that I have to leave. Because if I don't, I'll make good on every one of my unspoken admissions.

Distraction

Shades of pink smear the cloudless sky as the sun sinks into the shadowy depths of the horizon. I watch it in wonder, almost overwhelmed by the beauty of it all. People see the desert as lifeless, dry, and desolate. I see peace, stillness, and freedom.

I hear her approach, but I don't move, still watching as pink fades into the darkest of blues, allowing the stars to reemerge and shine. I imagine them twinkling in her teal eyes as she smiles. I'm just too afraid to look at her and see it for myself.

The slap of her sandals stops at the lounger beside me, and she takes a breath before sitting down. We don't speak. We don't have to. The stars speak for us.

"What do you see up there?" she whispers after several

minutes. We're bathed in darkness now, aside from the muted light coming from the main house.

"Space."

Ally snickers. "*Wow.* Such a profound observation, Mr. Drake."

I turn my head just in time to see her throw her head back and laugh, the sound so pure and unexpected that I find myself smiling.

"Not *space*-space. Not like the 'final frontier' or some shit like that. But space . . . room to breathe. To grow. To dream."

"Mmm." The sound is throaty and erotic as hell. "Poetic."

It is poetic for me, and I instantly regret my words. Seems like I can't stop the word vomit when I'm with her. There's just something about Ally that distracts me enough to forget myself, beckoning me like a siren's call to speak my truth. I just want to tell her . . . everything.

Maybe we were friends in a past life. Or lovers.

"Why did you leave me this afternoon?" she finally asks. I knew this question was coming, yet the words still feel like nails on a chalkboard.

"I had to."

"Why?"

I shrug. "I was distracted. And when I'm distracted, I can't do my job."

She frowns, and turns to her side, her front completely facing me. "You were distracted . . . by me?"

"Yes."

She hums a response but doesn't press for more. Instead she jumps to her feet, her sandals slapping against the pavement. "Hey, are you hungry?"

"Hungry?"

"Yeah. You weren't at dinner. I figured you must be hungry."

I shake my head. Sharing a beer or a bowl of ice cream is one thing, but breaking bread with the woman would be just asking for trouble. And I'm faring just fine in that department on my own, fuck you very much.

"I'm good."

Ally takes a step forward, close enough for me to see the floral pattern of her sundress from the corner of my eye. "Did you eat dinner?"

"No." I peer at her just in time to see her roll her eyes.

"Well, *I* want to eat something. And you're not going to make me eat alone, are you?" She flutters those dark auburn lashes, and her eyes grow as large and round as the moon.

"What about your ice cream?" I don't tell her that I already polished off that carton and had to send out for more.

"Nah. I need *real* food. I'm hungry."

"How can you be hungry? Wasn't dinner a couple hours ago?" I let my gaze sweep her slight frame, wondering where the hell she puts those bowls of ice cream she socks away every day. By society's standards, Allison would be considered thin, maybe even a bit skinny. Her breasts aren't naturally large or inflated with mounds of silicone or saline. Her ass is pert and small, just large enough to fit in my palms. And her hips are narrow, yet shapely and feminine.

Allison is a real woman. She isn't pumped full of filler or snatched and pulled to the point that she can't breathe. She's comfortable in her skin, and that makes me all the more intrigued by her, and confused by her reasons for being here. Women as confident as she is shouldn't give two flying fucks about being subservient sex slaves to douche-canoe little shits like Evan Carr.

"Yeah, it was. And while pan-seared Chilean sea bass in a dashi-soy broth is good, it's just . . . not satisfying. It's kinda cold and vacant. There's no heart in it. No soul."

I quirk a smile, and with a deep, resigning breath, I stand. And against my better judgment and the God-given sense I once possessed, I offer her the bend of my arm. "I'll be sure to tell my Michelin-starred, highly paid chef."

"Oh God! Please don't do that!" Allison laces her arm through mine without invitation as if the act were completely innocent. As if I hadn't nearly tasted her lips just this afternoon.

"No? I shouldn't fire her for serving such cold, soulless food? Or maybe I should can my sous chef, Riku. Good kid. He'll land on his feet eventually," I gibe as we stroll toward the main house.

"No, you shouldn't. That would make you a dick. And I'm quite enjoying the nondick you."

I turn to her, my eyes wide in mock mortification. "Non-dick me?"

"No! No, not what I meant! I mean, the dickless you. No! Um, uh, you without the dickiness!" Ally covers her rapidly reddening face with her other hand and shakes her head. "Oh my God, I'm hopeless. Cut out my tongue now before I make an even bigger fool of myself."

"You are oddly fascinated with dicks, Ally. Freud would've had a field day with you." I laugh, tears forming at my eyes. I pull her hand away from her face, and she quickly turns away. But not before I catch a bright smile and the sound of her cackling laugh. She has one of those laughs that make you laugh. It's not sweet or dainty. It's a raspy, full-on belly laugh. The kind that's sometimes accompanied by a snort. I chuckle even harder, and shake my head in disbelief. Yeah . . . even her snorts are adorable.

And *fuck me*. I'm using words like "adorable."

Our laughter tapers off as we make it into the house, and we silently shuffle toward the kitchen.

"I hope we don't get in trouble for being in here after hours," Ally whispers, her arm still locked with mine. I flip on the kitchen lights and give a half shrug.

"I hope not. I heard the boss is a dick."

She giggles and looks up at me, those animated eyes so alive with wonder. My gaze locks with hers, and I smile at the woman in front of me, like she is mine.

Now that we're here, alone, the halogen lights illuminating that tainted smile that I have no fucking right to wear, my lazy-ass Jiminy Cricket decides to intervene. I quickly unravel my arm from the warm comfort of hers and go to lean against a prep table. Ally doesn't notice, at least she doesn't show that she does, and begins to rifle through the large, stainless-steel refrigerator.

"Anything in particular you want? You know . . . something that isn't incredibly pretentious or requires a dialect coach to pronounce?" she asks, her head still in the refrigerator. She picks something up and brings it to her nose, then gags and puts it back. I stifle a chuckle.

Ugh. *Chuckling.* What am I now? A giddy-ass tween whose balls haven't fully dropped yet? I palm mine just to make sure my boys are still intact.

"Anything you want."

Ally emerges, holding up a wrapped wedge of Brie and a block of Manchego cheese like she just hit the jackpot. "Well, it won't be gourmet, but I bet I could make some kick-ass grilled cheese. Now . . . what are the chances of us finding just regular white sandwich bread?"

I make a face and shake my head. "Very slim."

"Eh. Then your soulless, hoity-toity bread will have to do." She winks. And the hot, heavy feeling from earlier unfurls within me once more.

"WHO WOULD KICK whose ass in a fight: Iron Man or Batman?"

Ally tears off a piece of her grilled cheese sandwich and

pops it into her mouth. We're both propped up on stools at a prep table, a spread of focaccia-bread grilled cheeses, green grapes, and red wine in front of us. Ally sits across from me, plucking off a few grapes and making a happy face with them on the metal tabletop.

I swallow a bite and wash it down with a sip of wine. "Why are Iron Man and Batman my only choices? Why can't I pick Superman? Or Spidey?"

"Nope," she says, shaking her head. "You can only pick between these two. Iron Man or Batman. And, ew . . . Spidey? Lame."

I take a bite of sandwich and contemplate my answer. "Fine. I guess I'd have to go with Iron Man."

"Why him?" She finishes her grape happy face then eats the poor guy's left eye.

"Well, he's got the suit—"

"Batman has a suit!"

"—and he can fly."

"Batman can fly!"

"But Batman can only swing from things from a bungee cord. He can fall. He does that a lot. He's a pretty great faller."

Ally frowns. "He is not a faller. He *glides*. He's an ass-kicking glider."

"With a rubber suit?" I smirk. "Because that is just *so* much more impenetrable than crystallized armor."

"Bullshit. Iron Man is only good because he has Jarvis. They should just rename the franchise Jarvis Man because the computer does all the work."

"Jarvis Man?" I raise a playful brow.

"You know what I mean. Or Jarvis and the Iron Ass-hat. They could be a team."

We share an easy laugh and take sips from our glasses. That's how things feel between us—easy. Uncomplicated with expectations or formalities. We're just two people who share a mutual love of grilled cheese and superheroes.

"Why only two choices?" I ask as I refill our glasses.

"Huh?"

"When you make questions out of these little random gems of useless information, it's only two choices. Mint chocolate chip or Rocky Road. Batman or the Iron Ass-hat."

"I don't know." Ally shrugs and picks at a crust of bread. "I guess, to me . . . Life is just a series of choices. We try to always make the best ones, but really we're just settling for the lesser of two evils. Or at least trying to."

She looks at me and a sad smile touches her lips. I don't know how to deal with it, so I just look down. *Coward.*

"Is that what you feel you've done? Settled for the lesser of two evils?" I don't elaborate, but she knows what I'm talking about.

"Honestly? I don't think the choice was ever truly mine to make."

I know I should just leave it at that, letting her words drift into another, simpler conversation. But, of course, I find myself needing to delve deeper into those turquoise waters. "Why do you say that?"

"There are things expected of me. Things I can only pro-

vide by marrying into an influential family and represent-
ing them in a certain light." She turns to me, pinning me
with those haunted, ocean irises. "We're all just trophies.
Shiny, plastic, useless trophies. Exciting at first, but we have
no real purpose other than attesting to someone else's grand
achievements."

I tilt my head to one side thoughtfully, my eyes trained
on anything but her and those sad eyes. "A diversion—
something pretty to distract from the real turmoil festering
just beneath the surface."

She nods, then asks, "Is that how you see me?"

I lift my gaze to hers and find her expression filled with
genuine curiosity—not anger or hurt. I shake my head. "No.
Not you."

"I had dreams, you know. Goals." She smiles, but looks
down, hiding its brilliance. "Now I'm no different than
them. I'm just like all those other women. Fighting, clinging on to the hope that we could be more than arm candy
at business functions or designer incubators. That we could
be truly loved for who we are, and not what we represent."

I don't respond, letting the words hang in the air until they
dissipate under the weight of Ally's pain. She stands and begins
to collect the uneaten food. "It's late. And you need your
beauty sleep." She winks at me, that carefree smile restored.
I help her discard the trash as she takes the dishes to the sink.

"Me? Beauty sleep? What makes you think I care anything about beauty?" I take a washed dish from her and dry
it with a towel.

"You're kidding, right?" She smirks, scrubbing a pan. "You possess beauty like most women possess shoes."

"Not following you." And I'm not. I could give a fuck about what's deemed beautiful by contemporary society's standards.

"Well, first of all, look at this place," she says, waving a wet hand around the room. "This estate is magnificent. Like paradise in the middle of the desert. Seems almost like a mirage."

I nod my head in agreement. Oasis is *my* oasis—my refuge. My escape from all the incessant narcissism and fuckery that comes with fortune. I didn't end up in the middle of the desert—as far away as I could possibly get from my original home in NYC—by accident. Eleven years ago, when I said good-bye to the noise, traffic, and permeating scents of piss and diesel fuel, I told myself that I would never, ever look back at my old life with a sense of fondness. A few years after that, I found Oasis, and I knew I was home.

"And then," she says, turning to me, her cheeks flushed pink, "there's you."

I smirk and look down to hide my own blush.

Yeah. I'm fucking blushing.

My entire life, I've been told I was strikingly handsome, and I've always believed it. Dark hair, cobalt eyes, and naturally tanned skin—I was the good ol' American Abercrombie prototype. That theory was confirmed soon after puberty when girls constantly defied their daddies and tarnished their good family names by spreading their legs without so much as a wink at propriety. As a kid, I knew about sex, but I wasn't really interested it. Not until my seventeen-year-old algebra tutor, Jessica, undressed me and swallowed my thirteen-year-old dick during a lesson on linear equations. It was an act of divine intervention that I passed the class with an A-minus, because I didn't do much more than study every inch of Jessica's body that school year.

Yet, hearing Allison even imply that she finds me attractive, let alone beautiful, makes me feel brand-new.

She hands me the rinsed frying pan, and I take it from her without looking.

My hand covers hers.

Now this is the part in every gag-worthy, chick flick where the guy and girl instantaneously lock eyes and sparks fly. Cue James Blunt or some other sappy cliché as they move in slowly, lips parted in preparation for their first kiss.

Fuck that.

See, that's the kind of bullshit that makes it difficult to have real, genuine connections. It's what gives these women a false sense of hope that their men are anything more than walking dicks with eyes and limbs.

I'm a guy; I should know.

And even though I am so goddamn distracted by her every quirky laugh and goofy grin, that I ache to spend hours tracing the patterns of her freckles while she's spread out beneath me, I'm smart enough to know that this is reality. This isn't some movie where the underdog wins the girl, saving her from a lifetime of heartache. This is real life, and in this episode of *Lifestyles of the Rich and Lonely* the good guy doesn't rescue the girl from her philandering husband.

No. He teaches her how to fuck him.

I pull my hand back and quickly dry the pan before stepping away from the sink. "This was . . . fun. Thanks for the sandwich."

"It was. Thanks for the company." She dries her hands on a towel and smiles. She's always smiling at me. I soak those smiles up like precious rays of sunshine, because if she really knew me, if she knew the truth, things would be different. She wouldn't only pity me—she would loathe me. I'm not sure which is worse.

I usher her out of the kitchen, flicking off the lights on the way out. The rest of the house is completely quiet and still, and only the pale moonlight illuminates her face.

"Good night, Justice."

"Good night, Ally."

I walk back to my little home, hating the stupid grin on my face. It hurts my cheeks, and gives me hope that I have no right to feel.

I kinda love it too.

Anticipation

I wait for them to file in and take their seats, noting the questioning looks as they take in the new additions to the room. It sinks in for a few, and curiosity turns into shock.

Ah, there it is. The pitter-patter of my little black heart. It's been a while, old friend.

It's like that zombie romance movie, as ridiculous as it sounds. The more I hang around Allison, the more alive I feel. The dark coldness of my heart begins to heat and bloom into something vital, and for once I feel . . . normal. Like somehow I belong.

The only difference is, I don't want to belong. Not really. I don't want to fit into Allison's world. I don't want to be defined by the media's perception of me, or an image cooked up by my publicist. I've never been good at coloring inside the lines, and I won't start now for some married chick I've known for five minutes.

That's why I know it's better this way. I'm not the good guy. To be honest, I'm the villain. Good guys wouldn't do what I'm about to.

"Ladies, we have an exciting session for you today. I know you're wondering about the changes to our regular instruction space. Well, today we have a special demonstration for you." I turn to the young lady on my right and place my hand on the small of her back. "This is Jewel. And this is her colleague, Candi. And they are going to show you the art of the striptease."

"You want us to be strippers?" Lorinda Cosgrove shrieks. She's lost the ugly muumuus and cardigans and traded them for something more formfitting and chic. She's learning. Whether she wants to admit it or not, it's starting to sink in.

"It's not about what I want. It's about what's going to happen with or without your consent. Men like strippers. They go to strip clubs. They get lap dances. Now, you can either cry about it or learn to do it yourself. And get an inside glimpse of what is so damn enticing about exotic dancers. Now, I suggest you pay attention, because during our final review, you'll be asked to do a little striptease . . . for me."

"No way," Shayla pipes up. "There's no way I'm taking my clothes off for another man."

"Not necessary, Mrs. Adkins. It's all about the journey, not the destination. The tease of a woman losing her clothing. *Anticipation*. Do you know how fucking hot that makes us? Waiting, hoping, praying that you'll show us just an inch of that smooth, silky skin?

"I've showed you how to get our attention, and now I'm going to show you how to keep it. Anticipation is what keeps us at home, dick hard, wanting *you*. Understand?"

They all answer with looks of shock and interest, so I fish out the tiny remote in my pocket and press a button. Booming bass lines and drumbeats fill the room, accompanied by the voice of Justin Timberlake.

Yeah. I put on JT.

Bitches love JT.

"Ladies?"

At my word, both Jewel and Candi begin to sway from side to side, rolling their hips with every move. Jewel slowly makes her way to the pole situated in the center of the room, her six-inch heels keeping time with the beat. Candi slides over an empty chair and turns to me to rake her fingers over my chest. She gives me a naughty smile before biting her red, bottom lip, then pushes me back to sit in the chair that happens to be facing the makeshift stage. She doesn't look away. Her big brown eyes stay locked on mine, giving me her full attention. Making me feel like I am the only man in the world that makes her wet.

Candi's red-tipped acrylic nails slide down my chest to my stomach. Her fingers explore the rigid planes of my abs through my white linen shirt, and she licks her lips in approval.

"Oooh, baby, you're so hard here," she coos. "I wonder where else you're hard."

The line is laughable, but she knows that's exactly the kind of shit that simpleminded fuckers want to hear. Her hands drift down to my upper thighs, just a breath from my cock. Her eyes flick down to my lap then back up, mischief gleaming behind dark eyeliner and heavy mascara. I lift a brow, challenging her. If she wants it, she has to come get it.

Candi giggles and her hands trail down the tops of my thighs before she stands upright. Hungry eyes still locked on mine, she begins to move, her own hands sliding over her curves. She palms her breasts, giving them a squeeze before caressing her flat, bare stomach.

I watch her as she dances for me in her sexy red lingerie, yet all I can think about is how daring that color would look on Ally accompanied with her red hair. How coy and mischievous she would act in front of me, moving those hips to the music. I close my eyes for a few beats, trying to blink away these thoughts and just focus on my job. And right now my job consists of sitting back and enjoying a striptease. Not fantasizing about another man's wife.

Candi can see the distance in my gaze and moves to stand between my legs. Body writhing, she reaches to her back to unhook her lace bra, letting it fall to the floor. Perfectly round DDs look back at me, not even drooping an inch with the lack of support. She cups her breasts and runs her fingers over her hard, light brown nipples. "Mmm," she moans, eyes nearly closed. "I want you to touch me."

I nod, but I don't give her what she desires. Instead, I look over at Jewel just as she slides down the pole, holding herself up only with her strong, shapely thighs. She spins, platinum-blond hair whipping around her face dramatically. She feels my gaze and looks to me, her expression burning hot and sultry. And with Candi now straddling my thighs, those perfect, doctor-designed tits bouncing in my face, Jewel performs just for me.

This is every man's dream—a topless woman riding his lap while another dry-humps a long, hard pole. I watch them, but I don't *see* them. In many ways, I'm no different from Candi and Jewel. We provide a service that is surrounded by sex. I know their angle. I know the only thing that truly gets them hot is cash. It's the same thing that motivates me.

They take their clothes off. I encourage women to do the same.

Jewel steps away from the pole and makes her way to Candi, who is still dancing, her back to my front. She grinds her ass on my dick, stirring it from rest, and I grip her hips, guiding her erotic movements. Jewel moves in close, pressing her bare breasts against Candi's, and they both moan. Their hands tangle in each other's hair, caressing hot, puckered skin and humid lace. They're putting on a show, touching each other with overexaggerated wonder and desire.

For their final act, Jewel pushes Candi back to rest on my chest, her face beside mine. Then her tongue snakes out, licking Candi's cherry lips before delving into her eager mouth. The kiss lasts for several seconds, both sets of their hands touching me, and each other, in ecstasy. Then, as if on cue, they stand upright, baring their near nude bodies shamelessly.

Eleven sets of eyes stare back in bewilderment.

Then, all at once, as if their brains have just simultaneously processed what they've just seen, questions, comments, and even expletives drown out JT.

"You want us to do *that?*"

"Oh my God, there's no way I'm kissing a woman!"

"Do we really have to take off our bras?"

"Hell no! My family would kill me!"

"I can't believe my husband likes that crap!"

"Wow, that was kinda hot!"

I put my palms up, hushing their flustered chatter to a murmur. "Ladies, I assure you—you will not be required to take off your clothes for me. But let me remind you that I have already seen each and every one of you in lingerie. Some in less than others. So please do yourself a favor and kill the false modesty. I probably know the female body better than you do."

A sardonic snort grabs my attention, and my eyes reflexively seek Allison. She looks back at me, her expression unreadable, and shakes her head slowly. I can't tell if she genuinely disapproves or is amused. I look away, telling myself that it's not my concern to find out.

"For the rest of the afternoon, Candi and Jewel will work with you personally on the art of anticipation. I'll oversee their endeavors, but please think of me as merely a silent shadow. You have no reason to be coy with me. This is nothing, compared to what you'll do for me over the next few weeks."

I find Ally's eyes again, her unblinking stare sparked with something new. Something dark and sultry. Something that's answering my challenge with a rousing *"Hell yes!"*

Maybe the graceful, meek gazelle that I thought I saw on Day One is not a gazelle at all. She is fierce and sexy. Confident yet restrained. I just need to get close enough to uncage her inner beast.

God, I love my job.

CANDI AND JEWEL divide the ladies up into two groups. They start out slow, demonstrating a simple, seductive hip roll before moving on to some racier moves. The ladies look on at the sidelines, too embarrassed to join in. I'm not surprised. It always takes a little time and gentle coaxing to break them out of their shells. Luckily for them, breaking them is my specialty.

I step up closer to Maryanne Carrington, pressing my front into her backside. She startles at first, then melts into me as soon as she feels my breath at her neck and my voice in her ear.

"Relax, love. You're all right. I've got you," I say just for her. I begin to sway my hips, gripping her sides and guiding her body to flow with mine. She's stiff at first, but at the feel of my firm touch and my voice gently cajoling her, her limbs loosen, and she submits to me. I work her body with mine, her softness giving in to my hard plains. She sighs and nearly sags against me, her head rolling back to rest on my shoulder.

"Do you feel sexy in my arms, Maryanne?" I ask, my lips at her ear.

"Oh yes. Oh, God yes," she pants.

"Good. I want you to feel sexy. You know why?"

"Nuh-uh."

"If you feel sexy, you look sexy. I need you to feel like this all the time. I need you to own it. And the only way you can do that is if you own your sexuality." I run my hands from her round hips to the front of her stomach. She shivers and presses in closer to me. "This is part of it. This is just taking that inner sex kitten and showing her how to display her goods. You can do that for me, can't you?"

"Yes. Yes, I can do that for you."

"Good girl. Now you see Jewel there?"

"Yes . . . ?"

"See how beautiful she is? See how sexy? You like the way she moves, don't you, Maryanne?"

"Um . . . uh . . ." Her body goes rigid against mine, but I keep my hands on her, manipulating it to heavy drumbeats.

"Don't lie. You like it, don't you? You wish you could move like that." I can feel every eye on us, but I keep my focus on her. "Tell me."

"Y-yes," she stammers. "I do."

"Good. That's what I want to hear." My gaze flicks up to Jewel, and she's already moving into place, coming to stand beside me. I place Maryanne into her skilled hands without missing a beat. We've done this a dozen times—seeking out the most resistant client and breaking her down. The other women will soon follow suit.

I step back as Jewel shows Maryanne how to use her body like only a woman can—to drive men fucking crazy.

I feel Ally's stare on me. I can hear the unspoken questions and visualize her forehead dimpled in frustration. But I don't look at her. If I do, she'll see it in me. She'll see what I was really thinking while my hands slid up Maryanne's hips. She'll hear whose name I really wanted to whisper, my voice raspy and thick. All my secrets will be laid bare for the entire world to see. And while I may not give two shits about appearances, I do care about my reputation. It's all I have.

So I walk until I'm out of those four walls, away from those excited voices and those treacherous thoughts that are so easily displayed whenever I look at her.

Away from that urge to smile whenever she smiles, and laugh whenever she laughs.

I step into my home just as the cleaning staff is finishing up. I dismiss them brusquely, needing to be alone in my thoughts and misery.

I told myself I wouldn't do this again. I'd be stronger than this. Yet even as I think it, I'm unbuckling my slacks and yanking them down, my briefs quickly following. I groan as cool air envelops my burning-hot flesh.

So hard. So damn hard it hurts.

I wrap a hand around my cock and squeeze, prolonging the needy ache. Life pumps through it, tortured by the promise of a relieving death. I stroke, feeling the veins slide underneath my thin, taut skin.

I can't even think about how wrong this is. Never in my life have I had to jerk off in the middle of the day, and I damn sure haven't done it in the middle of a session. I've never had to. But Allison . . . she has me off my game. Thinking about shit I shouldn't be thinking. Doing things I shouldn't be doing. And right now I just need to release it. I need to purge it from my body like a sickness, so I can get better. So I can get back to being me.

I try. Fuck knows I try. I rub my shit raw like a man possessed, urging the madness from my bones. But relief never comes. Fire doesn't erupt from deep in my gut. It just stays and kindles, building and burning to the point of pain.

With a growl, I stop, frustrated at my body's failure to launch. I can't do this. I can't go on like this. What the fuck am I supposed to do?

Fuck her. Fuck her and get it out of your system.

I shake the tiny voice from my head and busy myself by straightening my clothes.

Just do it. She wants it. You know she does.

I need water. Maybe I'm dehydrated. I make my way to the kitchen and down a glass of water. I refill seconds later. I'll flush it out of me. I'll drown this shit and move on.

You deserve her. Not him. YOU.

"FUCK!" I slam the glass down into the sink basin, shattering it into a million, tiny shards. I can't do this. I can't survive like this for another four weeks.

I pull out my phone and send a quick text.

Something came up.
Take over for me.
Then you and Jewel come see me when you're done.
xx

Infatuation

It's cooler tonight, and I can smell rain in the distance. Still, I dive into the pool, the cold water stinging my skin and paralyzing my joints. I swim through it, feeling my bones and muscles awaken. It's easier now that the heaviness in my gut isn't weighing me down. I can be mindless here. I can let the water drown the shame and wash away their scent. I know I have no reason to feel bad; I did nothing wrong or out of character. I did what any twenty-nine-year-old man would do with two exotic dancers in his home. I did what I've done before.

Candi and Jewel have been associates of mine for years. The three of us hooked up during some of my more boorish, formidable years and kept in touch. When it came time to enlist help with the program, I knew they were the ones for the job.

I should have cut off all physical association then, and I had, for the most part. But every so often, we'd have a few too many glasses of champagne, and we'd fall back into that familiar pattern—them fucking me, me fucking them, and them fucking each other while I watch, dick in hand.

Don't look so surprised. Yeah, I sleep with strippers. *Big deal*. What do you expect me to do with them? Play pinochle?

See, the great thing about Candi and Jewel is that business rarely blurred with pleasure. They'd do their job, we'd have a drink after, and most times they'd leave unsexed and well paid for their professional services.

This was not one of those times.

They did as I had asked, teaching the women their signature moves before they were dismissed for the evening. Then they were at my door with a chilled bottle of Dom and twin wicked gleams burning in their eyes.

"You look tense," Candi said, stepping inside. She eased my suit jacket from my shoulders and began to knead. Jewel popped the cork without spilling a single drop.

"I saw it too. You seem . . . different. Not as focused," she chimed in.

"Frustrated," Candi added.

Jewel returned to our sides with glasses of champagne. I downed mine in two gulps, threw my flute to the side and pegged her with a lustful, unapologetic stare. "Shut up. And take off your clothes."

There was no prelude required between us three. I didn't even expect them to do their usual song and dance to get me hot. They know what turns me on just as I know how to get them off.

And that's what I did.

There, in the middle of my living room, I bent Candi over the arm of the couch and took her from behind while finger-fucking Jewel. Candi came quick, like always. Just a stroke of her clit while giving it to her deep and fast, and she shattered beneath me in seconds. Jewel wanted to play. She straddled my lap, my latex-sheathed dick still glistening with Candi's sugary wetness, and mounted me. She moaned loudly, feeling her hypersensitive mound creating friction against my pubic bone. Candi sucked her friend's bouncing tits and played with her ass until I felt her insides tighten and shiver. Then she was screaming, crying my name so loudly I had to cover her mouth with one hand while I wrapped the other around her waist and bounced her hard, up and down on me, prolonging her orgasm.

When her cries quieted to whines, she dismounted and pulled off the condom. Then she and Candi took turns suck-ing me off, moaning against my dick as they tasted them-selves in the trickles that had slid down to my balls.

And that was it. No romance. No cuddling. Not even any flirty conversation. Just direct, to-the-point sex. We shared a laugh when Candi accidently put on Jewel's panties in her hazy afterglow. We made plans for next season's session. Then they were gone. Just like everyone else in the revolving door of my life.

And now . . . now I'm conflicted about it. Like I've been unfaithful or disloyal to someone. But to whom? Myself? Shit, if anything, I'm pretty damn pleased with myself. And feel a helluva lot better physically. Yet something deep inside me aches with regret. I can feel the loneliness closing in, squeezing my chest. I pant and wheeze with every stroke, but I don't stop. I don't give in to the water. I won't let it defeat me.

"YOU'RE WET."

I keep my eyes to the sky. "Yeah."

"But it's chilly out here. You have to be freezing."

"I'm fine." For the most part, I am. I've gotten used to swimming long after sundown, since many of the women like to sunbathe during the day. Plus, I'm too damn frustrated to feel anything besides frustration.

I hear the shuffling of Allison's sandals moving closer to me. And before I can lift my head to see what she's doing, she lays a sweater over my damp body. Her scent surrounds me, digging its way into my skin and hair . . . into *me*. She's not only affecting me, she's *in*fecting me.

I want to brush off her sweater, but I know it'd hurt her feelings. She's been rejected enough, and she doesn't need me pouring salt in the wound. And it's not her fault that I'm one rub and tug away from being downright infatuated with her.

"You left early today," she says, sitting in the lounger beside mine.

"Had to take care of something." I still don't look at her. I don't even thank her for the sweater. So damn conflicted in my feelings for her. Yet so angry with myself for harboring this sickness—this affliction—that forces me to be a somewhat decent human being and do the right thing. I don't want to hurt her, but I know I will eventually. There is no other option.

"Interesting class today."

"Yeah."

I feel her turn toward me. "Are you okay?"

"Yeah."

"Did I . . . did I do something wrong?"

"No."

"You just seem . . ." Distant. Cold. Exactly what I should have been all along.

"A lot on my mind." That's a lie. Now that I don't have any baby batter on the brain, my head is completely clear, and I can think somewhat rationally again. I can see how much of a mistake it is for us to carry on like this. She'll get attached. I'll let her. And then she'll go back to her husband. And where will that leave me?

"Wanna talk about it?"

"No."

"Okay."

It's quiet for a while, and I mentally prepare for her to get up and leave. When she shuffles to her feet, I close my eyes to cushion the blow of abandonment. Then I hear a loud splash, causing my eyes to pop open. I'm on my feet before I can even register what's happened.

"Holy shit, it's cold!" Allison exclaims, teeth chattering. Her hair is soaked, sticking to her face and neck, and her dress is completely drenched. This upper-crust princess who's probably never even worn the same garment twice has just jumped into a pool fully clothed. She smiles up at me as she wades toward the edge.

"Are you insane? It's cold out here! You'll get sick!" I say, waving my hands animatedly.

"Says the guy in dripping-wet shorts and nothing else."

"Seriously, Ally. You'll catch a cold. It's my job to keep you all safe and comfortable, and right now you can't possibly be either. Please don't make it impossible for me to do my job."

She rolls her eyes and splashes water in my direction. "Fine, fine. Spread on the guilt like mustard. I see how it is." She wades to the ladder, where I wait for her, hand outstretched, prepared to pull her into my arms—*ahem,* I mean, pull her out of the pool. *Yeah, yeah, that's right.*

"Give me your hand," I demand brusquely, irritated at her immaturity. A day ago, her playfulness was endearing. Now it's just a hassle.

She does as I say, those big, doe eyes locked on to mine, and goes to place a foot on the ladder, steadying her ascent with her hand in mine. And just as I think she's pulling herself up onto dry land, she pulls back. Hard. Harder than a little thing like her possibly should. Before our bodies collide, she jumps to her right, giggling hysterically.

Of course, all this is going down as I lose my footing at the edge of the pool and plummet, quite ungracefully, into the chilly water. I can still hear her laughing as my face and chest crack the surface with a splash.

"Are you crazy?" I shout, sputtering a mouthful of chlorinated water.

"Yes!" she croaks between chuckles.

"Oh, you think you're funny, don't you?" I ask, dropping my voice an octave. I can feel my face heating.

"Yes!" She's still laughing, still oblivious to my murderous expression.

I move toward her. "You think you're going to get away with this shit too, huh?" That catches her attention, and her eyes widen, the irises looking even bluer against the backdrop of the pool.

"It was just a joke. I'm sorry if I . . ." she stammers.

Closer now. Only a few feet separating me from her small, fragile body. "Just a joke. You think you're so fucking funny. You think you can just do whatever the hell you want."

"No, no, I don't," she says, shaking her head. She goes to move toward the ladder, but I block her with my body.

"You just do whatever you want, to whomever you want without consequence. Don't you, Allison? You have no regard for anyone else. The world revolves around you, doesn't it?"

"No, I didn't mean that. You have it all wrong about—"

Her words get caught in her throat as I move in as close as possible, my chest brushing hers. I can feel her nipples pebble with the chill, the cold, wet fabric clinging to her goose-pimpled skin.

My gaze lowers to her trembling lip, its usual pink color darkening to dusky mauve. "No, Allison. I think I have it all right about you."

She opens her mouth to respond, but the wind is stolen from her chest as I pick her up and sling her over my shoulder. She only has sense enough to shriek as I quickly make my way to the deeper end of the pool, a devilish smile on my lips. Then, sliding her body down to face mine, chest to chest, I scoop her up and toss her like a rag doll. She screams, arms flailing, red hair whipping water around like a sprinkler. Then, shoulders shaking, I let out a roar of laughter that surprises even me.

"What the hell? Oh, you are *so* dead!" she shouts, brushing her drenched locks from her eyes and mouth. Once she can see, she tries to wade over to catch me, and I quickly move away, still laughing hysterically. We're in a slow-motion ballet, running in liquid quicksand, trying to predict the other's plan of attack. Animated eyes lit with delight, Ally goes right just as I jump out of her path. She jukes left, and I catch her around the waist in a spin move, placing my front to her back. Then my fingers are sliding over her ribs, which are sheathed only in thin, wet cotton.

So many opportunities. So many alternatives. But I go with Option A. The only option that I truly deserve to have.

I tickle her.

I tickle Ally until she begs for mercy, until tears sprout at her eyes and her voice grows hoarse. I tickle her just to hear the sound of her laughter and the endearing little snorting sounds she makes between gulps of air.

I tickle her just have her in my arms.

"No fair! You're a much better swimmer than me! Off me, Ryan Lochte! Or I'll pull down your banana hammock!"

"Do you surrender?" I ask, going for the ticklish spot under her arms. She screams and thrashes like a beautiful, wounded animal.

"Never!"

"Fine by me." I really let her have it, and she throws her head back on my shoulder in hysterical exhaustion. "Give it up, Ally. I win! Just admit defeat, and I'll stop!"

"No! I'll just pee down your leg!"

I shake my head at her crudeness and move down to tickle her stomach. I'm a sick puppy. The prospect of this girl pissing on me from laughing so hard isn't totally revolting. It's funny as hell.

"Okay, okay! Not there! I give up! Uncle!" she screeches. We're both out of breath and panting. A sheen of sweat covers my forehead.

"Ah, so you're the most ticklish on your stomach. That's your kryptonite."

"Don't you dare tell anyone. Or use it against me!"

I've stopped tickling her, but I haven't let her go. She looks down, and I know what she sees: my arms wrapped tightly around her torso. I release her and take a step back.

"You're scary when you're mad." She turns around and a soft, thoughtful smile kisses her lips. "Well, when you're pretending to be mad."

I run a hand through my wet hair, sending droplets flying. "Yeah. My mom made me take drama one semester in high school. She always wanted me to be a movie star. Said I had *the look*."

"Well . . . she was onto something."

There she goes again. Subtly complimenting me and making me blush like a prepubescent fangirl. I hate it. *I love it*. I don't know what to make of it. I'm embarrassed by my reaction to her. Hell, I'm embarrassed by my mental ramblings.

I look away toward the edge of the pool, just to give my brain something else to focus on. "Well, we should probably get out and dry off. I was serious before. I don't want you getting sick."

"Fine, fine." She sighs. "You're lucky I'm too cold to feel my toes. I was about to kick your ass."

We climb out of the pool, and the cold night air instantly covers us like a frozen Snuggi. Ally shivers, and her teeth chatter violently. I jog over to the lounge chairs where I left her sweater, and drape it over her shoulders. But somehow, as I smooth the fabric over her freezing, wet skin, she curls into my chest and under my arm, burying her face just a breath away from my nipple. I awkwardly freeze where I stand, arm still jutted out to the side to avoid holding her close. To avoid what instinct and emotion are begging me to do. Fuck.

"Oh . . . God . . . so . . . cold." Tremors rack her small frame, and I reluctantly let my arm surround her to keep her upright. She's cold, yet something about her is inexplicably warm.

"Come on. Let's get in the house."

Now, a rational, mature man would've ushered her into the main house. It's closer, and that's where all her dry clothes are. She's cold, and warmth and comfort are only a few feet away. But the rational, mature part of me was deprived of precious oxygen and blood flow the moment I felt her soft, porcelain skin against mine, and her warm breath tickling my chest.

That's why I took the extra steps to my house, away from prying eyes and the prospect of saying good night. I wasn't done with her yet. I couldn't have her, yet I still wasn't done.

"Here, let me get you some towels." I release her from my arms and power walk to the linen closet to get fresh towels. I even grab a soft, flannel throw. When I return, Ally is standing in the kitchen, still shivering. I wrap her with two giant, oversize towels and put the throw around her, winding it around her body and creating the cutest, sexiest burrito.

Lame.

I wipe the water from my body with my own towel, then put on a kettle for tea. Then I excuse myself to change. As

I'm slipping on my sweatpants, I spy some old sweats that have grown too small, stuffed in the back of my closet. What the hell . . . what else do I have to lose?

"I brought you some dry clothes," I say, reentering the kitchen. Ally's managed to unravel herself enough to sit on a stool at the breakfast bar. "Just some old, ratty sweats I can't fit in. You don't have to wear them if you don't—"

"Thanks!" she says, jumping down off her stool and snatching the clothes. "Your bathroom . . . ?"

"Down the hall, two doors to the left."

I'm pouring tea into mugs when she reemerges, drowning in gray sweats that are three sizes too big for her. She's adorable. I turn away and place the cups on a tray before bringing them to the kitchen island.

"Thanks. You went to Triton Prep?"

I look over at the prep school emblem that she's staring at on the sweatshirt. "Briefly."

"Oh. That's where Evan graduated from. Did you know him?"

I drop a couple sugar cubes in my tea, keeping my eyes set on the tray full of mugs, sugar cookies, and madeleines. "I was only there for a year."

"Oh? What happened?"

I shrug. "Transferred."

"Okay." She busies herself, sipping her tea and nibbling a cookie. "I went to St. Mary's in Boston. But I'm sure you already knew that." She blushes, then looks down.

"I did."

She lifts her chin and her eyes find mine, burning with curiosity. "Triton is a great school. Probably the best in the country. Your test scores must've been amazing to get in."

I shrug again. Damn these shoulders. "They were all right."

"All right? If my parents hadn't been adamant about raising me outside the city *and* subjecting me to an all-girl hell, I'm sure my father would have been making a generous donation to get me in. Where'd you go after Triton?"

"Denton Academy."

"Oh. That's a good school." She tries to repress her smile, but I can already see it.

Denton isn't Triton.

I'm not Evan.

Just as I'm about to let the comparison worm its way into my head and hatch up a bunch of different reasons why I'll never be deserving of someone like her, Ally's face lights up, setting those cerulean eyes aflame. "Consider it a compliment. I've determined that the prerequisite for acceptance at Triton is that you must be at least one-third pretentious douche-nozzle. I think we've established the fact that this term does not apply to you. At least not one-third."

"Douche-nozzle?" I ask, raising a playful brow. "Are you sure you graduated from Columbia? Because I'm pretty sure that's not a word."

"Yup. With honors, buddy. And I would gladly explain the elements of a douche-nozzle, but I wouldn't want you to toss your cookies. No pun intended." She giggles, obviously pleased with herself.

I put down my mug and turn toward the refrigerator. "Well, lucky for me, I've got ice cream."

Ally makes a noise that quite frankly sounds like a mix between a squealing pig and a drowning cat. Either way, it makes me laugh, and I turn to gaze at her with wonder.

What is it about her? What makes every little quirk, every idiosyncrasy that would usually annoy the fuck out of me, seem so goddamn adorable? I laugh like an idiot when she's around. I worry about hurting her feelings or being too gruff. Hell, I've been eating ice cream like a hormonal chick with PMS! I just don't *get* it. What's next? Watching the newest Nicholas Sparks flick and drying each other's tears?

"You're not too cold for this, are you?"

Ally shakes her head vehemently. "Hell no. I could be in Antarctica, floating on an iceberg while ice-skating with a family of penguins, and I'd still want it."

I grab the pint and two spoons, handing her one. She digs in, and I quickly follow.

Ally scoops up a heaping spoonful and extends it toward me. "Cheers." We clink our spoons and devour that first creamy, cold bite of mint chocolate chip with identical *mmms*.

"So . . . if you had to give up one, would you rather sacrifice your sight or your hearing?" she asks, digging in for more ice cream.

"That's an easy one. Hearing. I'd definitely give up my hearing if I had to."

"Explain your case, sir."

"Well, for one, you can still communicate even if you're deaf. You can sign or read lips. And let's face it—we live in an age of excessive technology. I could just text or Instagram you."

"Yeah, but you'd never hear music. You'd never get to hear a child's laughter or the sound of someone saying 'I love you.' You'd miss out on so much."

I look at her, seeing her. Trying to make her see me. "But to not be able to see a pink sunset fade to purple or a million stars in the sky, stretching to eternity . . . you can't manufacture that. Technology can't create a smile so bright that it makes you smile even when you don't want to. It can't manipulate true beauty. It can try, but it'll never duplicate that exact shade of red, fiery hair. Or the pattern of cinnamon freckles on your nose. Or even the way your eyes change from blue to green like a mood ring. You can't forge what has been perfectly designed. That kind of beauty doesn't require sound or words or even music. It doesn't need anything else. Anything more and it would overwhelm you."

She doesn't speak, and neither do I. I've said enough. I've said too much.

Eventually we resume eating, confusion heavy in the air. I know she's wondering where that little speech came from—hell, even I'm not sure—but one thing is clear.

I've crossed a line. And whatever this thing between us is or was . . . I've tainted it with truth.

"Crap, it's late," she finally says, breaking the uncomfortable silence. She looks at me and raises a brow. "Save the rest for later?"

"Sure." I nod, wondering if there'll ever be a later.

I give her a bag to store her wet clothing and walk her to the door. She turns just before she crosses the threshold. "By the way, I would've picked hearing too."

She walks away, leaving me with her smile. She doesn't say good-bye. Maybe part of her never really left.

Sensation

Today on E! . . . Breaking news on playboy prince Evan Carr as a sex tape surfaces, starring the prince himself and an unknown woman. The video was leaked online just last night and has spread like wildfire, garnering nearly five hundred thousand hits in the last twelve hours. The mystery woman in the video is still unidentified, though it's evident that it is not Allison Elliot-Carr, Evan's wife of nearly five years. The pair has had a very public relationship, including rumors of infidelity on Evan's part. Neither Evan nor Allison was available for comment, yet sources close to the couple say that Allison has been absent from their Manhattan home for some time. Could this finally be the beginning of the end for the Upper East Side royal couple? Stay tuned for more on E!

Shit.

Shit shit shit.

I pull out my phone to dial, but it's already ringing.

"You hear the news?"

No preamble. Just straight to the point. That's my publicist, Heidi. I'm not surprised she's already on it. I pay her a small fortune to ensure that stories like these don't explode into full-on shit shows. As long as things stay somewhat quiet on the outside, I can do my job on the inside. But the moment things begin to fall apart in their absence, we run the risk of the wives catching wind and leaving. And exposing my identity. You see, Heidi also helps to maintain my anonymity. No one actually sees me until Day One, and they're required to sign NDAs to safeguard against exposure.

"Yeah." I nearly groan into the receiver. Yeah, it's a hassle to keep the lid on stories this public, but the fact that it's happening to Allison . . . shit. Shit shit shit.

"How do you want to proceed?" Heidi asks.

Under normal circumstances, a story like this would blow away in the wind as soon as a Kardashian sneezed, but the Carrs are prime real estate for gossip rags. And with a bastard like Evan dipping his dick into a different chick every other week, they feed the press like a smut-news soup kitchen.

"Contact his PR, but stay mum. We don't want the media to smell blood and we damn sure don't want Allison getting hurt in this."

"Allison?" I can hear the amusement in Heidi's question. She's as sharp as a tack and knows I never refer to clients so intimately. She's a shark, just like me. And sharks don't get comfortable. They don't slip up.

"Mrs. Carr. You know who the fuck I mean," I reply sternly. I'm still a shark. Regardless of how guppy-fied Allison makes me feel, I'm a shark, goddammit.

"Fine. You know this wouldn't be an issue if you would just listen to me sometimes. How many times have I told you—"

I press end.

I don't need this right now. Allison doesn't need this right now. And the fact that I'm aware of the demise of her marriage while she's been hanging out, eating ice cream with me, makes me feel kinda guilty. Yet not guilty enough to want to stop.

I dress for the day and head to the main house, more determined than ever to make everything right for her. To make her into the picture of erotic perfection so she will never have to face this kind of pain and humiliation again.

To transform her into the whore that Evan wants.

It's not fair to her—hell, it's not fair to me—but he won't stop. He'll never change his philandering ways. It's all he knows, all he's ever seen. And Allison, as smart and funny and fucking amazing as she is, will never leave him.

Welcome to the *real* game of Life, where we're all players, but no one ever truly wins.

The moment Allison enters the room and walks to her seat, I'm moving toward her. I grasp her shoulders and pull her into me, causing her to gasp with surprise. Those wide, sparkling eyes search my face for a motive for my sudden erratic behavior. I look back at her, searching for the same thing.

"Ally . . ." I swallow, suddenly nervous to utter the next words. Not because they're any more shocking than what I've said in the past. But because they're probably the truest, realest thing I'll ever let myself admit. "Ally, I need to touch you. And I need you to touch me too."

She doesn't answer, but her body, so soft and breakable in my firm grip, quivers with compliance. I let my hands slide from her shoulders and move down to her hands, where I lace my fingers with hers. Then I pull her to the front of the room without breaking my penetrating gaze. She doesn't resist me. Her feet move one in front of the other, matching my footsteps in a synchronized dance. She wants this. And maybe, on some level, she wants me.

My voice is loud and clear, but I speak only to her. "The act of lovemaking, of sex, is a feast for the senses. It isn't about just feeling, it's about seeing your lover writhing in ecstasy. Hearing her moan your name. Smelling her rich, musky arousal." I lick my lips in anticipation of my next words. "Tasting her on your tongue."

Allison's lips part, but no sound escapes. Her eyes linger on my mouth for just a beat, then flicker down to our locked hands. I'm hyperaware of what she and everyone else sees, and I force myself to pull away. I turn her body to face the class.

"I'm going to show you how to feel your partners with

your whole self. To explore the power of sensation and drive them wild before you even open your legs," I announce, my voice raw and almost choked with self-inflicted torment. "Pair up; it's time you got to know your housemates a little better."

I brush Allison's scarlet hair to one side and lean down to place my lips at her ear. "You're with me, sweetheart."

SOFT, SENSUAL MUSIC plays in the background. Every light is dimmed to a muted glow. And the women . . . blindfolded. Everyone is, aside from me.

"Start at the nape of her neck, slide just the very tips of your fingers to her shoulders. Yeah, that's right. Just like that, ladies. Now take turns trailing them up and down her arms to the inside of her palms. Slowly. Go slow. Remember: it's about the journey. Good. Now slowly move your fingertips to the top of her chest. Slide them down to the sides of her breasts. Yeah, right there."

They do as they're told, relying only on the sound of my voice and their heightened senses to guide them. I hear the ladies pant and gasp at the newfound sensation as they explore each other's bodies, but I can only see the one in front of me. The one that captured my attention the moment she walked into my life and set fire to my desert oasis.

My fingers stroke the bare skin at the hollow of her throat before sliding down to the tops of her breasts. I want to touch her so badly. I ache to let my hands keep going down this slippery slope to the hard, pebbled nipples that strain against her green silk blouse. She sucks in a breath, causing her chest to rise, and I swear she extends her breasts to me, aching for me just as I am for her.

"Lean in, ladies. Let her scent surround you. Don't be afraid to use all your senses. Tell her how good she feels in your hands. How sexy you feel touching her."

They all comply. I knew they would. We're going into Week Three, and the women are dying for physical contact. See, believe it or not, women are the more sexually uninhibited gender. While men are more vocal about their desires and get hard if a strong breeze whips through their legs, women can be aroused by almost anything. Gay porn, dirty talk, a gentle caress, a simple smoldering look . . . it all works to get them hot. As long as a woman is mentally open, so are her legs. But that's a different lesson entirely. To teach all the ways to attract and seduce a woman would take longer than six weeks. Hell, I'd need six months.

"Do you feel that? The way her heartbeat stutters when you graze her breasts? How humid her skin grows when you rake your fingers across it? That's arousal. She's hot for you. Congratulations. You've made a straight, married woman yearn for your touch."

I'm not ignorant of the fact that I'm just reciting Allison's reactions to *me*. There's so much more I could do to her, so many more ways I want to feel her squirm in my capable hands. I want to get closer, but I won't. And with my dick, hard and throbbing, begging to break free, I can't. So for now, I'll take this. It may be the only chance I get.

I step forward an inch so that our bodies just barely touch, our heat creating an undeniable friction that makes our skin pulse with electricity. Then I take her trembling hands and place them on my chest, stifling a groan.

"Your turn, Ally," I whisper only for her ears. "Touch me."

She sucks in a breath and bites her quivering lip. "How?"

My voice is low and raspy, wavering with my restraint. "Just like I touched you. Exactly how you want to be touched."

I watch as she takes a few breaths to steel her nerves. Then slowly, torturously, as if she wants to strip away every bit of self-control I have, she slides her delicate hands up to my shoulders, kneading the hard muscle sheathed in a white linen shirt. It's amazing how she can make such an innocent touch feel so dirty and sexual. It feels like she's undressing me, exposing me. Corrupting me.

"More," I rasp. My breath comes out in ragged pants, and my skin is on fire. Allison moves her hands down my arms until her fingers stroke the inside of my palms. Then she's touching my waist, my stomach. Her nails rake over the hard ridges of my abs, taking the time to feel each and every mound of muscle. I hold my breath, afraid that she'll continue her journey down south. I'm not ashamed of my body's reaction to hers, but I know nothing good will come of her feeling my hardness in her hands. And chances are, she wouldn't even know what to do with it.

"Talk to me. Tell me what you feel."

Allison swallows and her mouth parts. I watch as her pink

tongue darts out just enough to wet her lips. "You're so . . . hard," she whispers. If I hadn't been so focused on the sight of her tongue sliding over her lips, I wouldn't even have understood her.

"What else?"

"Um . . . uh. You're warm. Hot. You feel so strong under my hands. Like, I can feel every muscle."

"Keep going, Ally." It's meant to be a command, but my voice sounds like I'm pleading.

"And, um. So big. You make me feel small. And breakable. But I feel safe too, like your whole body could cover mine without crushing me." Her cheeks heat and bloom deep red. "It's stupid. I feel like an idiot saying this to you."

She goes to take off her blindfold and I stop her, placing her hands on my chest. "No, don't stop. It's not stupid."

A smile curves her pink, glossed lips, and she steps into me. Close enough for her nipples to brush the top of my stomach. Close enough for her to feel my erection nudging her.

She gasps, yet doesn't step away. I grin sardonically.

"Go on, Ally," I say, stepping even closer, letting her feel just what she's doing to me. Showing her that while I may make her feel small and meek, *she* has the power.

She inhales before sucking her bottom lip into her mouth seductively. Just like I taught her. "You smell so good. Like male and raw sex. Like sunshine and rainwater."

"Yeah? And what does that make you feel?"

"Hot." Her head lowers, but not before I see the red in her cheeks deepen even more. "And horny."

A flash of movement or light, or maybe even a voice, catches my attention, and I look up to find ten sets of uncovered eyes trained on us, each set displaying varying degrees of shock and outrage. My mouth goes dry, and I feel the blood drain from my face. I step away, yet not so fast that they could misconstrue my retreat as a sign of guilt.

"You all did a wonderful job. And I'd like to thank Mrs. Carr for being a good sport and trying some of our more advanced techniques." Without moving her body too much and revealing my massive hard-on to the rest of the class, I turn Ally around and remove her blindfold, keeping my hands chastely on her shoulders. She stays put, pressing her back and ass against my throbbing dick. I bite the inside of my cheek to keep from groaning.

"Let's break for an early lunch, shall we?"

We wait until the rest of the class files out, then Ally turns back to face me. Her cheeks are still pink, and even her hair looks disheveled, like she's been freshly fucked.

"Your mom was right," she says, looking up at me with glassy eyes.

"My mom?" I frown.

"You should've been a movie star. You're a damn good actor."

I raise a brow. "Maybe I should be telling you that."

Allison shakes her head and laughs nervously, looking down at her feet. "No. I can't act. Not even a little bit."

I pull her chin up, refusing to let her hide from me. "Then what was that?"

She shakes her head, her chin still secured between my fingers. Tears fill those wide eyes, and her lip trembles. "I don't know. I don't know what that was. I don't know anything."

Suddenly the need to possess her body is a distant memory. Seeing her so shattered because of me, because of this . . . thing, this undefined attraction that has her as fucked up in the head as I am, makes me realize just how careless I've been with her delicate emotions. She's been hurt, and somehow, in some way that I don't seem to understand, I'm hurting her too. I can see it, right in those sad eyes filled with tiny, drowning stars.

"Come here," I say, wrapping my arms around her. She buries her face into my chest for just a moment before she realizes what she's doing.

"No. No, I can't do this. Excuse me . . . I'm sorry." And with confused tears sliding down her porcelain face and a trail of fire at her back, the angel runs away from this lonely hell designed especially for me.

Stimulation

Days pass. Maybe a week.

It's all the same. Work. Swim. Sometimes I drink. Seldom I eat. Either way, nothing changes. Allison doesn't come at night. She hardly even looks at me. I feel like I've stained her, violated her in some way. Tainted her with wicked temptation. And for once, I'm relieved.

I couldn't stay away from her, and she wasn't put off enough by me to keep her distance. So maybe this was necessary. Maybe her physically seeing what I was capable of was just what she needed to permanently close whatever space she had left open for me in her life. Now she can remove the placeholder. I'm no longer on the guest list.

That's a good thing. That's what's best.

Still . . . it's shitty.

Feeling like I had some sort of connection with someone, even platonically, was something I hadn't experienced in years. Meeting Allison was like seeing a sunrise after being trapped in a dull, gray room with no windows. It was that first bite of ice cream on a treacherously hot summer's day. Without her, all is drab. Muted. Tasteless.

Lonely.

But I'm not complaining. The brooding, lonely role is one I play well. I'm an island, and I like to keep it that way.

That's why I couldn't figure out why the usual excitement surrounding this particular day just wasn't there. This had always been one of my favorites. The housewives would be particularly uncomfortable. The day's event tested each one of their boundaries and made them reevaluate their own desires. Seeing them like that—cheeks stained with embarrassment, mouths slack, squirming in their seats with arousal—was like living art to me. That raw emotion was what I lived for.

Yet now I feel indifferent about it, maybe even a little sad. Like doing this will be the proverbial nail in the coffin for Ally and me.

Ally and me.

Hmph. I can't even say that with a straight face.

I watch intently as they all file in, glancing hesitantly at the mechanism that sits in the middle of the room. A few whisper in curious speculation, others in excited anticipation. They can tell shit is about to go down, and who am I to disappoint?

"Good morning, ladies. Today we have a special guest joining us."

I nod toward the back of the room, and every head turns as a slender brunette in a red silk robe makes her way forward. I hold my hand out to help her onto the medical-style examination chair. "This is Erin. Erin has been with us for the past few years and is currently a medical student. She will also be helping us out today."

My voice drops to a husky baritone as if I'm letting them in on a naughty secret. "In order to give pleasure, you need to understand how to receive it. It's time we became intimate with the female body. With *your* bodies. Erin?"

On cue, Erin lets her robe fall open, exposing her naked frame. Pert, round breasts sit up without a hint of sag above a flat, flawless belly. Without hesitation, she spreads her legs and places her heels into the extended stirrups, revealing a bare, pink pussy. Hushed shrieks of surprise echo throughout the room, but Erin hears none of it. She's used to the reaction by now. And with me pretty much paying her way through med school while she works only four days a year, she could care less about a few judgmental hens who haven't clucked since before Miley Cyrus actually owned clothes and developed brain cells.

"Look familiar, ladies?" I ask, grinning evilly. "No? Probably because you've neglected your body, thus denying yourself the opportunity to learn about it. How can you expect your mate to fuck you right if you're not doing it yourself? No one knows what stimulates you better than you do.

"So, since I don't have the plumbing required to show you the ins and outs, so to speak, Erin will help me. First, let's start with the nipples."

Again, on cue, Erin palms the underside of her breasts, pinching her erect nipples between her thumbs and index fingers. Shocked murmurs resound around the room, which she answers by pinching her swollen buds and grinning.

"Your nipples are the most obvious pleasure points not located in the female genitalia. However, they are commonly neglected. Who likes their nipples stimulated?"

No one answers at first, but a hand eventually goes up. Lacey Rose, rocker wife and former sex kitten. Several more follow. I make it a point not to look in Ally's direction. Knowing that about her, knowing I could bring her to orgasm just by teasing her strawberry nipples, would drive me insane. Ignorance is bliss. And at least in my case, ignorance is necessary.

I focus my attention back on Erin, who smiles up at me. "Okay, good. Now, who likes to play with their nipples when they're alone?"

Fewer hands this time, but a couple women actually fess up.

"Excellent. Our friend Erin is going to demonstrate all the ways you can get off by nipple stimulation alone. Erin?"

The busty young brunette begins to pinch and knead her tan-tipped nipples, rolling them with her skilled fingers. She throws her head back in a moan and bites her bottom lip with practiced seductiveness. Then she brings her fingers up to her mouth, licking the digits before returning them to her swollen breasts. Even with her feet in the stirrups, she tries to close her legs in hopes of creating friction on her neglected pussy. I watch intently, fascinated by the way her sensitive pink flesh quivers with need. Erin looks back at me, her eyes begging me to touch her and put her out of her misery.

Aside from the creak of their chairs as they squirm, everyone is silent while they watch Erin stroke and caress herself. A few even unconsciously clutch their chests, starving to be touched.

Just as Erin is on the brink of bringing herself to orgasm, I gently tap the inside of her thigh, letting my hand linger on her flesh. She places her hands to rest at her sides, perfectly poised, save for her ragged breaths. "Very good. Now what can you tell me about what Erin just showed us?"

After a beat, a hand goes up. Lorinda Cosgrove, the dark-haired wallflower who is slowly blooming into an exotic tiger lily. "Um, when she pinched them . . . she moaned loudly?"

"Good, Mrs. Cosgrove. What else?"

Lacey speaks up. "And when she licked her fingers and wet her nipples, her back arched."

"Rolling them between her fingers made her knees shake," says another housewife.

"All great observations. What else?"

"When she watched you watching her, it made her hotter. She wanted you to touch her. You could see it in her eyes."

I freeze, forcing myself not to look in the direction of the voice. I was so close. So close to getting through this day without actually thinking about her. So close to not feeling like I was doing something wrong. But now that unwarranted guilt is creeping back, filling my head with illusions of morality. Making me think twice about my next move.

"Uh, that was . . ." I stammer. Shit. *Focus, Drake. Business before bullshit.* "So . . . right. Moving on. Next, Erin will demonstrate some of the more well-known erogenous zones, starting with the clitoris. Watch closely; watch the movements of her fingers. Note which areas are the most sensitive."

Without my prompting, Erin lets her hands travel down past her belly and between her thighs. First, she parts her sex, giving the women an in-depth view of her most intimate area. Then, with her other hand, she strokes her clit, moaning out her pleasure before applying more pressure.

My hand still on the inside of her thigh, I part Erin's legs wider, letting the women see every tight, wet part of her. "I get that most of you have had children and are not as young as Erin," I say over her fevered mewling. "But this is the type of pussy you all should aspire to have. Your job is not just to birth children and run a household. You are required to stay freshly waxed and groomed at all times. Your pussy should be pink and soft. If it's not, there are procedures to get it that way again. *This* is what your husbands want to see when you open your legs. No one wants to fuck Chewbacca. Groom your pussy as if you're Sharon Stone's crotch-shot stunt double."

Erin resumes massaging her clit, tracing circles around that swollen, throbbing button. Then she switches it up with rapid side-to-side movements before lightly slapping the emblazoned flesh, crying out with her climax. She looks up at me again with those needy eyes, shaking with the aftershocks of orgasm. I know what she was thinking about when she touched herself. I know she wishes it were my hands stimulating her silken skin.

I turn my eyes away, acting as if I'm engrossed in her quivering sex. "Clitoral stimulation can provide one of the most powerful orgasms you'll ever feel. And for many women, that's the only climax they've ever experienced. But there's one type of orgasm that, unfortunately, very few women have had the pleasure of experiencing. Of course, I am referring to the G-spot orgasm. Now, ladies . . . it's not the lost continent of Atlantis. There's no special code you need to crack this particular nut. Just patience and practice. And if you can find it, you'll be able to lead your lover to it."

I give Erin's leg a tap and she complies with my unspoken command, moving a hand only a few centimeters lower and dipping just the tip of her finger inside her pussy. She rubs the dripping-wet digit on her swollen clit before easing it inside herself again, this time sinking in knuckle-deep. She gasps at the intrusion, letting her muscles contract around her slender finger before easing it out a bit. Then she plunges back in, creating a slow, sinful rhythm.

"That's right, sweetheart. Slow and deep," I croon, massaging her thigh. "Add another finger. Fill yourself."

Erin does as I command, picking up speed with the addition of the second finger. I can hear the sucking sounds of her tightness, begging for more.

"Now curl your fingers up, baby. You feel that? You feel how it's throbbing for you? Begging for you? Milk it, baby. Milk that orgasm and come all over your fingers for me."

With a strangled cry, Erin lets go, and a rush of sweet nectar flows from her contracting pussy. Still massaging her thigh, I coax her down from her erotic high, whispering reassuring words of praise. When I look back at the crowd, every eye is glazed and unblinking, and every face is flushed scarlet.

"I understand that it may be difficult to vocalize our reactions to what we've just seen, so we'll be cutting today's class short. You're all dismissed to your rooms, where a special gift from our friends at Lelo.com awaits you. I want you to explore your own pleasure points. Find out what techniques stimulate you the most. And while you do this, utilize the full-length mirrors stationed in your suites. Watch yourself get off. See what *he* sees when he's pleasuring you."

Without much persuasion, the ladies hastily file out of the room, all silently pondering their homework assignment. Once we're alone, I turn to Erin, my expression burning with intensity.

"My house. *Now.*"

"WHAT THE FUCK was that?"

I pace the floor, trying to reel in my temper. Erin sits cross-legged on my sofa, sheathed only in her robe.

"What was what?"

"Don't play stupid, Erin. You know what you were doing."

She smiles, feigning innocence. "I don't know what you're talking about."

"Bullshit!" I shout, throwing up my hands. "You were giving me the *fuck-me* eyes the entire time. And don't think I didn't catch you moan my name."

She looks down at the floor to hide her forlorn expression. "Nice to see you were paying attention. You make me feel like I'm invisible to you."

I rub the back of my neck in frustration before moving to kneel in front of her. Erin may be confident and fearless, but she's still a woman. She still needs to feel desired. "Of course you're not invisible to me, Erin. I see you. Shit, I was touching you . . . talking to you in ways I shouldn't have been. For a minute, I forgot where I was."

She lifts her eyes and hope floods her face. "You wanted me, didn't you? You wanted to be inside me, right?"

I swallow, pushing down the instinctive yes in my throat. "I'd be fucking crazy not to want you, Erin. You're a beautiful woman. But you know I can't cross that line with you. Not now, not ever."

"But . . . but before we did—"

I shake my head, knowing exactly where this is going. "That was then, Erin. And it will never happen again. I told you that. Now, if you can't handle this arrangement, I can find someone who can."

Tears well up in her eyes and she shakes her head. "No. No, I'm fine. I'm sorry, I just . . ."

I kiss her on the forehead and climb to my feet. "Good girl."

For once, I'm actually not trying to be the villain. I like Erin, but not in the way that she wants. A few years back, I approached her in a Chicago bar; she was down to her last dime, looking for any rich bastard who would buy her a drink and hopefully be her sponsor. Despite being incredibly gorgeous, she reeked of desperation. I had to help her. It was my civic duty to do so before she got caught up with the wrong crowd.

"What's your name, sweetheart?" I asked her, sliding onto the bar stool beside her.

"Amy," she answered, smiling too brightly.

"Amy, huh? What's your real name?"

Her face fell, and she stared at the gin and tonic she had been nursing for the past hour. "Erin."

Without a word, I slid her a business card. No name. No information. Just a phone number. Then I slapped a hundred-dollar bill on the bar and turned and walked away.

Five minutes later, Erin was ringing my cell phone.

"There's a diner on Michigan Avenue," I answered without preamble.

"Which one?" she asked into the receiver.

"Whichever one you find me at." End.

Half an hour later, Erin slid into the booth where I was stationed; she looked flustered and irritated. I picked up my cup of coffee and casually took a sip before sliding her a menu.

"I'm not here to eat," she said, pushing it back toward me.

"Order. You're hungry. And don't lie and say that you're not. What we won't do is lie to each other. Understand?"

Her eyes grew wide, but she didn't argue. She was perfect for me. I knew she would be. I didn't have the time or patience to break in someone who didn't know how to submit.

I sipped my coffee while Erin devoured a large platter of eggs, bacon, sausage, hash browns, and toast. When she had eaten every morsel, I decided it was time to get down to business.

"Tell me your story."

Without much coaxing, Erin revealed that she was a first-year med student with no family and no means to support herself. She had lost her tiny, ramshackle apartment, and her small scholarship didn't cover much beyond the first year, let alone housing. She was stuck—either drop out and go back home to Idaho, or find other, less appealing ways to support herself. That day, she had decided that maybe her dreams of becoming a doctor just weren't going to come true.

"I have a proposition for you," I told her.

"I'm not a prostitute," she quickly interjected.

I smiled at her amusingly. "I would certainly hope not."

I showed her my hand, explaining to her what I wanted and how I would compensate her for doing it. There, in a small diner in downtown Chicago, I asked about her sexual history (two guys: an old boyfriend from Idaho and a one-hit wonder in college), her level of inhibition (she considered herself a "try-sexual": she'd try anything once), and her health background (squeaky clean: no glove, no love), all of which I had hardcopy proof of already. Then I paid the tab and took her back to my hotel room to sign all the necessary documents and begin the first phase of her training.

"Now, sweetheart, I need to know how far you'll go. You're not obligated to do anything you don't want to do, but there are places where I will touch you that will arouse you. That will arouse *me*. And I will want to fuck you. Hell, I want to fuck you right now."

She sat on the bed, long, smooth legs crossed and eyes hooded. "I want that too."

I touched her in places she never even knew were erogenous zones. I kissed her tight body until my lips burned. Then I fucked her long, deep, and hard until she soaked the sheets with her wetness.

As she looked at me lazily, her vision shrouded in afterglow, she smiled with delirious delight. "Oh my God. I don't even know your name."

I looked up at the ceiling, avoiding her tender gaze. "I'm Justice Drake."

"Mmm, Justice Drake. I like that."

I could already hear her trying out the name preluded by a *Mrs.* I shut it down quick.

"Yes. And that was for pleasure. However, anytime I touch you from here on out will be strictly business. Understand?"

Without so much as a kiss on the cheek, I left Erin alone in that hotel suite, sore and satisfied, with a few bills and instructions for the following week.

Illusion

I knew I should've sent Erin on her merry way the moment she started in with the waterworks. But truth be told, I'm not a complete bastard. I just sometimes like to let my inner asshole shine. He's much better at evading social niceties than I am.

So I let her dry her tears and even made her a cup of tea. Then I insisted that she pack up those perky tits and get on the first thing smokin' back to Chicago. But as luck would have it, I was quite possibly a day late and a dollar short.

"Call me when you land at O'Hare," I say, opening the front door for her to exit. I had been throwing hints all evening, and was about to resort to air-traffic control signals.

"Okay. Thanks again, Justice. You're always so good to me. I'd be lost without you." She stretches on her tiptoes and kisses me on the corner of my mouth. I'm just about to chastise her for crossing the boundaries, when all coherent thought and sense of speech are stolen from me.

Standing at my door, fire licking her shoulders in the cool, early autumn breeze, is Allison, her hand still raised as if she were preparing to knock.

"Ally . . . uh . . . hey." See, this is the part where the cheating husband shrieks out, *"It's not what it looks like! I can explain!"* while his pants are around his ankles and his dick is still rock hard.

But I'm not anyone's husband. And I can't cheat on someone that isn't mine. So . . . why do I feel like I've done something wrong?

"Oh, my apologies." She smiles tightly, stifling her discomfort. "I wasn't aware you had company. I'll come back later, Mr. Drake."

"No, no. Erin was just leaving," I tell her, holding the door open wider and nearly shoving Erin out of the way. "Please, come in."

"That's not necessary. I should've made other arrangements. I'm terribly sorry."

Allison turns to walk away, and I catch her elbow before she can take another step. She turns to me, animated eyes reduced to questioning slits, but she doesn't pull away. Fuck it. I'm screwed anyway. "Stay. Please. Stay, Ally."

She nods slowly, her gaze never leaving mine. I hear the muted rustle of silk and an irritated huff beside me. Dammit. Erin.

"So . . . I guess I'll leave now." She brushes past us brusquely, and makes a beeline for the main house to collect her things.

"Let me know you got in safely," I call out after her.

"Yeah, yeah." She waves without looking back. I know I should go after her and at least attempt to smooth things over before her wild imagination begins to cook up all kinds of rumor-inducing theories, but what would I say? And how could I even force myself to walk away, now that I hold this precious angel in the palm of my hand?

Erin will have to wait. Logic, morals, obligations will all have to wait.

"Come in," I murmur, holding my breath as Ally crosses the threshold. She follows me to the kitchen, where I retrieve our half-eaten carton of ice cream and two spoons.

"I can't stay. It's just . . . I, uh . . . ran into a problem with your homework assignment."

I bite my bottom lip hard to keep from chuckling. "Oh? Need a hand?" I turn just in time to see Ally's icy-cold glare. She shakes her head.

"See . . . coming to see you was a mistake."

"No, no, I'm sorry. Tell me about it. I sincerely want to help." I open the carton of mint chocolate chip and scoop up a serving, handing it to her. Ally pauses, contemplating her next move, before eventually exhaling her frustration and accepting the cold, creamy peace offering.

"It's nothing . . . I don't think." She eases the spoon into her mouth and hums her approval, letting her eyelids close in ecstasy. She slides onto a bar stool before sinking her spoon in for another bite. "It's just . . . okay, don't laugh. Promise?"

"Cross my heart and hope to die," I respond around a mouthful of sweet, frozen deliciousness.

"Okay, here goes . . . How do you know if you had an orgasm?" she almost whispers.

I frown. "What do you mean, *how do you know?*"

"I mean, how can you tell? Like, I'm not sure if or how I've . . . you know. And I've never . . . by myself . . . Oh God, this is too embarrassing!" She shoves the spoon into the carton and covers her face with both hands.

"Ally . . ." I stow my own spoon and place a comforting hand on her shoulder. Just an innocent shoulder. Nothing to see here, folks.

"I'm mortified! This was such a mistake!"

"It's not. That's what I'm here for. You can ask me anything, you hear me? Anything."

Slowly, she removes her hands from her face yet keeps her eyes trained on the countertop. "I swear, I'm not this clueless. It's just . . . there's only been Evan and we've never talked about whether or not I've . . . you know. So I'm not sure if it's happened, or if it did, what kind."

I nod, understanding what she's saying and suppressing the instinct to wrap her up in my arms and kiss her senseless. Her naïveté is incredibly inspiring. Oh, the things I could do . . .

"Well, Ally. If you have to wonder if you've ever had an orgasm, then chances are, you haven't."

Her eyes double in size. "Really?"

"Really."

"Are they that good? Like, will I be able to distinguish them from just regular sex?"

I grin, hoping that it comes off as more reassuring than mocking. "Think of the act of sex as a slow burn. There are highs and lows, of course. Some areas burn hotter than others. But for the most part, it just kindles until it's eventually extinguished.

"Now, achieving orgasm . . . imagine that burn building into a flame. And that flame growing into a wildfire. And that wildfire combusting into a fireworks display on the Fourth of July. Dozens of magnificent colors bursting, popping, sizzling. Lighting up the night sky with blinding brilliance. You can tell the difference between that slow, steady burn and fireworks, right?"

Ally picks up her spoon and digs around in the ice cream carton, avoiding eye contact. "Yes, of course."

"Then you know whether or not you've achieved orgasm." I pick up my spoon from the pint and lick the ice cream remnants before pointing it toward her. "So tell me, Ally . . . Did Evan ever make you feel fireworks?"

She's quiet for a few beats, so I know I've crossed the line. But instead of slapping me across the face soap-opera style or hightailing it out of my house, she laughs. She laughs that carefree belly laugh that illuminates the darkness of my lonely heart. The kind that is usually accompanied by a snort and/or tears at the tiny crinkles around her eyes. The kind of laugh that makes me laugh too, for no damn reason at all.

"No." She shakes her head, still laughing. "No, Evan never made me feel fireworks. Oh my God, how pathetic am I? Twenty-seven years old and I've never had an orgasm!" Hilarity overcomes her once more, and she slaps the countertop.

"Ally . . ." I say, catching my breath. "Ally, that doesn't make you pathetic at all. It makes him pathetic. He has perfection at his fingertips, yet he can't get you off? You were pure and untouched when you met him. Untainted. You gave him a beautiful gift. The least he could've done was make you come properly."

That gets her attention, and all signs of humor are erased from her expression. "I guess you're right. But it was just never a high priority to Evan." Her face falls, sadness creeping onto her delicate, porcelain features. "*I* was never a high priority."

I want to touch her so badly. I want to pull her chin up so she can see me . . . so she can feel the conviction in my next words. "Then why on earth would you want to be with someone who only makes you an option? When you clearly have made *him* your top priority?"

Her eyes meet mine, unmasked pain and confusion so evident in those cyan orbs. "Justice . . . don't—"

"I mean, why would you put up with that when you know you deserve so much better?"

She shakes her head. "I don't know. I mean, do I really deserve better? *Is* there better than this? We grow up seeing the leaders of our nation being cheaters and liars. We hear about deception destroying marriages every day. What's the alternative? Loneliness?"

No. Me. I'm *the alternative.*

But that would be a lie, wouldn't it? That would make me just as bad as Evan and every other piece of shit that's ever hurt a woman.

"Happiness," I say instead. "Friendship. Freedom."

"Ha, freedom," she half snorts. "Is there such a thing for us? When our lives are exploited for must-see TV?"

"Mine isn't," I state matter-of-factly.

"Yeah, that's because you didn't grow up as an Upper East Side sock puppet. You got to have a real childhood, with parents who didn't leave you to be raised by nannies and friends that actually liked you for you, and not for who you could introduce them to."

"Don't be so sure," I murmur, rolling my eyes.

"Oh yeah? Then how did you escape the madness? How did you avoid the paparazzi and fakeness and disillusions of grandeur?"

"Circumstance."

We both shrug and go back to raking our spoons over ribbons of mint and chocolate. I don't want to explain, and she doesn't want to hear an explanation. We're both comfortable in this illusion of safety and normalcy where spying cameras and incriminating tabloids don't exist.

"Okay, if you were on a first date with a woman, would you be more impressed if she ordered a salad or a big, juicy burger?"

I raise an amused brow at her unpredictability. "Huh?"

"Salad or burger? Which girl is gonna get the goods?" she says before plopping a dollop of ice cream on her tongue. I watch with rapt fascination as she licks the spoon clean, too absorbed to even attempt to answer her question. Ally catches my gaze and puts the spoon down, a mischievous smile twitching her lips. "Focus, Drake. Answer the question or I'll be forced to steal your ice cream stash and eat it all, locked up in my room alone."

I snap out of my trance and give her a half shrug. "What do you expect? I'm only human."

"Your sudden attack of ADD has nothing to do with being human and everything to do with you being a man. So put the testosterone on ice and answer the damn question."

"Fine, fine." I tilt my head from side to side, contemplating my answer. "I'd have to go with burger girl."

"Burger girl? Even though she smells like deep-fried animal carcass and has a case of the meat sweats?"

"No, no." I chuckle, shaking my head. "Because she isn't afraid to be what she is."

Both brows rise in confusion. "What she is? You mean bloated?"

"No, Ally." I smile. "Real. She's not afraid to show me who she truly is."

"Interesting," she remarks, tapping her spoon against her

lips. "Especially considering that getting you to show me who you are is like pulling teeth."

I look around as if she couldn't possibly be talking to me. "Um, I'm pretty sure you're in my house right now. And we've even quasi-swapped spit by sharing ice cream. You even wore my clothes!"

"But you're so vague! You're like a steel vault that I'm trying to tap into with a meat mallet."

"You have a weird obsession with meat today," I gibe, trying to resist a grin.

"Oh, you wish, buddy," she retorts, not even realizing just how true that statement is. Or maybe she does?

Ally props her elbow on the countertop, resting her chin in her palm with a sigh. "It doesn't matter anyway. Because you're full of shit."

"Ouch." I cringe.

"You'd totally pick salad girl. You'd pick her, bring her back to your place, then play her ribs like a xylophone."

Now it's my turn to laugh hysterically. "Oh, hell no! Definitely not."

"All guys pick salad girl. It's a proven fact." She nods confidently. "Burger chicks get no love."

What is it about this girl? She's so cool and cute and funny, and just . . . *real*. She's my burger girl. Everyone else is just salad—cold and unfulfilling.

We finish off the last of the ice cream before moving to the living room to channel-surf. Ally snatches the remote and instantly turns it to an old episode of *Friends* on nick@nite. It's the episode in which Monica and Chandler get married.

"I love these guys," she remarks, settling in at my side. I stretch my arm across the back of the love seat (don't even get me started on that word) and she curls into me even more. Holy fuck. *Please don't get hard, please don't get hard, please don't get hard . . .*

"Yeah? Why?" I ask, trying to distract my mind.

"Well . . . they're the ultimate BFFs. Six friends, living in the city, experiencing life together. From mishaps and misadventures to love, romance, friendship. I just love everything about them."

Ross threatens to kick Chandler's ass, and Ally giggles. I smile down at her as she watches intently, her face glowing with tenderness. It's like observing an extraterrestrial being, something so foreign and exotic and exciting that you just can't stop staring. You don't want to move, you don't even want to blink, for fear that they'll fade away into oblivion.

"I miss those days." She sighs as we watch Monica walk down the aisle. I know what she means, and something in my chest sinks. I want to pull away and let her live her memory alone, when she continues. "Not the wedding. Just that feeling of togetherness. Having friends to experience the highs and lows of life with you. I miss it."

I shrug. Ally feels the rise and fall of my chest and looks up with a frown. "You don't miss it?"

"I never had it."

"Oh, come on. No old friends from Denton Academy that you raised hell with? If memory serves me well, I remember Denton guys having quite the reputation."

I shake my head with a smile. Oh, I raised hell. Shit, I was legendary. But she'd never know that.

"I never had friends like that. I don't even have friends like that now," I tell her.

Ally lets her hand drift until it finds mine. She squeezes, her eyes smiling like they've just found a shiny, new penny. "Well . . . you have me. I'm your friend, right?"

Friend. *Friend.*

Is that what I am to her? Is there any other option?

I came into this with intentions of being something different. Her teacher. Her adviser. Her guide.

But then . . . then I wanted to be something else. Her friend, yes, but unconsciously, I thought that I would come to mean more. Something deeper.

Her lover.

I wanted to be this woman's lover. This married woman's lover.

As jaded and selfish and all-around fucked up as it makes me, it's what I want. And even knowing that it could never be, I still want the illusion. I want to dig my heart out with a teaspoon and set it aflame, when I can clearly see how loving her would destroy me. That this woman—this delicate little dove—would destroy *me.*

"You are." It's all I can say without giving way to my

true feelings. Without crashing into all the coulda–shoulda–wouldas that currently run through my head.

I squeeze the side of her arm and look back at the TV. Joey is officiating, and he tells Monica and Chandler to kiss once more. I laugh. Because that's what a friend would do.

Addiction

SEX, LIES, VIDEOTAPE, AND PREGNANCY RUMORS?

Upper East Side socialite Evan Carr was again caught with a woman, this time while leaving a secluded clinic in Hoboken yesterday, dressed in plain clothing, a baseball cap, and dark sunglasses. The woman, dressed similarly, appears to be the same one who appeared in a sex tape that surfaced a week ago.

Rumors of infidelity are nothing new for the twenty-nine-year-old Manhattan playboy, and sources say that the woman in the tape and photographs is actually wife Allison Elliot-Carr's best friend, Kelsie van Weiss. Both Kelsie and Allison

attended St. Mary's Prep and went on to study at
Columbia together. According to sources close
to the couple, Allison has indeed left their pent-
house home in the city and has checked into a
treatment facility for an addiction to painkillers,
allegedly sparked by her husband's cheating. No
word on the specific facility at this time, but stay
tuned for the latest breaking news . . .

I read the story again. Then a third time, hoping that I've
misread something. I mean, it's on the Internet. Shit gets
twisted, turned around, and lost in translation. This can't be
correct. So what if I'm still basking in the rose-colored haze
left by Ally's presence last night. Something this awful, this
disgusting, this hurtful can't happen to her. Not even a prick
like Evan could stoop *that* low.

I close the Google Alert on my phone and scroll to my
contacts. Heidi picks up on the first ring.

"I'm on it, Drake," she snaps over the blaring sounds of car
horns and shouting food vendors.

"Tell me this shit isn't true."

"What? You read Page Six, right? It's all over E! and
TMZ."

"I know." I silently scold myself for giving Evan too much
credit. Of course he would be this vile. It's his true nature.
That's what happens when two ain't-shit people procreate.
They birth ain't-shit kids that grow up to be ain't-shit husbands.

"Like I said, I'm on it. We've already leaked check-in information for Mrs. Carr. Even some photos of her enjoying a massage and a facial that we pulled from your security. Everything will check out on her end. As for Evan . . . nothing we can do there."

"And you ensured that the header was displayed on the documents?" For tax purposes, Oasis is technically an ultra-exclusive spa. Few people know it exists, and even fewer actually know its location. The pap wouldn't even know where to look.

"Yes, of course, Justice. This isn't my first rodeo, you know."

"Could've fooled me."

"And what's that supposed to mean?" Heidi asks, annoyance in her voice. When it comes to business, Heidi is about as no-nonsense as it gets. She isn't challenged often—she has no reason to be. Her reputation speaks for itself.

I pinch the bridge of my nose, feeling a migraine digging its way from my eyelids to my temples. Definitely not the way I had planned to spend my Saturday morning. "I thought I asked you to have someone on Evan?"

"And I did! We can't monitor his every move, Justice. I actually have other clients, you know."

"I don't give a damn about your other clients, Heidi. Take care of this." Knocking resonates from the front door, and I jump to my feet, anxious and irritated. "Look, fix this shit. The last thing Ally needs is bullshit addiction rumors. Do whatever you need to do." End.

I stalk to the front door, my patience diminishing with each step. Too preoccupied, I yank it open without bothering to look out the peephole.

Ally's gaze sweeps down my frame, eyes wide with curious delight, and those red locks illuminated by the bright morning sun. She's dressed in jeans, a green silk camisole, and a purple cardigan, more casual than I've ever seen her. However, I'm less than decent in soft flannel pajama pants . . . and nothing else.

"Well, good morning." She smiles slyly, sliding around me, her shoulder grazing mine. She's holding a brown paper sack and goes straight to the kitchen to set it down. She's comfortable here. She's comfortable with *me*.

"What are you doing here?" I ask, quickly closing the door, but not before checking to make sure no one followed her here.

"Yeesh, you're grumpy in the morning. For your information, I wanted to surprise you with something totally sweet and awesome, but I can leave if you want." She flips her hair dramatically and makes her way back to the door. I step into her path before she can even get close.

"Sorry, uh, I just wasn't expecting you," I say, gazing down at her, resisting the urge to take my finger and free her bottom lip from its cute little pout. "And I've had a rough morning. Please stay. I could use something totally sweet and awesome." I flash her a grin, just to soften her up. A face that gentle, that delicate, should never frown.

"Are you mocking me, Drake?" She smirks.

"Maybe. Depends on what you've got in that bag."

Ally smiles, and warmth sweeps over me. Not the heat I feel when I imagine her tight, little body under mine. But real, palpable, comforting warmth. Her smile is the sun—bright and infectious. I'd rather go blind from staring than be without it.

She turns back around and sets the bag on the counter. "Well, it's your lucky day, because honestly, this is as much of a treat for me as it will be for you." She begins to unpack her paper sack, spreading things on the marble countertop. "First—breakfast! Your friend Riku—who is a total, freakin' hottie, by the way—hooked me up with my favorite brunch food ever, fried chicken and waffles!" She uncovers a large Tupperware container and the mouthwatering scents of fried batter, spices, and syrup fill the room. My stomach rumbles in approval.

"You eat chicken and waffles?" I ask, stepping forward to get a better look at the piping-hot, deep-fried fare.

"Hell yes!" she exclaims proudly. "I can't even tell you how many times I've gone to Melba's in Harlem. You ever been?"

"Can't say I have."

She slaps my bare chest lightly and damn near squeals. "You have to let me take you! It's da bomb!"

"And apparently you have to go back in time to 1996 to eat there," I gibe, causing her to give me another playful slap.

She laughs, and I join her out of habit and necessity. Ally means well, but she could never know what she's doing to me. Making plans after our time here, as if I could actually have a place in her life outside these four walls? As if she and I could continue this . . . thing?

I'm not sure whether I should be pissed at her for giving me false hope or pleased by the fact that she wants me in her life. But when I look at her, so happy—happy with *me*—I can't feel anything but grateful for the charade, even though it will kill me when it's over.

Ally raises the dish until it's eye level, taunting me with the sweet, spicy aromas. "Shut up! Or you don't get any of this."

"Riku made that?"

"Yup. He was actually pretty surprised by my request. Guess the other ladies are too concerned with gaining an ounce to enjoy some real food." She shrugs. "Jeez, I see why you keep him locked up in the kitchen. He'd totally get molested by all these horny housewives if they saw him!"

I give her a half grin before turning toward the cabinets in an attempt to hide my flare of jealousy. I have no business feeling any type of possessiveness toward Ally. She isn't mine. But fuck it, I never copped to being rational.

"That's cool of him," I remark, with as much coolness as I can possibly muster.

"Yeah. Anyway, my plan is to fill you with fat and cholesterol, then I was hoping you'd be satisfied enough to humor me . . ."

I turn around with plates and silverware, just in time to catch a sheepish look on her face. "Humor you?"

"Yeah." She sets down the dish, opens her bag again, and gleefully reveals the next item, clutching it to her chest like it's her most prized possession. "*Friends* marathon!"

"You're kidding, right?"

Ally hugs the boxed set of DVDs and shakes her head. "I *never* kid about *Friends*. Come on, Justice! It'll be fun! I even brought sustenance so we don't have to leave your house for the entire day," she says, pulling out bags of chips, packages of microwavable popcorn, bags of candy, and a two-liter bottle of soda. "Just me, you, Ross, Monica, Rachel, Phoebe, Chandler, and Joey. And enough junk food to clog all of our arteries."

I pick up a king-size bag of peanut M&M's. "Where'd you get all this stuff?"

"I begged Diane to help me out, telling her I had some serious PMS cravings that would only be satisfied with carbs. I wanted to make you an offer you couldn't refuse."

I make a disparaging face and rub the back of my neck. Ally's expression falls in response. "Well . . . you're lucky clogged arteries are *so* in style this season."

Ally smiles and the sun burns my eyes. I just squint and smile too.

"OH MY GOD. That was . . ."

"Mmmmm." I rub my full belly and swallow the last, delicious morsel of crispy fried chicken, fluffy waffle, and sweet syrup. It's the perfect bite.

". . . amazing, delicious. Better than sex."

"I don't know about that," I say, wiping my mouth with a napkin. "Riku is a great chef and all, but nothing is better than sex."

"Meh."

I raise a brow. "Meh?"

"Meh. I mean, don't get me wrong, it's pretty good. But sex is just . . . I don't know. Just *sex*. I get why people enjoy it so much, but I just don't understand why we give it so much power. It's a physical act of love or affection, not love or affection itself. Relationships are about so much more than sex. They're about trust, loyalty, honesty, kindness, respect—all things that don't require a woman to spread her legs."

I peg her with a bewildered stare. "You *do* know who you're talking to, right?"

"Yeah, yeah, I know, Mr. Sexpert Extraordinaire. And I'll admit, you know your stuff. But don't you think there are other factors in a relationship, namely a marriage, which can impact sex? For instance, if your lover is sweet and sensitive and treats you like a treasure, don't you think sex would be amazing? Even if it's not that great physically?"

"No."

"No?"

"No." I push my plate to the side and prop my elbows on the countertop, leaning toward her. "I agree that all of those elements are necessary and required in a relationship, but to be honest, they all lead to sex. You see, we're sweet and funny and kind because we want sex. We sit through chick flicks, the theater, and ballet because we want sex. We wait patiently as you try eighty-three variations of a black peep-toe pump because we want sex . . . while you wear the shoes.

"Think of it this way: trust, honesty, respect . . . all those things are like the playoffs during football season. You need to be competing in them. They're necessary to get you where you want to be—the Super Bowl. Sex is the Super Bowl, Ally. And while those playoff games may have gotten you there, they really can't win the game for you. No one says, 'They played great in that game a few weeks ago, so it's okay that they're losing now.' It's how you play the game *that* day that matters. That's the only thing people care about."

Ally nods solemnly as she mindlessly swirls the remnants of syrup on her plate with a fork. "So . . . what if you don't have all the other stuff? What if there is no trust, no honesty, no respect? What if your partner loses *every single game*? Why on earth do they still feel deserving of sitting in the bleachers, let alone *playing,* at the Super Bowl?"

I look down where her hand continues to slide her fork through the sticky syrup. At the hand that displays her diamond wedding ring. Then I'm looking into her eyes, urging her to see me. To hear me. "Maybe you're just rooting for the wrong team."

She's quiet, but she holds my gaze, those wild eyes uncovering every complicated layer of my suggestion. I know she wants to ask me what I mean, and at this moment I can't lie to her. When she looks at me like that, like I somehow matter in her world, that I actually take up space somewhere in her thoughts, she can ask me anything. And I'd hand her every single one of my secrets on a silver platter.

"Come on," I say, standing to my feet and breaking our trance. I hold out my hand, offering the only thing I can provide her. The only thing I'm worthy of giving her: *right now.* "I want to watch *Friends* with my friend."

"I THINK THIS may be my favorite episode," Ally says with half a Twizzler dangling from between her lips. I pull off a piece and pop it into my mouth.

"That's what you said about the last five episodes."

"I know, but this one is the best. This is the one where they all go to Barbados and Monica's hair takes on a life of its own. And she's walking around with that little white hat on top of this massive mountain of black frizz. I die every time I see it!"

I shake my head and smile. *Of course.* My facial muscles haven't gotten this much of a workout since . . . since, well, ever. I look down at Ally curled up at my side like a cat, her bare feet tucked under her. I watch how she mouths her favorite parts of an episode and laughs, even though she knows the joke that's coming. She squeezes my thigh and looks up at me, giggling. Thank God I had sense enough to throw on a T-shirt and a pair of worn jeans.

"What?" She grins.

"Nothing. It's just . . . cute how addicted you are to this stuff. You've probably seen every episode at least ten times,

yet you still think it's funny. It's a little scary. But kinda adorable too."

"I can't help it." She shrugs. "It's my vice. Some people
smoke. Some people like booze or drugs. I'm addicted to
Friends reruns and ice cream."

"You're so badass."

"And sometimes, when I'm feeling really naughty, I watch
Friends while eating ice cream. Hashtag *BOOM*."

"Okay, that's *really* scary. And not in the way you think."

We both break into an easy, unrestrained laugh that causes
me to pull her closer, siphoning her warmth and goodness
like a fiend. I know I should stop. I know that no matter how
innocent I may try to make my actions appear, they are anything but. Yet I can't stop. I can't lose this now. I may never
touch an angel again.

"So, Justice, what's your vice?" she asks, reaching for a
handful of Sour Patch Kids. "And don't you dare say something stupid and healthy like swimming or running, or I
may have to reconsider this friendship."

"I don't have one."

She sits up and turns to face me, disbelief etched on her
face. "I call bullshit! Everyone has a vice. Come on, what's
that one thing you gotta have? That one addiction that makes
you psychotically happy? I promise I won't judge. Unless it's
something weird like goat porn. Or Crocs."

I roll my eyes and shake my head, stifling a laugh.

"Oh my God, is it something weird? It's goat porn, isn't

it? Or worse—Crocs! I bet you have a whole collection in different colors! Oh my—"

"I'm not into Crocs."

"—and here I thought you were a normal."

"Or any weird porn involving farm animals," I say over her sugar-induced rambling.

"Then what? Spill it, Drake."

I exhale and rub the back of my neck, trying to pacify her with an answer that doesn't make me look like a total jackass.

Sex.

Money.

You.

Even thinking of her as part of the series seems wrong, though it was both sex and money that brought her to me.

"Work," I resolve.

"*Work?* You're addicted to *work*?" She throws a Sour Patch Kid at me, pegging me in my shoulder. "What kind of vice is that? Lame, dude. *Lame.*"

"Hey, not my fault I haven't been corrupted by junk food and bad TV. And I like my work. It's important to me."

Ally twists her lips to one side, and her eyes narrow to small slits. "Um . . . You know what you do, right? You're not curing cancer or creating calorie-free cookies."

I lift a single brow. "But it's still important. It brought *you* here, didn't it?"

Her gaze falls, and I instantly feel like a tactless bastard for throwing her presence at Oasis in her face. I'm like a fish out of water . . . caring about people's feelings, thinking about what passes my lips before I just blurt it out. This isn't me. This isn't the Justice Drake that people know and loathe. Yet I don't want to be any other way with Ally. I like who I am when she's around. For once I can just . . . breathe. I can just be.

"I'm sorry. I shouldn't have—"

"No, you're right," she says, shaking her head. "You're right. I *am* here. And I'm glad I came."

"Why?" The question is out before I can stop it. It's been eating away at me since the day she set fire to my deserted paradise.

She shakes her head again, casting her eyes down to the few sugary remains of candy. "I came because . . . because I thought it was what Evan wanted. I thought it would fix what was broken. But I soon realized that you can't fix what's beyond repair. What was never really meant to be in the first place."

I don't want to read too much into her words, but I can't help that tiny shard of hope that lodges in the space between my rib cage and my chest. That small space that beats in double time whenever she smiles at me, all white teeth and soft, pink lips, like I'm the only one that can make her do that. Like I'm the only man in the world she's reserved those smiles for.

It's corny and sweet, and so unlike me in every way possible, but it's the truth. And after years of lying to myself and everyone else, honesty—as uncomfortable as it may be—is a welcome dilemma.

"And now?" I ask, causing her gaze to touch mine.

"Now?

"You said you were glad you came. Why? Why now?"

Scarlet kisses her cheeks and she grins, looking back down at her hands bashfully. "I've learned a lot. About myself and . . . sex. About what I like and what I want." She sweeps her eyes back to mine and gives me a naughty smile. I don't even think she knows it's naughty. But the way I can feel it, right down to the tip of my dick . . . oh yeah, naughty as fuck. "I've never been outwardly sexual. Hell, usually I just use humor to mask my discomfort whenever the subject comes up. But now I just feel more confident and free to explore this new side of me. And it's pretty damn exciting. So even if this trip is all for nothing, and Evan and I can't fix this . . . I'll know better for next time."

"Next time?"

"I'll know how to be a better lover. I can be what men want."

It takes every ounce of my self-control and common sense not to grab her by her shoulders and shake the shit out of her, telling her that she *is* what men want. That she was perfectly designed to be a goddess to every man whom she graces with her presence. There's nothing wrong with her—not a damn thing. But how do I get her to see that—to believe that—without looking like a fraud? Or worse: showing her that I actually am one?

"You know that no matter how amazing you are in bed, Evan will always be Evan, right?" *He'll always be a spineless, cheating bastard.*

She frowns, yet nods in agreement. "I know. I knew it the day I married him. Still . . . I thought marriage would change him. I thought I could change him."

"Common misconception among wives," I remark, grabbing a Twizzler. I tap her nose with the tip of it in an attempt to lighten the mood. She takes the bait, snapping at the candy like a hungry piranha.

"I know, I know," she says, chomping a mouthful of red licorice.

"And honestly, you shouldn't have to. He should want to change . . . for you. Because you're worth it."

My eyes still pinned on hers, I slide the candy between my lips, touching my tongue to the same place that she just bit seconds ago. Her eyes watch the movement, studying my lips as they wrap around the thin, red candy. It's like kissing her, tasting her. Feeding my addiction to her. It's not nearly enough, yet so much more than I should have.

Cue the 1980s porn music and dim the lights, because under normal circumstances, this would be the point at which I'd tell a woman to lose the clothes and bury her face in my lap. But Ally is no ordinary woman. And whether she's married or not, I could never treat her like I've treated so many before her.

Ally's face blooms red, and she turns back toward the television, nestling into the space—*her* space—against my side.

"I take that back," she says with a small yawn. "This one is my favorite."

The episode has changed, but the gang is still in Barbados. Monica gets Bo Derek braids and Ross hooks up with Joey's girl, Charlie. Joey can't even be truly upset because it makes sense. Ross is a better fit; he deserves her. He could never give Charlie what she wants. He could never truly fulfill her. He's Joey . . . womanizing, simpleminded, irresponsible Joey. He'll never change. They never do.

Passion

I pace the stage, waiting, watching the entrance to the theater like a hawk. I can feel my anxiety intensifying with every second, the remembrance of Ally's warmth searing the side of my torso. I haven't been able to feel anything else since she left my arms just as dawn lit the early-Sunday-morning sky, transforming it into a cotton-candy canvas.

We fell asleep sometime after Rachel and Joey finally hooked up. Ally was curled against my side like a small, wild cat, her knees drawn up on the sofa. With her hand fisting my T-shirt, that fiery mane falling into her closed eyes, she snored softly against my chest, using my body as her personal, heated pillow. I woke up just as the sun peeked over the horizon, just in time to watch quiet, lazy sunlight dance across her face. Even with my eyes hazed in sleep, she was glorious. Pure and reborn into a new day with new possibilities. New opportunities to be beside her and let her warmth smother the consequences that rest just beyond those jagged hills at the edge of my oasis.

The moment my eyes find her in the crowd, I can breathe again. My vision is clearer. I'm better when she's near, even when I deny myself the pleasure of actually looking at her. Most days, it's better when I don't. This is one of those days.

"I know you're all wondering why I asked you to meet me in our theater this morning. Well, today we have a special demonstration of sorts. However, before we get started, I'd like to know how you all 'handled' your homework assignment last session. Anyone care to share with the class?"

A sardonic smile rests on my lips as I watch them squirming in their seats while they imagine their bodies quaking from what they're doing with their own hands. I can't help it. I get off on this shit. No matter how I feel about Ally and the future that we can never, ever have, I can't change who I am. And who I am is not Ally's husband. So it shouldn't matter that I love what I do. It shouldn't matter that I get hard just thinking about a woman slipping her trembling fingers inside her slick pussy for the first time. And it shouldn't matter that I want sex, need sex, and plan to have sex as soon as I possibly can. My mind might be conflicted about it, but my body definitely doesn't feel the same. And after today's class, my mind may quickly follow.

Lacey is the first to raise her hand, and she climbs to her spike-heeled feet. She looks . . . different, to say the least.

Tight red cami, no bra, and a short leather skirt. Huh. Interesting.

"Obviously, that was not my first time," Lacey begins with an air of arrogance. A few of her colleagues roll their eyes and whisper insults under their breath. "But I did quite enjoy that toy. It was very . . . potent."

I call her bluff. "What'd you like about it, Lacey?"

"Um, it was . . ." She stammers, clutching the top of her exposed chest. A flush sweeps its way from that patch of humid skin up to her neck until landing on the thin apples of her cheeks. "It was powerful. Strong. Like the moment it touched me, I could feel myself lose control. But I didn't want to stop. I wanted to press it harder." She closes her eyes, speaking as if we're the only two people in the vast room. Speaking as if she's communicating something to me . . . her wants, her desires. "I needed something inside of me."

I take a step toward her, charging the auditorium with an unseen current. It seems smaller now, more intimate. "And did you put something inside you, Lacey?"

Her voice is raspy and full of need. "Yes."

"And did it feel good to you?" I match her affected tone. "Yes."

My voice dips even lower. "Did you come, Lacey? Did you come with your fingers deep inside your pussy?"

"Y-yes," she barely whispers.

"Good!" I state with a loud clap of my hands, releasing her from her lustful trance. Lacey's visibly shaken with the sudden change in the atmosphere, her shallow breaths quickening into a pant. "Now let's get started."

Had this been a regular day and a regular class, I wouldn't have let her off the hook so easily. I would've abandoned my place at the stage to stand behind her, close enough that she could feel my heat, but far enough that she would shiver with the need to be touched. I'd brush those bare shoulders lightly and watch with fascination as goose bumps instantly appeared. She'd tremble with expectation, but I wouldn't give her any more. Instead, I'd bring my lips to her ear, close enough that I could look down and see her nipples pebble under that thin tank. Then I'd whisper a command, just for her, my words both intoxicating and terrifying her.

"Show me how you touch yourself, Lacey."

She'd stutter all the reasons why she shouldn't, shaking her head adamantly. But her body . . . her body would grow hot with excitement. She'd get wet at the thrill of it. So fucking wet that I'd smell her, her wetness telling me that she wasn't even wearing panties to smother her spicy scent.

When my hand touched hers, still clutched to her chest, she'd flinch but she wouldn't pull away. She'd let me guide it between her swollen breasts and down to her flat belly, brushing the bit of exposed skin where the hem of her shirt rides up. Then I'd let her fingers play with the jewel in her navel, manipulating each digit as if that diamond-studded barbell was her clit. Demonstrating how I would stroke it for her.

When she began to pant and mewl gently, I'd finally put

Lacey out of her misery and guide her hand down farther until her fingertips grazed the tops of her thighs. And I'd whisper, "Go ahead, Lacey. Touch yourself. Show me how to please you."

But I wouldn't abandon her just yet. She isn't confident enough. She'd like to believe that she is, but I would feel the trepidations beating from her chest. So I'd ease that hand to the apex of her thighs, to that humid space that aches to be touched. She'd want me to do it, but I wouldn't, and that would frustrate her. So I'd tell her again, this time my voice gruffer, more commanding. "Touch your pussy, Lacey."

With embarrassed tears in her eyes, she'd sink her fingers between her folds, teasing her clit just as we had teased her jeweled belly button. She'd be humiliated and somewhat disgusted with herself, but she'd moan and let her head fall back on my shoulder. She wouldn't be able to help it. Because as mortified as she'd be, she'd be doubly turned on. And I'd stand there, a satisfied grin on my face, because I broke her. I'd unleashed the deviant that had been lying dormant within the walls of her inhibitions. And when she sank the first finger deep inside herself, while I and ten awestruck women watched in wonder, she'd feel it too. And she'd know that she could never be caged again.

That's what I'd do under different circumstances. It's what I've done countless times before. But the thought of touching Lacey doesn't excite me. It doesn't make the little devil in me rejoice at the opportunity to reduce her to a writhing mess in my theater. It kind of makes me sad that I ever thought it was kosher to do. And even feeling an ounce of remorse pisses me the fuck off.

The little devil sits on my shoulder, whipping his sharp, pronged tail to the back of my neck before jabbing it into my skin. *"Fucking soft,"* he hisses in my ear. I can't even be mad at him.

"OH YEAH . . . yeah. Right there, baby. Oh God, yes!"

"Stop!"

I get as close as possible to the couple positioned at the middle of the stage. They look up at me, their eyes hooded and hungry, yet they halt their movements. The man is still buried deep inside his lover's warm, wet pussy, and it's taking every ounce of his self-control not to thrust again. The woman's naked chest heaves with her labored breaths, and she leans back to rest on the odd-shaped, leather chair currently elevating her pelvis.

That's right.

We're watching people have sex.

How can it be that you're even surprised?

The couple is a husband-and-wife team who teach tantric yoga out in Cali. They've also been known to dabble in webcam sex shows, much like the one they are giving us today. Only difference is, I pay them quite a bit more than $2.99 per minute.

"Now you see the way Brad was thrusting into Laura? Tell me about her. What did you see her doing?" I say, addressing the class. As expected, no one says a word. "Okay, since you all obviously are not paying attention, I want you to watch Laura's hands. You'll notice that they are always moving— clutching the chair, pinching her nipples, grabbing Brad's ass, and pushing him in deeper. Still hands are a dead give-away to bad sex. You should be pawing at your lover like a hungry lioness. Make him feel like you are so overwhelmed with pleasure that you just can't keep still. Okay? Resume."

The couple picks up where they left off without missing a beat. Brad holds Laura's legs wide by her thighs and moves into her, slowly at first. Then he's gaining momentum, fuck-ing her like a man possessed. Laura croons his name, raking her nails over his bare chest.

"You see? Look at what she's doing," I say as her fingers drift down to stimulate her clit. "And you see how she looks at him? How their eyes stay locked on each other? What do you think that simple act represents?"

"Intimacy," someone calls out over the couple's moans.

"Right." I nod. "What else?"

"Togetherness."

"Passion."

"Exactly." I pace the stage as if there isn't a live sex show occurring just feet away from me. "There are two types of lovers, ladies. The kind who fucks and the kind who gets fucked. Always be the kind that fucks. No matter what posi-tion you're in, be passionate. Be engaging. Commit to the moment one hundred percent." I give them all an encourag-ing smile, feeling a tinge of pride at their progress. "Now let's see how well Laura rides."

Again, the two move together in a dance of synchronized perfection. Brad reclines on the tantra chair and Laura straddles his lap, slowly lowering herself onto his length, gasping at the depth the new position provides.

"How many of you watch porn?" I ask. Several of the women raise their hands without hesitation. I don't even look in Ally's direction to see if she is among them. "Good. Get used to watching it. You can learn a lot about sexual positions and acts that your partner may be interested in trying. Not all pornography is created equal, but there's truly something that can appeal to everyone."

Laura begins to buck faster and faster, fisting Brad's hair as she bounces wildly. He grips her hips and thrusts upward to meet her intensity before reaching around and slapping her ass.

"Don't be afraid of a little spanking, ladies. It can be pleasurable for both parties, and it doesn't mean that you're a masochist or any bullshit label like that. Your mate won't judge you. He'll think it's insanely hot."

Every eye stays transfixed on the licentious dance playing out within these theater walls. No one speaks; no one even blinks. It's erotically hypnotizing, like watching two animals in the wild, biting and thrashing as they try to dominate the other to sate their carnal need. I'm as fascinated as I am aroused by the raw visceral act. Maybe even more. It's basic human nature in its most beautiful form.

Laura cries out as she chases her orgasm, and Brad sits up to draw her nipple into his mouth, growling against the puckered skin. He's trying to hold back, trying to regain control so he can keep feeling her, keep fucking her. It feels too good to stop now.

Caught up in the frenzy of it all, I glance out at the audience to gauge their reactions, and everything just . . . stops. Laura and Brad fall away, their raucous moans quieting to a whisper. The women's heated pants of excitement, the squeaking of their seats as they cross and uncross their legs. It all fades to black, and I am immersed into pools of blue-green ice water, jostling me from my train of thought.

Ally looks at me—looks *into* me—eyes wild, and those flushed cheeks bleeding into her cascade of crimson hair. Her pouty lips part only a fraction, as if she wants to say something to me, but she just continues to stare. Maybe she gasps. Maybe she moans. Maybe she is just as lost for words as I am.

I know what's happening now just feet away from me. But I can't hear Laura as she screams with joy, bearing down on Brad as her pussy contracts. I don't see the way he jerks as her flexing inner muscles milk his orgasm. I can't care about anything beyond the fiery angel sitting yards away. Everything else is background noise. Muted, colorless, and insignificant.

She shifts in her seat and casts her glance down to her lap, releasing me from her hold. I glance to see Brad and Laura work to come down from their high, kissing and touching each other as their bodies quake with aftershocks. Yet I feel nothing. I've become numb to it all.

My gaze sweeps over the room, catching looks of confusion as eleven women await my instruction.

"Um, uh . . . uh . . ."

I clear my throat and try again, but the words just don't come out. Ally has stolen my breath and reduced me to a pathetic, stuttering mess. There's nothing left to say—nothing I trust myself *to* say.

So I do the only thing I possibly can do right now that won't jeopardize everything I thought I truly wanted.

I turn and walk away.

Reflection

I have to fuck her.

It's the only way. The only thing that will clear my head and get me back to where I need to be. So yeah . . . I'm going to fuck her. It's what she wants anyway, and it's what I need, that's for damn sure. I'll enjoy it; she'll love it. And once my balls aren't as heavy as my conscience, I'll move on and finish the job I was hired to do. Simple as that.

I'm in my living room, head in hand, internally freaking the fuck out about what I'm about to do. My finger hovers over the call icon, hesitation crawling all over my body like mites. *Just do it, you pussy. You know you want to.*

I do want to. *Badly.* But not for the reasons I should.

I have to fuck her. I *have* to.

Fuck it.

My thumb just barely grazes the phone icon, and the line begins to ring. Her voice greets me moments later, sounding both surprised and delighted. "Justice?"

"Yes."

"I'm so glad you called."

She knows what this call is about. Erin has been waiting for this moment for years. She could see it in me when she was last here—the desperation, the confusion. The guilt. She knew it would only be a matter of time before I came crawling back, craving her pretty, pink pussy and those perfect, perky tits. And what man wouldn't?

"How glad are you?" I ask, my tone low and husky. Unlike Jewel and Candi, Erin needs to be stroked and nurtured before sex. In all honesty, I could have just called the two strippers, but I was craving something else . . . something more intimate. Plus, that twosome is about as shrewd as I am when it comes to reading body language. They would see how I was deflecting from a mile away. They already had.

A pleased, erotic sound rumbles in Erin's throat. "So glad, Justice. I wish I was there so you could reach between my thighs and feel how glad I am."

That should at least pique my interest. Maybe even cause a little tingle down below. But nope. Nothing.

"Do you want to be here?" That's right. I'll play the game. A little cat and mouse will get my blood pumping.

"What do you think?" She plays her part flawlessly.

I'm just about to tell her to pack a bag and head to the airport, where a first-class ticket will be waiting for her, when a banging sound rattles my skull. Has Jiminy Cricket gotten off his green ass and decided to finally do his job? Or has that bug-eyed fucker cooked up an even better plan to sate our licentious needs?

Listen to my delusional ass. I really need to get out more.

The banging echoes through the space again, before I finally realize that it's not just a figment of my imagination. It's the door.

I make my way to the nearest window, where I peek through a curtain, my cell still pressed to my ear. I instantly regret my decision the second my eyes fall on her, so shiny and bright and alive.

I don't want shiny and bright and alive. I want dark, devious, and shameful. That's what people like me deserve.

"Uh, *hello*? Justice?" Erin calls out from the receiver. I ignore her and hasten to open the front door much more quickly than what most would deem proper for a man like myself.

Who am I kidding? I busted a Usain Bolt, then damn near hurtled over an end table, only to nearly break off the door handle.

"Hey!" Ally smiles.

Ally smiles. It's like a song lyric, or an ancient proverb.

"Hey," I exhale out of relief, as if I hadn't breathed easily since I'd last seen her. I hate how my body just knows her. How it reacts so differently to her than to anyone else. It gives her power over me, something no one has ever gained since the day I was banished from her world.

"Can I come in?"

"Hello? *Hellooooo?*" Oh shit. *Erin.*

"Let me call you back," I murmur into the phone. Ally raises a speculative brow.

"What?" Erin snaps loudly. "Who is that? Who's over there?"

"Maybe I should come back," Ally whispers over Erin's annoying screeching. I shake my head at her and hold up a finger as she tries to back away. Then I turn around so I can handle Erin properly.

"Who I have at my home is none of your concern," I say into the receiver, my voice so cold that frost damn near settles on the touch screen. "Do you understand me? You are an employee, and nothing else. But the next time you even think to open your mouth to question me, you won't even be that." I press end to keep from losing my shit and scaring Ally, ensuring that she'll never return. I turn back to her slowly, hoping—praying—that she's still there.

"Wow," she says, her eyes wide and sparked with amusement. "Look at you, boss man, cracking the whip. Ouch."

"Cracking the whip?" I smirk, stepping aside so she can enter. I stroke her cheek with a single finger just as she brushes past. "You wish you were so lucky."

"Mr. Drake, are you flirting with me?" she asks, spinning to face me with a hand on her hip.

I close the front door and lean back against it, crossing my arms in front of me. "I don't know. Depends on what you're here for." I grin, feeling the icy discomfort of just seconds ago melt away.

Reluctance shadows Ally's face and she looks down at the floor. "It's embarrassing. Which is stupid, seeing as I've already drooled on you, and you probably heard me snore. By the way, we'll just forget that ever happened, *capisce?*"

I push off from the door to stand directly in front of her and cup her cheeks in my hand, stalling her self-deprecating rambling. She's so soft, and I feel her face heat in my palms. It's like holding fire. "What can I do for you, Ally?"

She looks at me with wonder in those too-big eyes, and her lips part, causing my gaze to study the movement. This could be it. This could be the moment I confess my sins and kiss this beautiful angel. I could taste heaven for the very first time.

Do it. Look at her—she's begging you to.

Kissing Ally would be so easy. Touching her, holding her, tasting her . . . it'd be like breathing.

I want to breathe. I want to inhale her in every way possible. I want her life to sustain me, her heartbeat to synchronize with mine.

But I don't want to taint her. I don't want her to be like me. A cheater. A deviant. An outcast. She deserves better, and I'm not better. Not better than what she already has, which is Evan.

She doesn't want me. She has him.

The realization is like being dumped in a tub of ice water,

and I step away from her, removing my hands from the curve of her cheeks. Ally blinks rapidly as if she's been sleepwalking and knots her hands in front of her.

"So, um, yeah. I need your help."

I run my hand through my short-cropped hair just to give myself something to do. Then I go to the kitchen to get a drink for my suddenly dry mouth. I grab a kettle for tea. Nah. That won't do the trick. Juice? Water?

Wine. When in doubt, always go with wine. I hold up a bottle and she nods, so I grab two glasses and fill them with rich, velvety liquid. Ally meets me halfway to take hers.

"So like I was saying . . ." she begins before taking a large gulp. "I need help."

"I gathered that. Care to tell me with what? Because I'm pretty sure I could make a short list of things you need help with. Professional help."

"Hey now!" she shrieks with mock offense. "It took a lot of practice to be this magnificently awkward. Dude, I was awkward before awkward was cool. I'm a pioneer in the movement."

I chuckle before taking a slug of my wine. "Awkward was never cool. Only uncool people believe that."

Once again, we fall into that easiness. No expectations. No games. Just real, genuine companionship. I laugh at her corny jokes. She shakes her head at mine. Whenever I look at her, she smiles. And in turn, I smile too.

How could I have ever thought that there was room for more?

"So anyway. For real this time, I need help."

"With what?" I down the last of my wine and go to top off both our glasses.

"I have a confession to make: I'm a horrible dancer. I know what you're thinking—how can someone so *graceful* and *elegant* be a bad dancer? But it's true. Sad, but true. And ever since Candi and Jewel came, I've been really self-conscious. So I was wondering if you would help me, ol' buddy, ol' pal."

"Help you?"

She twirls a crimson curl around her finger. "Teach me to dance?"

I set my glass down on the nearest flat surface and throw my hands up so there's no misinterpreting my answer. "No!"

"Aw, come on! You said you were always here for whatever we need. And I need to learn how to drop it like it's hot. To shake what my mama gave me. To work my groove thang." Ally sets down her glass to clutch her hands together in front of her chest. Then she walks toward me with an impish grin. "Please, oh please, Justice Drake. Teach me how to Dougie?"

I can't even pretend to be put out by her. She's just too damn adorable, looking up at me, those eyes shining with innocent mischief. I smile and shake my head, knowing that I don't stand a chance against her ridiculous superpower.

"Fine," I exhale, rolling my eyes.

"Fine?" Those animated eyes dance with delight.

"Fine. I'll help you."

She makes that dying pig-cat crossbreed sound and jumps

up and down. Then she's grasping my shoulders. And it happens. Her lips are touching me—kissing me. It lasts for half a millisecond and she turns away just as swiftly as she approached, as if she doesn't even register what she's done to me. To her, it's just an innocent peck on the cheek. To me, it's enough to make my dick try to manually unzip my slacks, in hopes that it'll get a kiss too.

Ally makes her way to the Bose sound system situated on my entertainment stand and hooks up a little pink iPod she's retrieved from the pocket of her cardigan. "I have to be honest with you—I have no rhythm and have been blessed with the cruel gift of two left feet. So be gentle with me."

I raise a brow at her choice of words, but she's too busy scrolling through her playlist to notice. "How do you even know I can dance?"

She briefly gives me the side eye before turning a knob to adjust the volume. "I saw you with those strippers. I'm sure you know exactly what kind of dancing guys like."

Booming bass lines puncture the room, coupled by digitized drumbeats. It initially startles the shit out of me, before I'm nearly in stitches at her ironic song choice. Ally whips off her cardigan and swings it around over her head, laughing hysterically.

"Come on, Magic Mike! Show me how to ride that pony!"

And she's right—the girl cannot dance. Not to save her life.

She breaks into some remixed version of the funky chicken on crack before trying to twerk. And while that dance should not be performed by anyone—man, woman, or child—Ally in particular should never, ever try it. At first I think she's got butt cramps. Or her ass fell asleep and she's trying to wake it up. I can't even begin to ask what's wrong, too overcome with hilarity to form coherent words. Shit, even *I'm* snorting a little.

"Oh . . . God, stop! Stop! You're . . . killing . . . me!"

"What?" she asks innocently, still bent over and convulsing. She furrows her brow in concentration. "Am I doing it? Is it moving? I've been practicing for weeks!"

"Ally! Stop! You'll hurt yourself!" I bend over to place my hands on my knees, struggling to catch my breath. I look back up to see her clapping her hands, trying to get her ass to shake in time with each clap. I die laughing again, and tears roll down my face.

"Whatever. I got this. I got this shit. Miley ain't got nothin' on me!"

I'm cackling so hard that I'm coughing, nearly brought to my knees with exhaustion. "If you don't stop, I'm gonna choke! You're killing me with your horrible dance moves!"

Finally she straightens up and places a tiny fist on her hip. "Well, what am I doing wrong? How am I supposed to learn if you just keep laughing at me?" She's trying to give me the stern, serious face, but I see a smile at the corners of her mouth, clawing its way free. When she can't fight it any longer, she howls with laughter right along with me, until we're both on the floor, clutching our stomachs.

"I told you I couldn't dance!" she says, jabbing my arm

with her finger. We've spent the better part of ten minutes just catching our breath. Whenever I thought I was over my hilarity, I'd get a flashback of her bent over, her narrow hips willing her ass cheeks to move, with that look of sheer determination on her face. Luckily, the song has long ended and changed to something less unfortunate, or I probably would've hacked up my spleen.

"Holy shit, Ally. You can't. You really can't."

She rolls over on her side and looks at me, a few tears of laughter still in her eyes. "So do you think . . . do you think that's why Evan does what he does? I mean, if I suck at shaking my ass, I probably can't do . . . other stuff, right?"

I turn to face her, an odd feeling replacing the hilarity I felt just seconds before. It's something like sadness and sympathy and anger all rolled into one, and compressed into the hollow of my chest. It's too intense to feel, too complex to describe. But I feel it. I feel it for Ally.

"Come on," I say, climbing to my feet. I stretch out a hand to help her up. "I'd never be able to forgive myself if I let you believe that what you were doing was anything remotely close to dancing."

Ally lets me pull her up, smoothing her dress over her hips. "Well, then. What would you call it?"

I tap the freckled bridge of her nose. "Seizing."

"SO LIKE THIS?"

"Yeah, just like that. Dip your hips a little more."

"Like that?"

"Yeah. Good. Now grind your ass on me."

I know what you're thinking.

I'm obviously asking for it. I've got to be some kind of masochist who gets off on giving himself blue balls. But hear me out.

Ally needed help, and after seeing her so vulnerable and exposed, grasping on to any hope that she could recapture Evan's attention, I had to give it my best shot.

Plus, I just really wanted to feel her brushing her ass against me while my hands grip her hips. Hey, I'm only a man. Sue me.

"I feel stupid," she says with a huff. I feel her trying to slip away, but I hold her tighter, cursing the thin layer of soft cotton that keeps my fingers from touching her skin. I don't even care if she feels my erection pressing against her ass. On some level, I want her to feel it. Maybe she'll get an inkling of what she does to me.

"You don't look stupid, though. You should see yourself."

"Really?"

Hit with a sudden stroke of genius, I spin her around to face me. "Really. Let me show you."

I lead Ally to my bedroom just as the song changes to something slow and sultry, yet equally provocative. The room is dim, with only the light from the hall filtering in to illuminate our path. I switch on a bedside lamp, filling the space with just enough light for her to see what I see.

"Stand here," I command gently, positioning her in front

of the floor-to-ceiling, gold-framed mirror stationed beside my closet.

"You're kidding, right? You want me to dance in front of this mirror?"

I take my place behind her, barely leaving an inch between our bodies. "You wanted to see how sexy you look. Here's your chance."

Soft, muted light outlines the contours of her cheekbones and lips as she looks at me in the mirror. "But this is so . . ." Her voice is merely a husky whisper, but I hear her loud and clear. From this angle, I can see all of her. I can admire the flush of her skin and the way the color travels from her face to the tops of her breasts. I can see the way her eyelids droop to narrow slits when she sways her hips from side to side, like she's intoxicated by the energy flowing from my body to hers. And she can see the way my hand snakes around her waist to rest on her stomach, pressing her into me as I lightly push against her.

Ally's mouth parts, and something animalistic and hungry escapes her lips. She keeps moving, rolling her body with mine in time with the beat. The music is slow, yet the beat is infectious, like sex on Spotify. I feel the drums in my chest, the strings in my soul. My movements are as fluid and instinctual as if I was sliding into Ally right here, right now. As if I was fucking her from behind, here in front of this mirror, watching her come apart in my arms.

My hands move from her stomach to her rib cage, and I

feel her breathing become deeper as if she's gasping for precious air. Yet she looks completely serene in the moment. So much so that she lets her eyes slide closed as she loses herself to music and sensation. And as I watch her bite her bottom lip, her head thrown back on my chest, I lose myself in her.

This is where I should stop. Where I should make some stupid joke that'll break the palpable tension that has our bodies fused together, my chest to her back, my pelvis to the curve of her ass. It's what's smart and responsible. It's what I would do if this were another time, and another girl, and another lifetime. But all I have is now, and I can't see beyond the vision of her tight frame nestled into mine. I can't feel anything but my body fitting around her like a glove, and her hands sliding their way up to my neck before fisting my hair.

She turns her head toward mine, and her breath fans over my neck like a whispered kiss. I pull her closer, and my lips just barely graze her forehead. She doesn't flinch, just keeps moving with me, eyes closed. My lips move down to brush the soft velvet of her eyelid, then her warm cheek. And when she doesn't make a move in protest, space and time diminish under the weight of this moment. This single moment that could very well destroy everything, yet crushes all consequence into a speck of dust too infinitesimal to even acknowledge.

My lips find hers like they've known them forever. Like they've never kissed another set of lips that were this soft, this sweet. They submit to me, and my tongue touches hers, gently at first, as we learn each other's taste. Then we're all hunger and passion as Ally turns her body to face mine, allowing my mouth to connect wholly with hers.

We communicate without words, settling for throaty moans and grasps of clothing and hair. I push her up against the mirror, cradling her face so I can taste her deeper. She brings a thigh up to my hip and I gladly grip it, lifting her body up with my palms. Ally wraps her legs around my waist, locking them at the ankles, and giving my hands access to the skin revealed by her gathered dress. I should be gentle and take this slow, but I'm starving for her. Too famished to think about stopping now or coming up for air.

My fingers digging into her ass, I grind my rock-hard length into her thinly sheathed sex. I fuck her through cotton and lace, while my mouth makes love to her jaw and neck. Damn these clothes; I want them off. I need to have her skin on mine; I need to make her moan from more than just my kiss. I need my lips and tongue to taste the parts of her that are so damp and humid that I can feel the heat through my slacks.

"Wait."

I can't tell if it's a whisper or a whine, or even just my imagination. Jiminy Cricket and his cock-blocking ass can go to hell.

"Wait, Justice. Wait! Stop!"

Cold water floods my veins, extinguishing the white heat burning in my groin. I slowly place Ally down on her feet and take a step back so she can straighten her clothing into its once perfectly pressed state. So she can erase any evidence that I was between her legs, reducing her to a disheveled mess of ravenous tongue, frenzied hands, and impassioned moans.

I close my eyes for a beat longer than a blink and exhale my frustration, trying to will my pulse to slow. Ally is frantically trying to smooth down her hair. She touches her lips and stills, as if the memory of them merged with mine is just now pouring into her consciousness.

"Oh my God," she whispers. "Oh my God, what did we just do?"

"Ally . . ." I step toward her with my arm outstretched, but don't dare to touch her. "Ally, it's okay. It's not as bad as you think."

She finally looks at me for the first time since before I stood her in front of the mirror. The first falling stars melt and slide down her cheeks, her lip trembling. "I'm *married,* Justice! This is exactly as bad as I think. I'm not some kinda . . . whore . . . that just kisses guys that are not her husband. That's not me! None of this . . . none of this is me!"

This time I grip her shoulders, commanding her attention. "Ally, this *is* you. This is who you are. You can be as awkward and silly and goofy as you want with me. I don't care about your hair looking perfect or what labels you wear. I don't give a damn who you know or what school you went to. And I definitely don't give a fuck about Evan, who wouldn't know how to be loyal and honest if he had a fucking gun to his head. *So fuck him.* And fuck feeling guilty for finally taking control of your desires. You wanted to kiss me, Ally. You wanted to kiss me just as badly as I wanted to kiss you."

"No," she says, shaking her head adamantly. She brushes my hands away and turns, giving me her back. "I don't want this. I don't want to be a cheater."

"You're not a bad person, Ally. There's nothing wrong with feeling the way that you do."

She shakes her head again and nearly runs out of my bedroom. I'm right on her heels, refusing to let her dismiss the living, breathing desire that's been between us since Day One. "You can't run from this. You can't just act like there's nothing between us."

She bends down to collect her sweater, still shaking her head, refusing to face me. She's not just dismissing the kiss— she's dismissing *me*. She's done with me. I'm not worth a response, or even a glance. I've been discharged from her service. She doesn't need me anymore.

Pain-laced rage boils just under the surface of my skin, and I stalk behind her as she tries to scurry to the door.

"Really, Ally? After all the time we've sat here—right here in this fucking living room—talking, laughing, and just *being,* you want to act like I don't even matter? Like what we both felt didn't matter? Tell me it didn't matter, Ally. Turn the fuck around and tell me you didn't want that to happen back there!"

Her hand is on the doorknob and she leans forward, her forehead pressed against the door. I can't help it. I can't stand this distance between us. I can't lose this angel only to be forever cast into hell alone. In a final act of desperation and insanity, I wrap my arms around her, completely covering her body with mine. I want her just as immersed in me as I am in her.

"Please, Ally. Just stay," I whisper urgently, kissing the shell of her ear. "Stay, or tell me you don't want this. That I'm a fool for wanting you like I do."

I hear the click of the door lock and hope splinters like broken glass, falling away into the land of broken dreams and stolen moments. A land where Ally's smiles are brighter than the sun, and her laughs are the sound track of pure, untainted happiness.

"You're a fool," she croaks, pulling away from my arms. From *me*. "And I don't want this."

Part of me stands at the door, waiting for her to come back. Hoping that she'll change her mind and choose me. *Choose us.*

The other part of me lies at the bottom of a pool, drowning, while a million tiny stars look down at me in pity.

Affliction

*T*oday's lesson is actually very simple. So let's get straight to the point, shall we? Open the cases in front of you."

I wait for the sounds of metal latches and the horrified intake of eleven breaths, but I don't look at any of them. I don't make eye contact. Not today.

"What are we supposed to do with these?" Lorinda. Or maybe Maryanne. Or . . . fuck if I care.

"Suck them."

"What?" Another Mrs. Fucktease von Clueless.

"You're going to learn how to suck them," I say louder, my voice carrying throughout the room. I close my eyes and count to ten in an attempt to get a handle on my shit.

"Now, if you'll all be so kind as to remove the dildos from

your case and, using the suction cup at the bottom, attach them to the table in front of you, we can begin."

"You really expect us to do this?" another woman asks, her whiny voice making me cringe. "It's disgusting and degrading."

"And that's exactly the train of thought that forces your husband's dick into your nanny's mouth."

"That's sick!"

"That's the fucking truth." I massage the back of my neck and take a leveling breath. The room is completely silent, save for the sound of incessant pounding in my skull.

I'm hungover.

And not, like, a little hungover.

I'm a lot hungover.

Plus, I look like shit. I didn't shave and only had time to hit the hot spots in the shower before class started. My simple tan slacks and white linen shirt are unpressed and my hair is just finger-combed. And my mouth tastes like a raw oyster that's been sitting under a desert sun all day.

Like I said, I look like shit. And I probably smell like I bathed in that fifth of Jack instead of drinking it, now that it's seeping out of my pores.

I swallow against the dryness on my tongue, but to no avail. "Look, if you want to learn how to do this shit and do it right, I'll teach you. If you're too hung up on stereotypes, or think Jesus won't love you because you gave a little head, then there's the door. So what's it gonna be, ladies? You want your husband to look at you as a housewife? Or as his own, personal whore? You choose."

No one answers, yet they all stay deathly still in their seats, staring in delightful horror at the eight-inch, flesh-toned dildos in front of them.

"Good." I nod with a grimace. *Fuck, that hurts.* "Let's begin."

"Don't be afraid of it, Maryanne. It won't bite you."

I watch as the matronly woman slides her trembling lips over the tip of the silicone penis. Her pink tongue gives it a lick before she eases her head down, taking it into her mouth completely.

"Good. That's good. Let it touch the back of your throat and gently suck as you pull out slowly."

She complies, looking up at me with big, brown eyes, seeking validation. I pat her on the back and nod before moving on to the next housewife.

"Shayla, use your tongue, baby," I croon, resting a warm hand on her shoulder as I squat down next to her. "Lick the tip when you pull up. Swirl it around the head. Imagine tasting those little drops of precum. That's how you know he's ready for you; you're making him feel good. Now, when you ease it back into your mouth, put pressure on the underside of his shaft."

Just like Maryanne, Shayla does exactly what I say, even letting her eyes close as she imagines the feel of a hot, pulsing cock sliding between her lips. I almost smile with pride when a moan rumbles the back of her throat. She feels it too. The thought of bringing a man to his knees with her mouth is getting her hot. Shit, it's even getting me a little hot.

Beside Shayla, Lacey is trying to suck the plastic off her rent-a-dick.

"Slow down, Lacey. Slow. Sensual. Take your time." I place my hand on the back of her head and push it down slowly, forcing her to match my tempo. "Slow, sweetheart. Just like that. Taste every inch; savor it. Put more of it in your mouth, baby. Yeah . . . all the way to the back of your throat."

·I gently grip her hair when she lets out a muffled groan. "Okay, now a little faster. Suck it harder, baby, but still be soft. Put that pretty, wet mouth all over it."

Pulling her hair a bit, I speed up until Lacey's head steadily bobs up and down. When she takes hold of the dildo and begins fisting it enthusiastically as she sucks, I let go and take a step back, admiring the little monster I've created.

I actively engage the women as they explore the art of oral copulation, getting off on their obvious discomfort and inexperience. This is exactly what I need to distract me from the pressure at my temples, and the rage resting at the back of my neck. Not to mention the niggling ache in my chest. I shut it out. I shut it all out, focusing only on my work. Which is exactly what the fuck I should have been doing all along. Not humoring a silly woman while she cries about her cheating bastard of a husband and failed fraud of a marriage. Not sitting through dozens of episodes of mindless drivel and eating lard while she nestles against my side like the cocktease that she is. And not letting her lead me to believe that I was anything more than the hired help, damn near the equivalent of a gay BFF.

How did I get to this point? How in the fuck did I lose sight of what I am and what I stand for so easily?

I can't even really blame her. She's simple and vapid and shallow. She couldn't drown in the depth of her petty thoughts. So I can't hold her responsible for the state that I'm in. *I* let this happen. *I* let her in when I swore that such a thing would never happen. I should've known better. I knew what type of person she was since the day she made it clear that I was an outsider. A nobody. Not even good enough to be fucking honest with. I was a shiny new toy to play with, then discard when she grew tired of me.

My thoughts lead me to the mahogany desk she's stationed at, but I don't look at her. I only know it's her by her shoes—those same sandals that slapped against the pavement when she'd intrude on my nights by the pool. The same sandals that she'd slip off before tucking her feet under her ass and curling her body next to mine.

I hate those fucking sandals. I should have told her that. No man wants a woman who wears sandals. They want women who wear heels. Platform stilettos. Heels that look damn sexy when they're sitting on our shoulders or wrapped around our waists. Ain't shit sexy about sandals. They're one tier up from flip-flops, which are barely a step away from Crocs.

Fucking Crocs.

"You're doing it wrong," I blurt out gruffly, before my little reflective moment takes a turn for the worse.

"What?"

I still don't look at her. I just keep my eyes trained on those sandals and her little, pink-tipped toes peeking out of them. Even her toes are adorable.

Humph. Adorable.

I've never been a fan of *adorable*. Chubby-cheeked babies are adorable. Puppies are adorable. Sometimes even little old ladies named Ethel. None of those things equate with *sexy*. So neither should she.

"I said, you're doing it wrong," I say more sternly.

"I heard that." Her voice is small and sad. Just like she is. A small, sad, adorable woman. "What am I doing wrong?"

"Everything."

"Everything?" She sounds defeated. Like she wanted so bad to succeed at this so she could give Evan the blow job of his life, ensuring that he'd never stray. Like she wanted to be the Superhead of the Upper East Side and boast of her talents on a billboard in Times Square.

"Yeah. You're doing everything wrong." Sorry, Super-head Junior. No book deal for you.

I start to turn away, somewhat satisfied with myself, when her small, sad voice stops me in my tracks.

"Can you teach me how to do it right?"

Can I teach her how?

Can I teach her *how*?

I bite back my initial response—which would probably consist of me telling her exactly where she could go, how she could get there, and with what shoved up her tight, frigid ass—and take a moment to breathe before formulating a more professional response. "If you need extra help, Mrs. Carr, I suggest you make an appointment during business hours."

"An appointment?" I can hear the confusion and hurt in her voice.

"Yes. An appointment. That's what clients make when they find that they require more assistance than usual. When their inexperience stifles their progress. I can't give you extra attention just because you seek it, and take precious class time away from others. That would be *foolish* of me, don't you think?" I answer tersely, giving her back her own words.

Her face contorts as if I've just slapped her, her eyes twice their size and mouth agape. "What are you doing?" she whispers, though it's already too late. We have an audience. And right now these gossipmongers smell fresh shit to stir. Still, I lean in close, invading her personal space and stealing her air. I want her to be as uncomfortable as I am. I want her just as exposed and humiliated and wounded as she's made me.

"I'm doing my job, Mrs. Carr. Exactly what your has husband paid me to do."

BY THE TIME I dismiss the ladies for the day, I'm exhausted, both mentally and physically. Everything hurts. I can't think of one part of me that doesn't ache with every step I take back to the refuge of my home. And it's not just my body that feels it. I'm too tense, too edgy. I feel like I could explode at any given moment.

I know I fucked up in class when I spoke to Ally in that nasty way, but shit, she needed it. She needed to see who I am . . . and what she's reduced me to. As much as I hate it, she caused the mess that I am right now. So, bravo, Allison Elliot-Carr. You've single-handedly fucked up my day and given me blue balls. And you've reminded me why I despise people like you . . . why I hate the world you come from, and why I've emancipated myself from it.

Thank you, Ally. It's bitches like you who create cold-hearted bastards like me.

"Hey!"

I hear the slap of those damn sandals again, and my skin goes clammy and hot. I try to shake it off and keep walking, ignoring her approach.

"I said hey. You wanna tell me what the hell your problem is?"

"Make an appointment, Mrs. Carr," I bark out without turning to address her as I fumble with the lock at my front door. Goddammit, I don't have time for this shit.

"I don't give a damn about your appointments, Justice. Why are you acting like this?" Her voice is right here, right behind me. I can nearly feel her warm breath at my back. With her this close, her heat mingling with mine, I can't even respond. I'm too tired for this shit. Too exhausted to even try to make sense of what's happened between us. Maybe I imagined it all. Maybe Ally was completely innocent with me and her feelings strictly platonic. I could've misread her signals. Shit, maybe she really *did* look upon me as her gay BFF.

"Hey," she says softly, placing a hand on my sweat-dampened back. "Talk to me."

I didn't realize how much I could miss a simple touch until I didn't have it anymore. It's so easy to let her back in. To let her wiggle her way back into my arms and smile up at me like she is the moon and I am every star in her sky.

When you spend your life in the dark, looking up and wishing for something better—something brighter—you don't realize just how lonely you are. Not until the sun shines, shedding light on all the empty spaces and filling them with beautiful warmth. But when the sun abandons you, everything seems darker and colder than before.

Emptier.

Lonelier.

I force myself to push open the door and step inside, not even sure if she's trailing behind me. When I turn around, she's standing in my living room. I want her to stay; I want those smiles and that maniacal laugh and those cheesy jokes. But I don't want this feeling that will return full force when she leaves. I can only do this once, so for all intents and purposes, I'm going to do it right.

"What do you want, Allison?"

She hesitates, looking around the room to stall for time. I turn back around and begin to make my way to the bedroom. "Let yourself out."

"Wait," she calls out. "I just . . . please, Justice. I can't leave things like this."

I face her with a huff, my annoyance as palpable as the friction crackling between us. "Like what?"

"I know I hurt you and—"

"I'm not hurt."

"Oh." She looks surprised, like she'd expected me to agree. Like she just knew that she was that fucking important to my happiness. She nods as if she's just realizing that she isn't. Not even close. "Well, I know I shouldn't have led you on to believe we . . . that there could be more than friendship between us."

I take a step toward her, a mocking smirk on my lips. "Is that what you thought it was?"

"What do you mean?" She frowns.

"What—you thought I was your friend? You thought I actually liked you? That I wanted our acquaintanceship to grow into something more?" I laugh sardonically, the sound harsh and too loud even to my own ears. "Allison, you are a client. An obligation. Not my friend. I don't have friends, and if I were looking for one, I surely wouldn't seek it in you."

"What?"

I move in fast, anger and aggravation guiding each step, until I'm a meager inch from her face. Fear sparks those turquoise eyes and she gasps in surprise, those soft, sweet lips trembling. I imagine biting them, sucking them into my mouth and tasting that trepidation.

"Did I fucking fail to make myself clear? You're not my friend, and you never will be. Are you friends with your maids? Your driver? The person that walks your rat of a fucking dog and picks up its shit? You paid me for a service, and I provided it. End of story."

She finally finds the good sense to take a step back, disgust etched onto that beautifully blemished face. "Why are you acting like this? How can you say that we were never friends, Justice? I told you things. *Personal* things. And you acted like you genuinely cared. You were so attentive and nice—"

"Nice? *Nice?*" I shout, the sound piercing my cranium. The pain is nothing compared to the ache spreading in that cold, hollow space in my chest. The space the sun no longer touches. "I'm not fucking nice, Ally. Ain't shit nice about me."

She squints like she's just now seeing me for the very first time. "So it seems."

"Good." I turn back around, expecting to feel triumphant. Yet that empty ache just keeps spreading until it's in my throat, choking me. I can barely breathe, but I can't let her see that. I can't show her what she's done to me . . . what she's doing to me now. "You can leave," I croak, through the pressure on my vocal cords.

I stand stock-still until I hear the click of the door behind me. I exhale, releasing a sound that's too broken and ragged to have possibly come from me. I don't feel like myself. I feel like an impostor has crawled its way into my body, sheathed itself with my skin, and is now controlling my actions like one shifts gears in a car. *He* said those things to Ally, not I. Yet I'm the one who's left to deal with the fallout.

The pressure in my chest and throat rages on like rising bile, and I work to strip off my clothing, desperate to wash away the remains of her on my body. The water in the shower is hot, but I don't feel it. I don't feel anything, yet feel everything all at once, emotion and sensation overwhelming me to the point of numbing pain. It's all too much to digest, all too much to keep perfectly contained under my cloak of detachment. I'm failing at the one thing I've always done so well—not giving a fuck.

I taste salt in the water that sprays over my face as another broken sound heaves from my throat. I lean up against the shower wall to prepare to be sick, although the nausea isn't in my stomach. I slam my fist against the water-slick tile and choke out a frustrated curse. I need relief. I'm breaking from the inside out, and if I don't purge this sickness from my body, it'll consume me like a cancer.

I run my fingers over my length and watch through blurry eyes as it awakens at my touch. It hardens almost instantly, and I exhale with relief at the first stroke of my hand. It feels good, almost good enough to eclipse the pressure in other regions of my body. Eager to chase that feeling, I cup my heavy balls with my other hand and a deep, throaty moan escapes me. I close my eyes and give myself over to pleasure and nothing else.

My strokes grow urgent and desperate, and I pant loudly

with painful exertion. I feel relief closing in, shooting from the base of my spine and penetrating my muscles with white heat. Sensation prickles my thighs and crawls its way to my groin. It sinks into my balls and tightens into a hot, throbbing knot, stealing every ounce of strength from my body in preparation for release.

Just a couple more strokes and I'll be free. I'll be emancipated from whatever bullshit feelings I ever had for Ally. Everything we had will soon be washed down the drain until it's dissolved into nothing.

If I hadn't been so consumed with the feel of my hand squeezing this affliction from my cock, I would have known I wasn't alone. I would have at least sensed movement on the other side of the shower door. I would have felt those cerulean eyes on me, my most vulnerable moments on display through the frosted glass. And I would have anticipated the cool air hitting my bare back as the door slides open behind me.

Possession

I bite back the groan on my tongue and open my swollen eyes, but I don't turn around to face my intruder. I know she's there, but I can't let her see me like this—eyes reddened with tears and dick hard and throbbing in my hand. She already sees me as a savage—someone to corrupt her perfect, little existence and replace it with something wild and deviant. Maybe I am one. Maybe I really am the villain in this piece. It wouldn't be the first time.

The door slides closed, and I sigh with relief and exasperation. She's seen what she needs to see. She'll go back to Evan, realizing that her place was with him the entire time. And me . . . I was just a placeholder.

Warm hands wrap around my waist, and I flinch at the unexpected feel of soft skin, such a contrast to my own. I look down at her delicate hands on my stomach as Ally runs her fingers over my abs. I want to ask her what she's doing, but I'm too afraid she'll stop. I just want her to touch me, even if it is a lie.

Her hands sink farther, and I jerk when she wraps a palm around my still-hardened length, swollen from lingering on the brink of release. "Ally," I groan through a sob. I can't tell if it's one of pleasure or pain.

"Shhh," she whispers, her lips on my skin. "Just let me do this. Please."

She kisses my back as her hand slowly strokes my dick. It pulses wildly under her fingertips, excitement and antici-pation running through the rigid veins. Her fingers caress the tip before she twists her wrist and takes it all into her hand, squeezing with perfect pressure. With the warmth of her skin gripping my blistering heat, the slickness of the hot water, and her lips trailing kisses down my back, I'm drown-ing in sensation.

She feels so good here, touching me, exploring the most intimate parts of me. With her hand still fucking me, her other reaches around to cup my balls. She twists her hand around my dick with each stroke, and then gently pulls with the other. Stroke, pull, stroke, pull. It's not painful, but the mix of sensations is driving me insane. The rotating grip of her hand on my dick makes me want to come, spurting my seed all over the shower wall. Yet the gentle pulling at my base forces me to hold back, prolonging the intense pleasure.

I'm fucking astounded.

The need to touch her, to kiss her, becomes overwhelming, and I reluctantly turn around to face her. I watch those eyes grow wide with wonder as she takes in my naked body, my dick standing tall and proud. It brushes the middle of her belly, still covered by her dress, now soaked completely through. It clings to her wet body like a second skin, and her auburn hair sticks haphazardly to her face and neck.

"Justice . . ." she whispers, her gaze taking in every inch of my frame. Her lips tremble, either from fear or from being wet and cold. "You're . . . you're beautiful."

I wrap her in my arms, and the moment my lips touch hers, I feel revived. I haven't breathed since she walked away from me the night before. I didn't know I was a dying man until I had her life on me—in me—tasting of hope and forgiveness. She winds her arms around my neck, and my hands make work of stripping off her soaked clothing, eager to feel her skin slipping against mine. I push her up against the shower wall and pull away just long enough to whip her dress over her head. Her bra is next, and the tiny scrap of lace that is her panties quickly follows.

I know I should go slow and take my time with her; I may not get another chance to kiss an angel. But with the taste of Ally on my tongue, and her soft, smooth skin pressed against mine, sharing my heat, I can't even think about stopping.

Reading my mind, she wraps her leg around my thigh, and we're right back to where we were nearly twenty-four hours ago—me between her legs and her ankles locked at my waist. Yet without the barrier of our clothes, my dick slides right against her soft slit. All I have to do is bend my knees a bit and thrust, and I'll be inside her.

As badly as I want to be buried balls-deep within her walls, I want to make this last. I want Ally to remember this moment forever, even if it is a fluke. Even if I never touch heaven again. I want her to remember that I commanded her body like no one else, and gave her what she craves. What she's never been given before.

With her riding my waist, I suck a pebbled nipple into my mouth while plucking the other with my fingers. Ally gasps loudly and digs her short fingernails into my shoulders. My other hand holds her up by her bare ass, and I let it slip down farther, finding her wet entrance. With my dick rubbing rhythmically against her clit, I insert the tip of a finger inside her pussy, causing her to cry out. She's tight, yet I feel her throbbing, begging for me. I push in deeper and begin to finger-fuck her slowly, still teasing her clit with my cock while laving her breasts with my tongue.

I'm an excellent multitasker.

When I push in a second finger, I feel her walls quiver, approaching orgasm. She pants wildly, moaning, scratching at my hair and shoulders. I pick up the pace of my hips and fingers, and suck and nibble her nipples even harder.

"Wait, wait, oh God," she whines.

"What?" I answer against her puckered nipple. I slow down, but I don't stop. I couldn't stop even if I tried.

"Something's wrong with me. I feel weird. Oh . . . no . . . it's too strong . . . oh."

I resume my rhythm and smile slyly against her heated skin. "Nothing's wrong. You're coming, baby. You're coming for *me*."

I press the tip of my dick directly on her clit and hold it, and her snug pussy pulses out of control. With a strangled cry, Ally's body goes rigid, before a flood of her wetness completely drenches my fingers and collects in my palm. I ride out the waves of her orgasm, easing the friction on her clit and letting my mouth trail up to hers to kiss her deeply, swallowing her little mewls of pleasure.

She pulls her lips from mine, her face flushed and eyes sleepy. "I saw colors. So many colors popping, glittering my sky." Ally smiles, and light touches every cold, empty space within me. "Fireworks."

I slip my fingers from her still-shivering sex and put them in my mouth, savoring her taste before the water can wash it away. "I'm not done with you yet."

With her still in my arms, I turn off the water and slide open the shower door. She squeals and laughs when the cold air hits us, burying her wet face into the crook of my neck. I laugh right along with her as I awkwardly make my way into the bedroom, dick still rock hard, and her tight frame wrapped around me like a spider monkey. We flop onto the bed, dripping wet, and I pull the covers over us as I nestle between her thighs.

"Justice, I just want to say I'm—"

I place a finger over her lips before she can finish. "Shhh. Don't. It's me who should apologize. But not now. I don't want to think about anything else but this. Nothing else but your body and what I plan to do to it for the rest of the night."

She kisses my finger and grasps my hand to slide the tip of the digit between her lips, nipping at it playfully. "Do your worst, Drake."

I kiss her deeply, consuming every bit of her mouth. She wraps her arms and legs around me, and my dick slips between her folds, my swollen head nudging her wet slit. I rock my hips back and forth, reigniting that delicious friction we had the shower, and Ally moans against my tongue.

"Oh God, put it in. Put it in, please," she whines.

"Put what in, sweetheart?" I smirk, looking down at her hungry expression.

"*It.*"

"It?" I shake my head and press in a little farther, my tip right at her entrance. "What's *it*, Ally? If you want *it*, you have to say *it*."

She squeezes her eyes tight, and a beautiful flush paints her cheeks. "Your cock. I want your cock in me. *Please*."

Gritting my teeth, I drive into her—probably harder and faster than I should—but shit, I'm as anxious as she is. Ally's eyes pop open with shock and her lips round into an O. A strangled cry gets stuck in the back of her throat.

"This?" I pant, the feeling of her tight body enveloping mine almost too much take. "Is this what you were referring to?"

She nods her head frantically, trying to swallow a whine. "Yes. Yes. Now shut up . . . and *fuck me*."

The words ring in my head like a sweet melody, as if Ally's just opened Pandora's box and unleashed every lustful desire within me. I pull out to the tip and push back into her, feeling the tightness quiver and stretch for me.

God, she feels good. *Too* good. So good that every nerve ending within me is flashing bright red, signaling me to stop. I pull out quickly, before the feel of her dissolves every ounce of common sense I have left.

"What?" she rasps, an almost pained look on her face.

"Fuck," I grit in frustration. I reach over to the nightstand and retrieve a condom from the top drawer. Ally's eyes grow large at the sight of the little shiny package.

"Oh," she whispers, trying to look at anything but me as I tear it open.

"Yeah." I slip out the latex and position it over the head of my dick, still glistening with her sweetness.

"Wait." Ally's hand is over mine, pulling the condom away. "Wait. You don't have to . . . you don't have to use it. I trust you. And I hope . . . I hope you trust me too."

I sit back on my heels so I can assess her face clearly. "I do. I trust you, but . . ." Fuck. How do I say that it's Evan that I don't trust? That I shouldn't do this because of his sketchy-ass habits?

"We always use condoms," she says, reading my mind. "Always. I don't trust him. But . . . Justice, I trust *you*."

I toss the condom aside, not giving a fuck where it lands, and lie back over Ally's body, hungrily sucking her tongue while I slowly push my cock into her. She hums her appreciation, smiling against my lips as I rock my pelvis upward, ensuring that I graze that sweet spot. She works her own hips with mine, meeting me thrust for thrust, sucking me deeper into her.

Why is she here? I wonder to myself as I slide my hand under her ass, positioning it so she can take all of me.

I mean, I'm glad as fuck that she came, but Ally has no business being here at Oasis. There's nothing wrong with her. Not a goddamn thing. The way she moans and mewls while kneading and scratching my back; the way her soft thighs squeeze my waist, telling me to go deeper; the way her body moves perfectly with mine, as if we were made to do this. As if it was specifically designed to meld with mine . . . Ally doesn't need any help in learning how to be a good lover. She already is. She's already more than I could ever hope for. And part of me always knew she would be.

Fire licks up my thighs and ignites embers at the base of my balls, and I know that all sense of control will be relinquished inside her walls soon enough. Her pussy begins to quiver, coaxing that ball of fire from me. I feel her getting wetter for me, ready to extinguish my fire with her own flood of surrender.

One hand under her ass and the other reaching down to

rub her clit, I pick up the pace of my thrusts, eager to drown in her warm waters. Ally cries in ecstasy, and her fingers find her breasts, which she begins to squeeze and pinch. I lean over and suck a hardened nipple into my mouth, then lick the other as Ally presses them together, offering them to my tongue and teeth.

I fuck her entire body, submerging her in sensation. She's hoarse from moaning, screaming my name. Chanting how good I fucking feel. How deep I am. How she wants me to keep going and never stop. Never, ever fucking stop or I-will-fucking-die-please-oh-please-don't-stop.

Her back arches off the bed until only her shoulders remain on the mattress, and I feel her explode from the inside out. Her eyes are shut tight and her mouth is open, but no sound comes out.

"Yeah, that's right, baby," I say gruffly, still pushing inside her. "Keep going. Keep coming for me."

She's gorgeous. Savagely beautiful. I just want to watch her fall apart over and over again until she's too numb to move. But seeing her so vulnerable and wild while her insides tremble around my dick has my own orgasm seizing my spine. I want to slow my thrusts, but it's already too late. My back is tight, and my fingers are gripping her hips, driving into her one last time. I crawl as deep inside Ally as I possibly can, singeing her womb with my hot seed. Marking her pussy so there's no denying that not only have I been here, but I possessed it.

I collapse on top of her, exhaustion covering me like a

heavy cloak. Only my shaky elbows keep me from crushing her petite frame.

"During which week is that lesson taught?" she asks, a sleepy grin on her lips. I kiss them, tasting the sun.

"No lesson, baby. Something that damn incredible can't be taught."

"COKE OR PEPSI?"

"Coke."

"Pepperoni or sausage?"

"Pepperoni."

"Action movies or comedy?"

"Is there a point to this?"

"We should talk. I like getting to know you. So answer the question, Secret Squirrel."

"Action. Now shut up so I can feed you."

I slide the cold spoon between her lips, and she licks it clean of every bit of ice cream. "Mmm. Figures you'd pick action."

I steal a bite for myself, the icy treat tasting even better after working Ally's body like her own erotic personal trainer. "Why's that?"

She props her elbow up on the pillow and turns her naked body toward mine. My eyes zero in on her perfect breasts, lolling to one side and resting on my shoulder. "Well, considering you have the name of a superhero and all . . ."

"Superhero?"

"Never fear! Justice Drake is here!" she announces in a corny timbre, pumping her fist in the air. "Ready to slay the villains of Scottsdale with double-headed dongs and acid lube lasers!"

We both laugh until tears form at the creases of our eyes. Until snickers taper off into soft mewls and touches. Then we're chest to chest, skin to skin, and I'm devouring her mouth, the ice cream forgotten. Ally parts her thighs for me, and I roll my body on top of hers, cradling her face so I can kiss her deeper.

"I'm never going to get used to this, am I?" she remarks as I gently suck the skin under her chin.

"Do you want to?" I ask, before licking a trail from her neck to the space between her breasts.

"No. I want this excitement, this newness and fun . . . I want it to always be like this."

Can it be?

The question is right there on my tongue, but I smother it with Ally's puckered nipple, making her moan my name. All the questions and consequences will have to wait. None of it matters when she's in my arms. And I don't even know how long that can last.

"Hey," she says, letting her fingers slide up the back of my neck to grab a handful of my hair. "You're trying to distract me from the task at hand."

I let my palm drift over her stomach until it's cupping her swollen mound. "I thought this was the task at hand."

"Ooooh, good point."

I flick her clit gently, knowing that she's still sore and sensitive, while I scoot my body down farther to position her thighs on my shoulders. When I replace my fingers with my tongue, Ally makes a garbled sound that resembles a cursed growl.

"What's that, babe?" I ask, her clit on my lips. I take it between my teeth, just barely nipping it. "I couldn't hear you."

"Fuck you," she whispers through a moan.

I suck her flesh harder before flicking my tongue over it to ease the sting. "Oh, such a filthy mouth, Allison. Maybe I should fill it with something so you can't say such naughty things to me."

She gasps as I insert a finger into her and resume licking her clit. "Don't you dare stop. Unless you want your head to be permanently dented from my thighs squeezing it like a walnut."

"But I thought you wanted to talk, baby?" I insert another finger and fuck her with them hard and fast for only a few seconds before removing them. "I shouldn't do this. We should talk."

"If you stop what you're doing, Justice Drake, so help me God, I will tie you to this bed and go all *Misery* on your ass!"

I laugh, letting the vibrations transfer from my mouth and tickle her sensitive flesh. I enhance the feeling by inserting my index finger and licking her in slow, lazy circles. "Okay," I say, kissing her soft folds. "You talk. I'll lick."

"You really expect me to be able to form actual words? Sentences? That make sense?"

"Do you want me to finger-fuck you and suck your clit until you come so hard in my mouth that you pass out?"

Her eyes grow wide with delight. "Yes, please."

"Then talk to me, baby."

I devour her sex like it's my last meal before a beautiful death, savoring her sweet-salty flavor. I'm so hungry for her; I feel like I haven't eaten in weeks and only Ally can sate my need. Her knees shake against my ears, and I remove my fingers to grip her thighs, opening her wider for me. Then, with a maddening rhythm, I alternate sucking her clit and fucking her with my tongue. I want to taste every bit of Ally. And when she comes, not a drop will spill over onto the sheets.

"Talk," I command, when she's too overcome with pleasure to utter a coherent word.

"God! Oh, you . . . oh God."

"That's flattering, but call me Justice." Suck. Lick. Stick.

"Justice." She's so breathless, my name sounds like a soft breeze. "Justice. You son of a bitch. How dare you . . . how dare you do this to me."

"Do what, baby?" Suck. Lick. Stick.

"*This*. All . . . this. Now I know . . . I know what I was missing. And I can't . . . I can't be without it. I can never go back."

My rhythm falters, and I groan against her quivering flesh, trying to bury myself in it. What does she mean by that? Never go back? Does she want to stay with me and leave Evan? Is that even an option for her?

But mostly, shit . . . Is that even an option for *me*?

I know I want her body more than I want my next breath. And I know that meeting her, basking in her smiles, and wanting her on me like a second skin has forever changed me. But can there ever be more? Can I spend every night counting her freckles, like I once counted the stars? Can I replace my sunrise with the vision of her sleeping beside me, fiery hair, wild and tangled all over her face? Can I swim in those too-big turquoise eyes and drown myself in her laughter every night?

I think the bigger question is: *How can I not?*

There's no doubt that I want to be with Ally. I knew it the day I knocked on the door to her suite. It wasn't those walls closing in on me; it was fate. And if Ally is my fate, losing her—being without every quirk that makes her so uniquely flawless—will be fatal to me. And that's what terrifies me more than I could ever admit.

So if all we have is now, I'm going to make her remember. I'm going to become a permanent stain on her body that she'll never be able to wash away. And when she closes her eyes and squeezes her thighs together, I'm going to ensure that she's imagining me here. Like this. Setting off fireworks within her slick, sweltering heat, like the Fourth of July.

Ally cries out with her release, cursing me and praising my name as she crumbles in my hands. And, just as I promised, I suck and lap up every drop of wetness seeping from her pulsing sex, prolonging the violent waves of climax. She begs me to stop, but I don't. She only thinks she's dying right now as I lick the stray droplets running down her ass. Little does she know, I claimed her life the moment she broke inside my palm against the shower wall.

That was the very second she became mine, no matter whose last name she bears. And every time she came thereafter, I was just marking myself deeper and deeper into her skin like a tattoo. Carving out a space that would only be for me.

Justice + Ally.

Confession

"Call in sick tomorrow."

I grin sleepily and kiss her forehead. "It's already tomorrow."

"Then call in sick today."

"I never call in sick, even if I'm sick."

"Please? I don't know . . . I don't know how long I can have you like this. I'm not ready to let it go."

I squeeze her body into mine and breathe her in. I just want to memorize this moment. Her scent, her taste, her softness. I want it infecting my mind like a tumor, growing and influencing every thought and action.

Ally kisses my bare chest, her lips so warm and delicate, like the brush of a feather. "Please?"

One arm still tucked under her body, I reach over to grab

my phone. "There," I say after tapping out a text to Diane. "I'm sick today. So sick. I wonder if someone will nurse me back to health."

I feel Ally smile against my nipple. "Are you asking me to play Naughty Nurse, Mr. Drake?"

"I don't know. Are you down for some sexual healing?"

She kisses me again. "Most definitely. But later, okay? I really do want to talk to you."

I roll my body toward her and position my arm so she can rest her head on my biceps. "About what?"

"About . . ." Her gaze goes glassy and distant. "Next."

"Next?"

"What's next?"

I swallow and take a few breaths to collect my thoughts. I can't ask this woman to leave her husband. I can't tell her to ruin her lavish lifestyle in exchange for one of exile and isolation. This isn't what she knows. Financially, I could give Ally whatever she wants, but socially? She'd be like me. An outcast. A fallen star that once shined brighter than a million diamonds.

I can't be certain that a life with me would be enough for her. I can't be certain that even *I* would be enough for her.

"What do you want to be next, Ally?" I hold my breath.

Her eyes sweep over my lips, my chin, my neck, then back up to my face. "I don't know. The future is scary. I just know that I've never felt this way before. I've never been so out of control and reckless and totally wrapped up in a person . . .

ever. But then again, what if all this is just a temporary high? What if the taboo of it all is what's driving us together?"

I brush her cheek, just so I can keep touching her. I need to remind myself that she's here. Here with me. Not him. "Is that what you think this could be?"

"Honestly? No. But I've been wrong before. And that's cost me my freedom. Walking away without repercussions isn't an option for me. My life would come crashing down."

I stay silent, because anything I could say would be static— just background noise. She's right. She can't just walk away. No matter what Evan does to her, no matter what he does with his little weasel prick, Ally has to play her role. The supportive, loving wife. Strong, resilient, and tolerant. A perfect picture of grace and elegance.

"Justice?"

I smile through the infection of my thoughts, feeling them seep into my conscience. "Yeah?"

"Do you want me to walk away? Do you want me to leave him?"

My lips part, the answer burning my tongue. I swallow it down before answering. "I want you to do what makes you happy."

She kisses my lips in response before nestling into my chest like a sleepy cat. My lips are in her hair, and I wrap both arms around her body, refusing to let her go.

I could make Ally happy. I could fill the void that her departure from the upper crust would create. But then what?

What would that mean for my business? My reputation? Would I be exposing myself and reinciting the witch hunt that led me to seek refuge in my lonely desert years ago?

I feel her breaths growing deeper and heavier, so I let my own tired eyes slip closed. "Please don't leave me, angel," I whisper, somewhere on the edges of sleep and the most beautiful dream. "I don't want to be in the dark anymore."

DRESSED ONLY IN soft, flannel pants, I pad out to the kitchen, led by the scents of bacon, eggs, and toast. And coffee. Oh, sweet, wonderful coffee.

A hot breakfast and fresh coffee would be enough to make most men salivate, but the sight of Ally fluttering around in one of my prep school sweatshirts and nothing else, with a messy bun on top of her head, is just downright delectable. The thick, gray cotton is about five sizes too big for her and slips over a bare shoulder, exposing the top of her breast. I waste no time making my way over to cover that delicious patch of skin with my mouth.

"Good morning." She smiles, her attention on the pan of fluffy scrambled eggs on the stove.

"Morning. You weren't in bed when I woke up."

"I was sticky and hot, so I needed to shower. Plus, I was too hungry to sleep. We only had ice cream for dinner." She turns her head and gives me a soft kiss.

"Speak for yourself. I ate more than that."

A blush paints her cheeks, and I can't resist kissing the one closest to me, feeling her skin heat under my lips. Soon they're trailing down her neck and to the sensitive area under her ear.

"Hey!" she squeals. "Some of us are working with scalding-hot food here! Go sit down; your breakfast is just about ready. And your coffee's on the counter."

I give her bare ass a pinch before doing as I'm told.

"Oh, today's paper was on the counter when I came out here. I hope whoever brought it in didn't peek in on us. Holy shit, could you imagine?"

"Nah. My people aren't like that," I say, sipping my brew. I push aside the *Arizona Republic* and pick up the *New York Post,* thankful that it's still neatly folded. Ally didn't read it.

I stop at the top story on Page Six, and blind rage has me seeing red. I can clearly read the headline—see his fake, solemn mug looking pathetic as fuck—but I can't digest it. I can't accept it. It's a myth, a lie, like the fucking Easter Bunny or Santa Claus.

MANHATTAN SOCIALITE EVAN CARR: "I'VE MADE MISTAKES, BUT I'M READY TO RECONCILE"

Evan Carr, grandson of former governor Winston Carr, broke down yesterday and opened up about his tumultuous marriage to wife, Allison Elliot-Carr, cheating and pregnancy rumors, and how he hopes to make things right.

"I love my wife," he told sources. "Ally is my life. And I would never, ever do anything to intentionally hurt her. I know I have a lot of work to do, but I'm going to show her that I can be the husband that she deserves. Even if it kills me."

Earlier this month, Evan had been sighted with a woman believed to have been Allison's gal pal, Kelsie van Weiss, though he did not confirm or deny the accusations. However, he doesn't deny any claims of infidelity.

"I messed up; I know that. I was disloyal to her, and now I'm paying the price. But I'm prepared to do what it takes to earn her trust. I would do anything for her."

Mrs. Carr is currently vacationing alone at an exclusive resort spa, despite earlier rehab rumors. She is completely healthy and anxious to reconnect with her husband when she returns.

I read the story again, dissecting every word. It's bullshit. It's all bullshit. Evan was reeled in by his equally fucked-up father and was basically spoon-fed those manufactured lines of regret. He probably has the song and dance memorized, considering he's spewed the same rubbish more than once.

"Hey, can I get that after you're done?" Ally asks, startling me from my murderous thoughts.

I look down at the paper in front of me. Evan looks so distraught, so remorseful. He looks exactly like a loving husband would look when he's missing his other half. "Sure." I nod. Then, most unfortunately, the mug in my hand, the one I'm tipping to my lips, suddenly slips from my fingers, and covers those blasphemous pages with hot coffee.

"Shit!" I hiss, jumping off my stool before the scalding liquid can hit my bare skin. I grab some napkins and sop up the mess, folding the ruined newspaper into a ball. Ally rushes over with a dish towel just seconds after Evan's face is marred beyond recognition.

"It's okay," she says, drying the countertop while I discard the mess. "I'll get you another cup."

"No," I reply, coming up behind her. I kiss her neck while my hands snake up the oversize sweatshirt that stops at the middle of her thighs. "You sit. I'll take care of the rest."

Evan may play the rueful husband in front of the cameras, but I'm the one putting cream and sugar in Ally's coffee. I'm the one serving her breakfast, even feeding it to her while her smooth, bare legs rest in my lap. And I'll be the one spreading her body out on my kitchen breakfast bar and covering her swollen sex with my mouth while she chants my name like a prayer.

Ally may be Evan's by law, but she's mine by nature. And in a battle between lions, no one gives a fuck about what's lawful. It's all brute strength, cunning, and instinct. Three things I've utilized my entire life to survive.

WE'RE SITTING ON the couch, kissing like horny teenagers, while the TV plays in the background. Ally insisted on borrowing a pair of boxers before sitting down, although I was more than happy to let her scent permeate the butter-soft leather.

"So what do you want to do?" she asks, straddling my lap.

I nudge my hips forward so that the hardened bulge under my thin pants presses against her mound. "I can come up with a few things."

She rolls her eyes and purses her lips, stifling a smile. "I'm sure you could. But seriously. Let's do something fun."

"Like what?"

Ally reaches over to grab my phone, and I nearly jump out of my skin. However, she doesn't slide the unlock icon, and instead pulls up the camera.

"Smile," she says, taking a picture before I can react.

I grab her by the hips and tip my head to the side. "What are you doing?"

"Taking home a souvenir. I'm going to send these pics to myself. Come on, give me something I can work with." The whir of the camera sounds three more times as she takes shots of my face, chest, and abs.

"Mmm, very nice. This'll do nicely in my spank bank." I snatch the phone away before she can get another candid shot of me, causing her to protest. "Hey! I wasn't done yet!"

"My turn for a souvenir," I reply, turning the camera on her. She instantly covers her face with her hands.

"Are you crazy? That's exactly what I *don't* need. *Half-nakey pics of the sullied socialite while she vacations alone with an unknown man.* The tabloids will spin it to make it look like I was spread-eagled on the couch, sucking a cherry-red lollipop while making a sex tape."

"Now, that's an idea." I smirk, the visual in my head making my mouth water.

"I am *not* pulling a Kim Kardashian, Drake. So hand it over."

I snap a pic of her lips pressed in a hard line and her hand extended. "Ally, these are only for me. For my pleasure. I'd kill someone before I shared these photos. I just want to be able to look at you . . . always. If I can't keep you, at least let me have this."

Her gaze falls to her knotted fingers resting against my stomach, and she sucks in her bottom lip. "Okay." Her eyes find mine, and she gives me a solemn smile. "Okay, you can have this."

I capture images of her looking at me through those sad, peculiar eyes. A wisp of red unravels from her bun, and I take the opportunity to snap a photo of her tucking it behind her ear, her gaze far away and thoughtful.

"What are you thinking about?" I ask, studying her through the lens.

"How I can't remember ever having this much fun. And being this happy. And how I'm terrified of what the future holds."

Tears collect along the rims of her eyes, and I stroke her cheek, forcing her to look at me. "Don't think about that right now. Let's just keep having fun and being free. Let's be happy together for now and not think about tomorrow."

I kiss her hungrily, snapping an erotic selfie of the moment.

In another place, at another time, it'd be my home screen. And Ally . . . Ally would be the first number on my favorites contact list. And when she would call me to tell me about her day, or to relay a funny story, or just to say that she'd be coming home to me soon, her blinding smile and happy face would light up the screen, those cyan eyes sparkling like the brightest, boldest stars in the sky.

She pulls away just far enough to bring her body into the frame, a mischievous smile on her lips. The naughty little minx is back, and I have every intention of capturing her and never letting her go.

"Take your shirt off," I command, my eyes fixed on the screen that is displaying her blush.

"What?"

"Your shirt. Lose it. I need a little something for my spank bank too."

She tugs at the hem of the sweatshirt, revealing just a peek of skin. "I swear to God, Justice, if you show anybody—"

"Trust me, Ally. You trust me. Remember?"

"Yeah." She nods. "I do." And with that, the sweatshirt slides over her torso and is on the floor, her beautiful breasts just inches from my hungry mouth.

Ally covers her chest with her hands and looks away. "I look ridiculous, don't I? You're used to Big Boobs McGee shaking her Double Ds in your face. And here I am . . . the rack of a twelve-year-old. I'm practically a husky boy with moobs."

The camera whirs again, before I lower it so Ally can see

the seriousness etched on my face. "Please don't ruin this for me by comparing yourself to a boy. Or any adolescent, for that matter. What did I teach you, Ally? Sex appeal isn't about having big tits or a round ass. It's not about your dress size or even how skimpy your clothing is. It starts inside here." I graze her temple gently, and Ally shivers under my touch. Then I trail my fingers to her chest, prying her fingers from her breasts. "And here," I say, splaying my hand over her heart. "Here, Ally. If you feel sexy, you'll be sexy. If you believe it, so will I."

When her hands are balled at her sides, I resume my intensive study of her body. I zoom in on the cluster of freckles on her nose, and the tiny mole on her left breast. The heart shape of her lips, the bottom one just a fraction bigger than the top, giving her a permanent pout. The way her waist appears so small and narrow, yet solid enough that I'm not afraid of breaking her when I'm inside of her to the root.

Ally is art. She may appear simple and understated to the untrained eye, but to me, she's a rare, exotic piece that should be cherished and appreciated.

"Lift your chin," I instruct, recording the image of her slender neck.

"I better not see Mary-Kate and Ashley on the Internet, buddy."

"Mary-Kate and Ashley?"

"Yeah. My girls," she says, gesturing between her breasts. "Small, maybe a little sad, but cute."

I lean over and cover her left one with my mouth. "Who is this?"

"Ooooh. That's Mary-Kate. She's the smaller, perky one."

I move my tongue to the right one, flicking the nipple before sucking it entirely into my mouth. "So this one must be Ashley."

"Yeah," she answers with a gasp. "Which one do you like best?"

I toss my phone aside, and it tumbles from the couch with a clatter. I don't even care. Not when both of her breasts are in my hands, pressed together so both nipples stand erect to me. "I don't know. I need to taste them both."

Ally's eyes flutter closed as I thoroughly suck and bite the pebbled skin, careful to shower equal attention on each one. She moans my name and rocks her hips, running her cotton-sheathed sex over my bulging erection. I can almost feel the small wet spot saturating her borrowed boxers through my pajama pants.

"I need to be inside of you," I say against her heated skin. "Right now, baby. I need to fill you right now."

I lift her off my lap so she can kick off the boxer shorts, and I quickly do the same with my flannel pants. Then she's straddling my lap, the tip of my dick at her entrance. We both suck in a breath at the sight of it—our bodies joined together, pulses racing inside our most intimate parts. Hearts beating together in perfect harmony. I grip her under her ass and thighs to guide her descent.

"Slow, baby. Look at me while I fill you one inch at a time."

Ally's glazed eyes touch mine, lust shining bright and wild within them. I ease her down just a bit, just enough so that my head is nestled inside her, and watch the emotions play out on her face. Surprise. Pain. Complete and utter ecstasy.

"More?" I ask.

Ally nods, struggling to keep her eyes open and trained on me. "Yes. More."

One more hard, glorious inch. Her walls contract and expand, but she's still tight and a little swollen from last night. Even with her dripping wet, I feel her walls squeezing me like a vise grip.

"God, baby," I grit out, restraining myself from just driving into her. "More?"

"Yes, yes. Justice, please," she whines.

She cries out when I give her what she craves. She begs for even more, and I can't resist complying with her wishes.

"Oh, this is too much. Too . . . too . . . much. I can't hold on," she sobs.

"Just a little more, baby. Stay with me."

I ease her down onto the last few inches, thrusting up to meet the jolting movement, and I feel Ally break apart all over my lap. Her insides suck and pull at me, and I bounce her up and down in a fast, unrelenting rhythm. Her walls keep quaking, and she rides out the never-ending orgasm, crying my name, her face buried in the crook of my neck.

"Shit," I grit out, when my own climax clutches my spine. With her pussy still contracting, my release draws tight at my groin. I lift Ally off before it's too late and set her on shaky legs.

"Taste yourself, baby," I pant hoarsely, holding the base of my dick. "Taste how sweet you are. Suck yourself right off me."

Her eyes grow wide with shock and delight as she takes in the sight of me stroking my glistening wet cock. Reluctantly, she licks her lips and slides down onto her knees between my legs.

"Don't be afraid, baby. Trust me; you'll love it."

Ally's gaze flicks to mine, desire burning hot and bright. She wraps her hand around mine before slowly bringing her lips to the slick tip, and I groan loudly when I feel her pink tongue snake out and lick circles around my head.

"You like it?" I ask her, my voice thick with overwhelming need.

"Yes," she answers breathlessly.

"Then lick it all, baby. Don't waste a drop."

I pulse violently as she slides my hardness between her lips and onto her tongue, until it touches the back of her throat. She takes me slowly at first, getting accustomed to the foreign feeling. Then she's sucking me hungrily, vibrating my dick with her moans while still squeezing me at the root. I buck my hips upward, eager to meet release.

"So close. So close, baby," I croak. "Touch yourself. Play with your clit while you make me come."

She doesn't hesitate this time, and a hand disappears between her legs. I feel the exact moment her fingers meet her soft folds, because she sucks me harder, more enthusiastically. Seeing her so turned on by her own flavor, my cock in her mouth and her hand stroking her pussy, makes the heat at my core burst and expand into a glowing hot ball of liquid fire, which snakes through my body faster than I can stop it. With an agonized growl, I grudgingly pull Ally's mouth away just as the first spurt is purged from my body. She watches with rapt fascination as cum spills onto my tight belly, and I jerk and shiver through the category-five climax.

"Wow," she whispers, her lips red and swollen. I groan in response, unable to do much more.

As if I could be even more enamored by her, as if she could possibly do anything to intensify my infatuation, she leans over and licks the salty, milky trail of my surrender that is cooling on the rigid muscles of my abs. I cradle her face lovingly and stroke her hair, overwhelmed with emotion in this moment, and too raw to even begin to put it into words.

It's the ultimate act of submission, yet Ally dominates every muddled thought, every sensation coursing through my body, and every single, ragged breath in my lungs.

Soft purrs tickle the inside of my thigh while her head rests on my leg after she's devoured every drop of me. I lift her into my arms and cradle her against my chest, both our naked bodies sticky with sweat and arousal.

"You should've recorded that for your spank bank," she says, once our breaths have slowed to normal.

"What makes you think I didn't?"

"True. Just Photoshop some bigger boobs on me. The Olsen twins need some meat on their bones."

"Shhh. You're perfect, angel," I whisper in her hair. "Perfect just the way you are."

Consumption

$\mathcal{I}$t's funny how you never realize how much you hate sleeping alone until you're forced to do it.

There. I said it. I hate sleeping alone.

Or maybe I just hate sleeping without Ally tucked into my side, her red, disheveled mane falling into my face and smothering me in slumber. Or her drool trickling onto my chest, or her spontaneous bouts of snoring scaring the shit out of me in the middle of the night.

God. I fucking love it.

So much so that I couldn't sleep a wink after she slipped out my front door, leaving me satisfied, yet still hungry for her in every way, shape, and form.

"People will start to talk," she said, sliding on her sandals. Those ugly-ass sandals. God, I fucking love them too.

"Let them talk."

"You're cute." She smiled before touching her lips to mine. "Cute, but not careless. You know how people love to talk. And those women haven't had a piece of juicy gossip to feast on in months."

"Fuck them," I answered, wrapping her in my arms, refusing to let her go.

"Mmm." She ran her nose from the base of my throat up to my chin. "I like it when you don't shave. Scruff is sexy on you."

"*You're* sexy on me," I replied, letting my hands drift down to squeeze her ass. It fit perfectly in my palms. "Stay. Don't go."

"You're diabolical, Mr. Drake," she said, shaking her head. She kissed my lips and unwound my hands from her body. "Tonight, okay? I'll come by right after dinner. I'll even skip the panna cotta, so you better have some ice cream for me."

"I'll have more than that for you."

She turned around and smiled at me just before she reached the door, and all I could do was bask in that smile like it was the warmest, brightest ray of sunlight I'd ever seen. I would go blind before I stopped staring at her.

"Tonight," she said. "We'll have tonight."

I wish I had made her stay. I wish I hadn't told her that I needed to talk to her, that it couldn't wait another minute, that there was something she needed to know about me before we went any further. But I just stood there, dumbfounded, staring at that trail of fire until she disappeared into the main house.

Even with the lack of sleep, I can't wait to get to class this morning. I shower, shave, and throw on my clothes with more zeal than I've ever felt. I don't even bother to do my daily ritual of checking Google Alerts, Page Six, or all the other gossip rags. None of that matters anymore. Not when the memory of Ally's body under mine, trembling with the aftershocks of orgasm while she mewls my name, is permanently burned into my skull.

I've barely stepped inside the great room, when Riku approaches me, trailed by my head of concierge, Diane, and a few members of my staff.

"Dude . . . are you okay?" he asks, concern engraved in his face. He squints his slanted eyes, making them look black under his dark brows.

"Yeah." I frown, taking in everyone's anxious stares. "What's going on?"

"Haven't you checked the news? I've been texting you."

I fish my cell out of my pocket and press the home button. Completely black. I must've forgotten to charge it after Ally and I took naked selfies yesterday. Shit, that's not like me.

"Phone's dead. Why? What's up?"

Riku looks around, stalling nervously as a few of the housewives trickle into the room for this morning's lesson. My gaze goes straight over his shoulder, past everything and everyone else, in anticipation of seeing Ally.

"You should really check the news, J.D.," he says gravely. "Heidi is on her way down."

"Heidi?" That gets my attention. I've worked with her for years, yet have only actually seen her less than a handful of times. This obviously isn't a social visit.

"Yeah. Flight got in early this morning. She'll be here any—"

"She's already here," a voice says from behind me. Heidi DuCane, the HBIC of the PR world and renowned pit bull in a skirt. Heidi is probably the only person on earth whose cold demeanor can make me shiver. The ice queen's penchant for perfection and for getting results is what has made her the most-sought-after—and highest-paid—publicist in the business. And her sharp, Nordic features and statuesque frame have definitely made her the hottest.

I take in the tall, leggy blonde holding a sleek briefcase at her side and nod at her approach. Heidi's flawless face is screwed into a scowl that would make even the toughest alpha male wilt on sight. Riku shrinks back into the kitchen before she stops in front of me.

"Charge your fucking phone, Drake," she says without preamble. Then she turns to make her way across the court-yard toward my house.

I look back at Diane, feeling a few inches shorter. "Dismiss the ladies. Tell them to review in their suites, then they're free to enjoy the day."

When I look up, she's there, stealing the breath from my lungs and replacing it with what feels like helium. I feel like

I'm floating when she's around, so high that I can kiss the sun. She looks back at me, frozen in place, those cherry lips slightly parted as if she's just gasped or moaned. It takes everything in me not to stride over to her and find out for myself.

"Stand by. I'll be in touch," I mutter to Diane without looking at her. Then I turn away and step back into my cold, dark reality.

"THIS IS FUCKED, Drake. Seriously. How could you let this happen?"

Heidi paces the floor of my living room in six-inch Louboutins, a smartphone in each of her hands. She brings one up to her ear and barks out an order, but I don't hear it. My eyes and ears don't move past the scenes playing out on the television screen. Variations of the same headline play over and over again as people try to speculate and dissect the bit of information they've been given on a silver platter.

BREAKING NEWS: SEX DOCTOR TO THE STARS REVEALED!

MALE SEXPERT TRANSFORMS SOCIALITES INTO SEXPOTS

$250K TO SLEEP WITH YOUR WIFE?
YOU WON'T BELIEVE WHO HIS CELEB CLIENTS ARE!

A REAL-LIFE DR. FEELGOOD? HIS PATIENTS UNMASKED.

WHO IS JUSTICE DRAKE?
CELEBRITY CONSULTANT OR SEXUAL PREDATOR?

Who is Justice Drake?

Who *is* Justice Drake?

Even I can't answer that question.

"Justice. Justice!" I turn toward the sound of Heidi's aggravated voice, but I don't look at her. "Did you hear what I just said?"

"They don't have anything. Just a name. All they have is a name," I answer almost robotically, ignoring her question.

"Yeah, but who knows who leaked it? And it's only a matter of time before they have more."

I turn back to the TV just as the scene changes, displaying a new headline: *A SEARCH FOR JUSTICE.* Clever.

"Justice . . . I've got my hands full dealing with irate clients. You promised them complete discretion, and now they're scared this will get out." She walks over to me and places a slender hand on my wrist. It's the first time Heidi has ever touched me. Her skin is softer than I imagined, more delicate. Even with the hard exterior, Heidi is a woman through and through. I briefly wonder about her love life. Is she married? Dating? Gay or straight? Is someone making her toes curl regularly?

"Hey," she coos with a pained smile. "You have to make a decision here. The curtain is closing. Time to send the players home."

"No." I'm on my feet, fists balled at my sides.

"No? Justice, did you hear what I just said? We breached the contract. You will lose everything if you don't fix this shit right now. Send the women home, refund their money, and disappear before someone reveals your identity."

"I don't give a fuck. I can't let her . . . I'm not ready to. I can't send them back yet. I'm not done."

"Jesus Christ! Listen to yourself!" she says, throwing her hands up in exasperation. "I can't represent you if you don't listen to me. We still have time to fix this if we act now. It's not like you're actually fucking any of these women."

My eyes pierce hers reflexively, wide with guilt. Or fear. Or maybe a mixture of both. She reads my expression like the back of a cereal box.

"Holy fuck, you didn't. Tell me you didn't, Justice. Tell me right this fucking minute!"

"Heidi, it's not like that . . ." I croak. But the words don't sound convincing even to my ears. Apparently, Heidi doesn't buy my statement either.

"I can't believe you. I knew it. I *knew* it. Since the last time we spoke. I just didn't want to believe that you'd ever be so careless. You of all people, with your rules and control and anonymity. You would never do something so stupid."

"I can fix it."

"You can't do shit. Who is she, Justice? Which one is it? Maybe there's still a way to salvage this mess. If I know who she is, we know how much to offer for her silence."

I stay quiet. Partly because I won't betray Ally like that, and partly because I'm too much of a coward to tell her that

I don't want to fix this. Now that the secret is out, I can breathe. I don't have to hide who I am anymore. I don't have to hide how I feel.

"Name, Justice. Now."

I look up at Heidi, feeling like this is the beginning of the end. As much as I try to fight it, I know it's over. I know that the sun has set on Ally and me.

"We can't pay her off. Her silence is not for sale."

Heidi arches a meticulously shaped brow. "Everyone is for sale, Justice. You should know that better than anyone."

"Well, she's not. Not Ally."

"Ally? As in Allison Elliot-Carr? *The* Allison Elliot-Carr? For fuck's sake, Justice, why did you have to diddle the richest bitch here? You're right; there's nothing you can offer her that she doesn't already have probably stashed in her coin purse."

"Like I said, it's not like that. She wouldn't take any money anyway."

"And how would you know? Are you two supposed to be in love or something? Do you think, even for one second, that she would leave her life of excess and luxury and take up with you? She has Evan, Mr. Sexiest Man Alive according to *People* magazine. Even Oprah would hit that. No offense, Justice, but what would she want with you?"

I don't respond, because I don't have an answer. Heidi is right. Compared to Evan, I'm a pauper. And that's never really bothered me . . . until now.

The bottom of the television screen is scrolling the words

BREAKING NEWS. Heidi turns up the volume just as Giuliana Rancic begins her diatribe.

"The media is buzzing after it has been revealed that an unidentified man, known as Justice Drake, is actually the sex therapist to the starlets. And apparently, he has some high-profile clients. It's been confirmed that earlier reports placing Allison Elliot-Carr, wife of Evan Carr, at an exclusive spa were indeed false, and that she has been at an undisclosed location with this celeb sexpert. When we reached out to the Carr camp for questioning, they replied, "No comment." The question now is, did Evan Carr actually hire a man to sleep with his wife in order to make her a better lover? Stay tuned for more on this story . . ."

I switch off the TV. I don't need to hear any more.

"You see?" Heidi says, gesturing toward the blank screen. "Bits and pieces are falling into place. And now they have the Carrs involved? This is bad, Justice. Even you have to admit that."

"I know." My head is in my hands, rubbing my temples.

"Let them go. You can start over somewhere else, get a new alias, new staff. It's best to get out now before you're forced to."

I look at Heidi, but all I can see is Ally. All I can see are those sad eyes smiling at me for the last time. She'd go to her corner of the world, and I'd stay safely tucked away in mine.

"I can't," I whisper, and I know in that moment that I will. I can't keep her. The mirage is just that—something so beautiful and desired, it can't possibly be real.

Light knocking at the door lifts my heavy head and has

me sprinting to answer it. I open it without checking to see who's there.

"Ally." It's like I've just breathed after being underwater for hours.

"I'm sorry to interrupt . . ." She peers around the frame, and when her eyes grow wide, I know what she sees: a tall, leggy blonde with a killer body, heels, and a pencil skirt that looks like it was painted on. "Um, uh, I can come back."

I grab her arm before she can escape me an inch. "No. Stay." *Stay*. If she only she could feel the weight of that tiny, minuscule word. "Heidi was just leaving."

"You've got to be fucking kidding me," the sex-on-legs publicist mumbles behind me. She makes her way to the door, stopping to press her red, glossed lips to my cheek. "You've got twenty-four hours, Drake. Make a decision," she whispers before turning her icy gray gaze on Ally with a tip of her head. "*Mrs*. Carr."

Ally and I watch as Heidi struts away, hips swaying in sync with her spiked heels. When Ally turns back to me, she looks pensive.

"What?" I ask her, pulling her into my home and into my arms.

"She's . . ."

"Tall? Cold? A little scary?"

"*Gorgeous*. And yes, a little scary. She's like the female version of you."

I shake my head. "You think I'm scary?"

"You were." She wipes the glossy imprint of Heidi's lips

from my cheek and replaces it with her own. "But I believe in facing your fears. Now you're about as frightening as a kitten. Who was that, anyway?"

"Publicist."

"Everything okay?" She frowns with concern.

"Of course. Just some paperwork that needed to be signed in person," I lie seamlessly.

"Oh, I hope I didn't interrupt." She looks back at the door and frowns again. "She doesn't suspect anything about us, does she?"

"Would it bother you if she did?"

Ally shrugs and turns back to me, her gaze unfocused. "I don't know. I mean, I know, but I'm not really sure how I feel about it."

"You don't know how you feel about us." It's not a question.

Her eyes touch mine, searching. "No. Yes. I do—of course I do—but I feel like it's wrong to feel this way. Like I'm a horrible, disgusting person to harbor these feelings because of my situation. And if I acknowledge them, they'll take over. They'll consume me. *You'll* consume me."

I step in as close as humanly possible. Close enough to feel her heartbeat stutter against my rib cage. "I want to consume you, Ally. I want to devour every bit of you until there's no you and there's no me. Until we're nothing but sensation and exhaustion. Until you see music and hear colors." My lips are just a breath away from hers, longing for a taste. "You don't have to define your feelings for me, Ally. Let me do it for you."

She opens her mouth to speak, but I smother her words in a searing kiss. Her response isn't necessary. What we have, what I feel for her, goes far beyond rational explanation. When I pull away, there are sad stars in her eyes.

"Why did that feel like a kiss good-bye?"

I kiss her again just to keep my mouth from admitting that she's right The beginning of the end. The very start of the saddest good-bye in history. Because after tonight, she'll walk away from me and go back to him, holding a piece of me in the palm of her hand. And whenever I look up at the sky at night, wondering where she is, if she's happy, if Evan laughs at her corny jokes or smiles along with her smiles, that empty space left behind within me will ache with remembrance. Because her light once filled it. She filled *me* in a way that nobody on this earth could. And I'll never feel whole again.

We don't speak as I lead her into the bedroom. Our eyes stay transfixed on each other as we slowly undress. When I touch her, she shivers, yet her skin is burning under my fingertips. I wrap her in my arms, wishing I could cover her in a way that would make her disappear in me. They can't take away what they can't find.

"You're so small," I whisper in her hair.

"You're just so big. But I like it."

I hold her until the pain of my erection becomes too great to ignore any longer. She slips a hand between us and squeezes my cock, hearing my thoughts and making me groan without a shred of dignity.

"So big," she repeats with a satisfied grin. "But I like it."

"It likes you too."

Then there are no more words, all signs of jest erased as I lay her down and cover her body with mine. I kiss her mouth, her neck, each of her pert breasts, the dip of her navel. When my tongue finds the apex of her thighs, she opens for me automatically. I drag a thumb through her folds before pressing her clit. She shudders, and I repeat the motion, slowly trailing my thumb down through her pink flesh, tracing her sex with precision before bringing it back up to apply pressure on her sensitive bud. By the time I give her my tongue, she nearly breaks apart.

"What are you doing to me?" she pants, teetering on the edge of orgasm.

"Exactly what I taught you," I reply. Then I send her flying into oblivion, giving her my mouth and fingers. Sucking her until her release trickles down my chin. Until she pulls me up by my shoulders, begging me to stop.

"Oh God," she sobs. "I can't take any more. Too much."

I kiss her so she can taste herself, my tongue snaking with hers as we share her arousal. I'm perfectly aligned with her entrance, still slick and hot, so I slowly push until the head of my cock is nestled inside her. Ally gasps at the intrusion, and I trace her lips with my fingers before hooking two inside her mouth. I delve in some more and watch the emotions play out on her face, all varying shades of carnal insanity. When I'm submerged to the hilt, I pull out so suddenly that she whimpers, and I flip her onto her stomach.

"Up you go," I say, elevating her ass and hips and bending her legs in a way that causes the soles of her feet to touch. I admire the way her sex contracts, begging me to fill her once more.

One hand on her hip, the other on her shoulder, I enter her from behind, slowly at first. I'm so deep at this angle that I can feel her heartbeat in her stomach. The sheets rumple under her tight grip, and Ally grits out a curse.

"Is this okay?" I ask. I don't even know why I'm asking. I've never asked for anything I've wanted, and I damn sure didn't care enough to do it during sex.

Ally nods into the pillow, eyes closed tight. "Yes. Better than okay."

I pull out to the tip and plunge back in, pulling her back into me by her shoulder. We both moan in unison, and her knees tremble.

"Good?" I don't know why I'm asking again. I know it's good. I can *feel* it's good for her.

"Yeah," she rasps between whimpers.

All restraint is cast aside, and I let go, thrusting into her with ravenous intensity. I lean forward and kiss her back, smothering my groans of pleasure in her skin and hair. She turns her head, and my lips instantly find hers.

If this was a different time, and I was a different man deep inside of a different woman, I'd look into her eyes as my body dipped and rolled into hers. She'd stare at me lovingly and caress my jaw, a look of pure ecstasy on her face. I'd sweep her hair to one side over her shoulder and drag my tongue across her neck to her ear. And when her back began to arch as the first tingles of orgasm seize her body, I would whisper "I love you" because I'd want those words to be the only thing she heard when she came for me. Only for me.

Regardless of my feelings for Ally—and there *are* feelings—I'm not that man and she's not that woman. And all the time we have is right now. Uttering those words would only spark confusion and conflict for both of us. So I swallow both our moans of surrender as I give her the parts of me that I can give. The parts of me that quiver and pulse until pain and pleasure become one and the same. Until heat and cold race up my spine, and my joints are too flooded with sensation to move, and I release it all into her—the fear, the anger, the bliss of just having her in my arms—it's all hers.

I'm hers.

SOMETHING STIRS ME from sleep, but I try to fight it. I don't want to move, I don't even want to breathe. But it sounds again from the living room, and I know I have to leave this bed and the warmth of Ally's body.

Fuck. My phone.

Dim light filters through the blinds, and I realize that we've sexed and slept the day away. There was talking, some eating, even some hydrating, but mostly our time was spent kissing, touching, and pushing our bodies beyond pleasure.

As gently as I possibly can, I unravel my arm from under Ally's frame. She stirs, murmuring something unintelligible before resuming a soft snore. I shake my head and laugh silently to myself as I make my way to the living room. Before Ally, every woman I had ever been with looked like a supermodel even in slumber. Hair and makeup somehow stayed meticulously in place. Part of me didn't believe they ever truly slept, just fluttered those long-lashed eyes closed and posed like wax statues on the bed. But with Ally, everything is different, more real. Her red hair is in knots all over both our faces. She snores a bit, not loudly, but loud enough that I know she's asleep. And a little drop of drool settles in the corner of her mouth.

Maybe all women really sleep this way. I don't know. I've never stuck around long enough to find out.

I follow the chimes resonating from my phone and find it on the coffee table. Missed calls and text messages from Heidi. One from Diane, checking in. Another from Riku asking me if everything is okay. I ignore them all and zero in on the half-dozen Google Alerts clogging my screen.

BREAKING NEWS . . .

THIS JUST IN . . .

SHOCKING TRUTH REVEALED . . .

Same bullshit, different headline. But all I can see is a face, a name. A wolf in sheep's clothing, crying false tears of remorse and longing.

EVAN CARR'S SHOCKING REVELATION:
"I SENT MY WIFE TO THE SEX DOCTOR"

In a press release earlier today, a regretful Evan Carr revealed that he sent wife, Allison Elliot-Carr, to celebrity sex therapist Justice Drake under the pretense that Drake was an intimacy professional, NOT a sexual deviant.

"When we first were told about Mr. Drake and his practice, we thought it would help Allison build her confidence and get in touch with her sexuality," said the socialite. "We signed up under the assumption that the treatment would be positive for our marriage. Little did we know what Justice Drake was really about. I would never have put my wife in this situation had I known."

A tearful Carr went on to say that he was doing everything in his power to locate his wife and bring her back. "Her place is with me," he says. "Not with some quack that sold us a lie. I can't even imagine what he could be doing to Ally and God knows who else."

Evan Carr provided details about the registration forms, saying that the women would be sent to an undisclosed location where they could have no contact with the outside world for six weeks. When asked about Justice Drake's identity, Carr shook his head.

"No one has ever seen him. I can't even be sure
that he's a man. All contact has been through his
PR person or e-mail."

Drake's publicist, Heidi DuCane, was unavailable for comment.

I dial the elusive blonde next, my heartbeat pounding
painfully in my head.

"You're lucky I have shit to do," Heidi says after picking
up on the first ring. "I wanted to storm your little love nest
and drag your ass out of there."

"Where are you?" My voice is gruff with sleep and aggravation.

"Headed back to New York, but had to make a stop first."
She pauses to give someone instructions to a hotel on Michi-
gan Avenue, presumably a driver. "Something came up and
I want to check it out."

"You're in Chicago?"

"Yeah. Art is meeting me here."

I exhale heavily and lean back on the couch. Arthur Cam-
bridge III is my attorney. If he's involved, something serious
is up. "What's wrong?"

"You're being blackmailed, Justice. A few hours ago, I was
sent an audio recording of you having sex. I don't know who
it was with, but the woman was very vocal. She kept calling
you by your name. Know anything about that?"

I close my eyes and rub the tension collecting in my temples. "No. How do you know it's not doctored?"

"We checked it out. It's authentic. However, my team was able to trace the IP address back to Chicago."

I almost smirk. "You have a team of hackers, Heidi?"

"Doesn't everybody? And even if the recording was made years ago, we can't take that risk. Not with the press calling for your head on a platter. I'm texting it to you now. Listen. Call me when you're done."

A message chimes a second later and I hang up with Heidi to open the attachment. Heavy breathing. Moaning. A sweet voice singing my name as I instruct her to fuck then suck me.

I don't need to hear any more. I was there. Just yesterday, I was there.

I call Heidi back, and she answers immediately. "I have a pretty good idea who's behind this, and I'm sure you do too."

Erin.

Stupid fucking Erin.

I think back to when I took Ally right here on this very couch. I remember telling her to take off her shirt and then capturing her flawed beauty through the lens of my camera phone. Then my mouth was devouring her pink-tipped nipples and demanding she take off those ridiculously oversize boxers. And then I was deep inside her, losing myself to pleasure, my phone forgotten.

How the fuck did Erin get a recording of that? Hers was the last number I dialed, but the screen was locked. Had she called? Did we accidently graze that evil, little green icon while Ally rode me like a cowgirl?

"We're going to bury her," Heidi continues. "Her grand-children will be paying you their lunch money."

I shake my head in frustration. "How much is she asking?"

Heidi makes a tsking sound. "Two million, which techni-cally won't kill you, but still . . ."

"Give it to her."

"What?"

"Tell Art to give it to her. Give her the money."

Heidi's voice goes a pitch higher than I've ever heard it. "You can't be serious! That bitch is in blatant violation of contract, and you want to reward her? She has nothing, Jus-tice. There's no way she can prove it was you—"

"It doesn't matter, Heidi. None of it matters. Retrieve the evidence, give her the money, and do what you need to do to ensure she disappears."

The line goes quiet for several beats before Heidi chuck-les. "You've gone completely mad, haven't you?"

I chuckle too. I don't know why. My business is crum-bling at my feet, I'm being blackmailed by a girl who didn't have two nickels to rub together before she met me, and I'm having an affair with a married woman whom I can't shake. I am mad. Mad, yet I've never felt more normal. More tied to the life I left behind—Ally's life.

I hear light shuffling behind me, and I look up in time to see Ally leaning against the doorjamb, wearing one of my sweatshirts, sleep and sex sparkling in her eyes. She smiles at me, and a feeling too strong to fully contain bursts in my chest before sinking into the pit of my stomach.

"Take care of that for me, Heidi. And what we talked about earlier . . . I'll do it. I'll send them."

Her voice takes on that soft, feminine sound again. Like she pities me. Like she cares for me. "Got it. This'll be good, Justice, and everything will be okay. You can start over, rebuild. You can be whoever you want after this."

I don't have a response, at least one that I can voice, so I just hang up. Heidi is used to my terseness. I'm like that with everyone. Everyone except Ally.

As if she can hear her name ringing melodically in my head, she slinks over to the couch just as I set my phone on the end table. I grab her by the waist and pull her onto my lap as she squeals. I bury my face in her hair, trying to soak in as much of her scent as I can, while I can. I can smell myself on her, mixed with her perfume and sweat.

"I didn't mean to wake you," I say against the smooth skin behind her ear. "I was just about to come back to bed."

"I'm tired of sleeping." She sighs.

I look at her, my brow raised sardonically. "You're *tired* of *sleeping*?"

She pinches me on the arm. "Oh, you know what I mean."

I snatch her hand and kiss her palm. Then we're quiet, as we watch shadows grow before our eyes, dusk fading into night.

"Can I ask you a question?" Ally asks, her voice small in the vast silence.

"Don't you always?"

She pinches me again. "Knock it off! Can you be serious for five minutes?"

I give her a level stare. "*You're* asking *me* to be serious?"

"Ugh!" She tries to shimmy out of my arms, but I wind them around her tighter.

"Okay, okay, I'm sorry. Ask me anything. Seriously this time."

Ally nods toward shadowed, white walls. "You don't have any pictures up."

"That's not a question."

"Shut up, will you, and let me finish." She smiles and shakes her head, before laying it on my shoulder. "You don't have any photos, and you've never really talked about your family. And since you already know all about me and my life, I thought . . ."

"You want to know about my family."

"Yes." She turns toward me, a tearful apology in her eyes. "I want to know you. We only have a little over a week left together. It's not enough, Justice. I need to soak up as much of you as I can."

I take a deep breath and position her body so I'm forced to look at her. So I'm forced to see the judgment and regret that will soon undoubtedly appear on her face.

"My story is nothing new; you've heard it before. My father never loved my mother. He was charming, rich, powerful, and an impeccable liar. She was gentle and naive, thinking that her love for him would change him just enough to make him feel something for her. She was too good for him, yet too stupid to see it and leave him alone."

She gives me a soft smile. "Sounds about right."

"She didn't, of course. And soon he found himself a shiny, new toy to feed his ego. My mother had served her purpose, and so had I. His relationship with me ended with theirs."

"Where is your mother now?"

"Somewhere grieving her broken heart, probably a dirty martini in hand. She never got over him. When he sent us away, I told myself that it was his loss. But it was ours too. I lost that warm, compassionate woman who was just too optimistic for her own good. The one who'd tell me how I'd grow up one day and be a movie star and marry the most beautiful woman in the world, and give her half a dozen grandchildren. I lost her, and she lost herself. She lost her reason to live."

Ally cups my cheek and looks at me like she can see right through my impassive exterior. Like she can actually see the broken pieces of me that are glued together by lies and deceit.

I muster a weak smile and remove her hand. "Don't feel bad for me. I don't."

"But it has to be lonely."

"How can I be lonely?" I smirk. "I'm constantly surrounded by beautiful women and a very efficient, if not overbearing, staff."

"It's not the same, Justice. Everybody needs someone."

"I don't."

"Yes, you do. We all do."

I grasp her tighter, pulling her so close that my lips graze hers. "Then who do you need, Ally?"

Her animated eyes search the parts of me she can see, this close up. She opens her mouth to answer, yet doesn't say a word. And I realize, I don't want to hear the answer. I don't want to hear that she needs anybody else but me. So with my fingers knotted in her matted mess of hair, I kiss her despite my fears. I kiss her so she can taste just how much I want her, how much I *need* her. Although it's more than my heart can stand, I kiss that angel as I feel every vital part of me being crumpled into dust.

Every kiss is a good-bye. Especially the ones that kill you.

Eruption

"Oh my God, I can't believe I'm doing this. I can't—I can't, Justice."

I look up from the Ferragamos I'm slipping on my feet and furrow my brow at the red-haired goddess before me. "Ally, it's not as bad as you think."

"How can you be so sure? I've never done anything like this. Ever! Oh my God, I feel sick."

Panic sets in. "Wait . . . what exactly are you talking about?"

"The walk of shame!" she answers, throwing her hands up. "I knew I should've gone back to my room last night. All I need now is raccoon eyes and bedhead. Ugh!"

I stand up to wrap her in my arms and touch my lips to

her cute little pout. "First of all, you're beautiful. And it's still early; no one will even see you. And, no, you shouldn't have left. You wanted to stay with me just as badly as I wanted you to."

"You're right—I did want to stay." Her expression softens before her forehead falls on my chest. "This is so hard. Why is this so hard?"

I kiss the top of her head. "Because it's supposed to be. Because things like this are meant to torture us until we bend and break. You just need to figure out if all of this is worth it."

She looks up at me, and every dark corner in my heart is filled with blinding light. "You know, when this all began, I felt guilty. A part of me still does. And I'm disgusted with myself for feeling downright devastated, because I know that this can't last." She closes her eyes and shakes her head from side to side. When she looks back at me, those cerulean irises are drowning in tears. "And I'm trying not to think about it. I'm trying to just enjoy the little time we do have together. But dammit, it hurts, Justice. It hurts because I'm already bending and breaking. And there's nothing I can do to fix it. If all we have is now, I know I'll never be whole again. And, God . . . it's worth it. *You're* worth it. I'll gladly stay broken for you."

Every emotion inside me battles its way to the surface, and I open and close my dry mouth, willing the feelings not to spill out. Here we are, two lonely, broken souls lost to our own desires. I was born into the life she lives, and all I want to do is take her away from it. To steal her from everyone she loves and knows, and possess her smiles and gentle heart. But I can't say that. I can't tell her how badly it hurts when I think about her leaving me. I can't describe how much she's completely altered the man that I thought I was, and how broken I already am. How I'm breaking right now.

"And I'll stay broken for you too."

Ally smiles. And a lifetime of loneliness and pain disintegrates under the brilliance of that smile. So I smile too, because any time with her, whether it's a day or an hour, is worth it.

"I wish I had you before . . . before you left New York. I wish I had met you first. But then again, it wouldn't even have mattered. I would have found you eventually."

"Why do you say that?"

"Because . . . because you're my lobster," she whispers.

"Huh?" I ask, raising a questioning brow. Did she say . . . *lobster*?

She just shakes her head, wearing a tight-lipped grin. I lace my fingers with hers, kissing her knuckles before ushering her out of my home for the very last time. That once cold, sterile place that housed my secrets and solitude. The space she filled with more warmth than the sun.

"Come on. Time for class," I say as we cross the threshold.

Stay, Ally. Don't go. Leave him and stay with me.

That's what I should have said.

"First, I want to say how much of a pleasure it has been to have the opportunity to teach you and guide you all toward healthier, more fulfilling sex lives. Not only that, it's been a pleasure getting to know each and every one of you. You all have been great . . . always willing to learn and improve, even when you weren't one hundred percent comfortable or convinced. And I just want to say thank you."

I take a deep breath to steel my resolve and glance out at the eleven confused faces staring back at me. I'm proud of them—all of them. And it truly hurts that I have to utter my next words in order to protect them. "That's why I regret to inform you that the course will be ending a bit sooner than expected, and you'll all be heading home."

"What?"

"Why?"

"Did something happen?"

"Did we do something wrong?"

The questions hit me all at once, and I make a motion with my open hands to calm them down. "Ladies, I assure you, you've done nothing wrong. It's just that some issues have surfaced that require my immediate attention. Of course, you'll all be issued a full refund and—"

"Why are you doing this?" The voice is broken, just like me. I can't even look in her direction.

"Like I was saying, a full refund will be—"

"You can't do this. You can't just send me away. You can't do this, Justice!"

I open my mouth to explain, but Diane rushes in, saving me from another cold, rehearsed line.

"Mr. Drake, we have a situation," she mutters only for my ears. I give a stiff nod before turning toward the class.

"If you'll excuse me for just a moment."

I'm leading Diane to the back office that mostly houses locked file cabinets of client information and things of that nature. That's when I hear it. A voice I haven't heard in over a decade. A voice that shouldn't be here.

I turn to Diane, whose dark, bronze skin suddenly looks ashen. "I tried to explain," she shrieks. "Mr. Drake, what's going on? The staff is worried . . ."

The voice grows louder, more annoying. It echoes through the foyer and pierces my eardrums with the pain of remembrance. I duck into the sitting area right off the great room before I can be seen.

"Isolate the situation, Diane." My voice is calm and level, but truth be told, my entire body is on red alert. "Make sure the ladies don't know."

But just as I say the words, I know it's too late.

It's too late.

Take a bow; the curtain's closed. It's time to go home.

"Ally Cat, come here, baby."

I look around the corner just in time to see Evan Carr pull Ally—*my Ally*—into his arms. He touches her wild, red mane like he's afraid it'll bite, his brow furrowed at its newly freed state.

"Wow, you look . . . different." He assesses her clothing, her sun-kissed skin, her swollen lips, still tingling with the taste of me. Ally returns his stare with bewilderment.

"Evan . . . Evan, what are you doing here?"

"I missed you. And with the scandal surrounding this Justice Drake guy, I knew I needed to bring you home."

By now, the other housewives have trickled in. Diane tries to usher them back into the great room, but her efforts are futile. The damage has already been done.

"Scandal? What are you talking about?" Ally frowns. It doesn't look right on her, and something within me shudders at the sight, longing to trace her lips and ease them into the smile that I know and love.

"The guy's a quack, Ally. A fraud. He fooled us all just to get in the pants of dozens of innocent, unsuspecting women." Evan flippantly runs a hand through his tousled, dirty-blond hair as if he *isn't* defaming my character and my business.

"You know that's not true," Ally replies sternly. She pulls her wrists from his grasp.

Evan moves in close as if he's about to kiss her, yet stops just a millimeter away from her lips. "Yeah, but we have company. And we want to make this good for them, right?" Then he places his lips on hers, just as a camera whirs and a blinding flash covers the room in fluorescent light.

Evan brought the paparazzi.

This fucker is doing this for publicity. Not because he loves and misses his wife. Not because he is concerned for her and the welfare of ten other women. He's doing it all for press.

A cameraman steps out from behind a pillar and snaps several more shots of the couple, as well as the interior of the house.

"Where is this Justice Drake anyway?" he shouts, drawing more eyes and ears. "Where is the big, bad sex doctor now?"

It takes everything in me not to step out from the shadows and confront him. To show him just who the fuck I am. But that's exactly what he wants. He wants that reaction so he can profit from it. I can see it now: EVAN CARR EXPOSES SEXUAL PREDATOR JUSTICE DRAKE. Fuck that. I won't feed his little shit show.

"Leave him alone," Ally commands, nervously looking around. "Just . . . forget about him. I'll go get my things and we can leave."

She pushes away from him and begins to make her way to the staircase, toward me. I can see the trepidation in her eyes as she scans the hall. Maybe she's worried I'll see her with her husband. Maybe a tiny part of her feels like she's betraying me by being with him. Or maybe the worry etched in her face is a result of her shame. I don't know and I don't give myself time to debate the whys and hows, before my hand is grasping her elbow just as she slips past me.

"Justice, what are you—"

"Don't go." The words are out before I can stop them. And they keep coming, all my doubts and discretion smothered in desperation. "Don't leave with him, Ally. Stay with me. Please. You don't belong with him."

Her animated eyes search the hopelessness in mine. "I can't just . . . What are you saying?"

I take a step toward her and grasp both her shoulders. It's now or never. If I don't try, I'll never get another chance. "I'm saying that I don't want you to go. Ever. I'm saying that I can't live without the sun shining down on my face, and I can't dream without the stars kissing me good night. I can't be without you, Ally. So . . . here we are: your two choices. Pick me. Choose *me*."

I don't even realize that the entire room has gone silent, save for my determined breaths and the sound of my heart-beat racing out of my chest. But when I hear his voice, I know that my plea has been heard loud and clear.

"What the hell is going on here?"

I feel Evan approach behind me, but I don't turn around. My fixed gaze is still trained on Ally, waiting for an answer, a sign. Anything that'll tell me that she'll stay.

"Evan," she breathes, though her eyes are on me. "Evan, I, uh—"

"Is this him? Is this Justice Drake?" he spits, his words laced with accusation and amusement. I feel him right behind me, and I know that I have to show myself. I can't stay hidden in the shadows any longer.

Had this been a cheesy sitcom or soap opera, this would be the part where the camera fades to black for commercial. Or maybe it would be the end of the episode, leaving viewers on the edge of their seats, ensuring that they tune in next time.

But this isn't TV. There are no closing credits to follow the look of pure shock and disgust on Evan Carr's face when I turn to face him. No heart-racing sound track plays in the background, signaling the transition into a nail-biting climax.

This is life. My life. The life that chewed me up, spat me out, and discarded me without a second thought.

"Sean Michael? Is that you? What are you doing here? And what the hell are you doing with my wife?"

I don't say a word. I can't. I just stay tight-lipped as cameras flash and whir in front of us, our audience holding their breath in anticipation. My joints and limbs are frozen where I stand, until I feel Ally's soft, delicate hand grasp my forearm. She steps into view beside Evan, her confused expression rivaling his.

"Justice, what is he talking—"

Evan nearly pushes her aside to take a step closer to me. "Wait a minute. Wait one goddamn minute . . . *You're* Justice Drake? You're him?" He barks out a sardonic laugh and throws his hands up dramatically. "You've got to be kidding me! Sean Michael is Justice-fucking-Drake. And apparently, he wants to steal my wife from me. *This* is rich."

Every muscle feels so tightly bound in aggravation that I can barely move. I don't even realize how long I've been standing there, staring murderous daggers at Evan's theatrics, until Ally forces her way into my line of vision.

"Justice, what's going on? Please, talk to me." Concern mars that beautifully flawed face, and I instantly feel guilty because I'm the cause of it.

I open and close my mouth, trying to find the words to explain, but Evan, being the selfish prick that he's always been, steals the moment away from me. One hand on Ally's back, he waves the other in my direction. "Ally Cat, darling, meet Sean Michael. My father's bastard, and my half brother."

And all the fear, the shame . . . it all comes bubbling to the surface, overflowing with my secrets and lies. I can see the repulsion on her face as she looks at me, hurt and betrayal in her eyes, lit up by the flash of half a dozen cameras. She doesn't feel wronged by Evan, her husband, for keeping such a massive secret; she feels wronged by *me*. As if all of this is my doing. As if I forced his father—*my* father—to cheat on his wife with a young, naive housemaid and birth a son, just two months after Evan was born.

"You're his brother?" she whispers in a broken voice. "You're a Carr?"

"Half brother," I say, finding my voice, as if it makes my omission any less shameful. "And, fuck no, I'm not a Carr."

There's fire in the water of her eyes. "So all this was a lie? Just a way to settle some score with Evan?" She shakes her head, her lips twisted in disgust. "Oh my God. You picked me, didn't you? You just wanted to use me as a pawn! You purposely made me fall . . ."

I try to reach for her, but she steps away. "No! Don't you dare even *think* that. Yes, I knew about you, but—"

"But what? How will you explain this one, little brother?" Evan interjects smugly. "You know what? I can't decide what makes you a bigger asshole—the fact that you preyed on my wife, or that you're trying to weasel your way back in where you obviously don't belong. You and your mother were paid handsomely to stay away from us. You think changing your name somehow voids the contract? Father's attorneys will have a field day with your ass!" He pulls his cell phone from his pocket.

"Father's attorneys? Don't you mean *your mother's* attorneys? Since you're so fond of hiding behind her skirt, you should know good and well that her conniving ass orchestrated that plan to try to bury us."

Evan shrugs. "True enough. But you see, the thing about marriage is that they're united. They are one. And *we're* a family. You and your whore of a mother will forever be on the outside looking in."

There are no thoughts. No intervention from Jiminy or any coaxing from that little narcissistic devil pressing at my temples. Just red fury and a blur of movement as I snatch Evan by the throat and slam him against the wall. I don't hear the women shrieking with fear as they watch, or the clicking of cameras capturing this moment for all time. I don't feel Ally tugging at my arm, begging me to stop, or even Riku trying to pull me back before I do what I've wanted to do for decades. There's only blind rage numbing my hand as I apply more pressure to his strained throat and watch those denim-blue eyes, so much like mine, widen with fear.

I'm going to kill him.

I'm going to fucking kill him.

My childhood was stolen from me because Evan's mother refused to allow my father to accept me. And when he arranged for me to attend the best prep school in the city, even that was taken away because Evan felt "uncomfortable" with my presence. And now he's stolen my happiness. I don't give a fuck if Ally is his by law. She's mine, right down to my bones. She was always meant to be a part of me. And Evan wants to take that too.

So I'm going to take his life, like he and his bitch of a mother tried to take mine.

"Please, Justice, don't do this! Please, you don't want to do this!"

Ally's voice cuts through the blood whooshing in my ears, but it sounds so far away, like a distant memory. I squeeze Evan's neck tighter, and he tries to scream, but no sound escapes.

"Where's your mommy now, Evan?" I spew through a painfully clenched jaw. "Who's gonna save you from me now, huh? Huh? Answer me, asshole!"

A garbled whine escapes his trembling lips, and I squeeze his neck so hard that my knuckles turn white. I bring my face closer to his, ensuring that he can see the rage in my eyes, and that I can see the fear in his. "What was that? I can't quite hear you through all your crying, Evan. You gonna tell your mommy on me? You gonna lie and say I was mean to you, like you did when we were kids? Or how about you tell her I've been rummaging through your shit and taking your things?"

A wicked smile curves my lips, and I bark out a forced laugh before leaning forward to whisper harshly in his ear. "Well, actually, I did take one thing of yours. I took it over and over again, until she screamed my name and begged for more. Until she came so hard that she *fucking sobbed*."

"Stop it! Please!" Ally screams. "Somebody do something!"

"Come on, man." That's Riku's voice. It's far away, yet closer than before. I can feel his grip on my shoulders, pulling me back to reality. "Everybody's watching. Don't ruin your life for this fucker. He isn't worth it."

"Please," a broken angel cries. "Please don't. Please don't do this."

Her voice just keeps replaying in my head, begging me to stop. Begging me to spare her precious husband. Hell yeah, hurting Evan would make me feel better, but it would also destroy her. A part of her would die with him. And by making her a widow at the age of twenty-seven, I know that she'd forever hate me. And that . . . that would destroy *me*.

I loosen my grip on Evan's throat and let Riku pull me back, allowing Ally to swiftly move to aid her husband as he crumples to the ground, coughing and sputtering. She brushes his hair from his sweat-dampened forehead and caresses his beet-red face, crying for him. Crying for the life she nearly witnessed fade away by my own hands.

Someone rushes to help Evan to his feet, and with Ally pressed against his side, they usher him toward the exit.

"You didn't take her," he tries to spit over his shoulder in a strained whisper. "You just paid for her with every fucking dime you own."

I don't respond. I don't even give him a second look. I just keep watching, as Ally makes her choice. Evan is the lesser of two evils. And I'm . . . I'm just less.

He's the star in her life. I was just the understudy.

Just before she crosses the threshold, she turns to look at me one last time. Sunlight filters through a single teardrop sliding down her cheek, turning it to crystallized sorrow. I want to go to her, capture it in my palm and kiss it away until it dissolves into nothing. But her tears are not for me. They're because of me.

The anguished angel slips away from me, fleeing my singular hell as fire trails behind her. Stars burn and fall from my sky, and the clouds cry, darkening in sorrow.

The sun is gone. I've lost her forever.

Desertion

Dear Justice,

Happy (belated) New Year.

I'm not sure if you've been receiving my e-mails, but as your publicist—and I still am your publicist, like it or not—I feel the need to keep checking in with you. You know, to update you on what's going on here. And to let you know that we're all worried about you.

There, I said it. I'm worried about you.

Last I heard, you were in Tokyo, and then holed up in a chateau in France. Your mother has been in touch, and told me that you were in Poland briefly, visiting your grandparents for the holidays. She's a lovely woman, by the way. She even told the story of your unfortunate former name. Sean Connery and Michael Douglas, huh? Can't say that I blame her.

Anyway, after Poland, the trail went cold. That was three weeks ago.

Look, I get it. You're pissed at the world right now. But at least let me know that you're alive so I know I'm not writing a corpse.

I doubt you've been keeping up with current events, because if you were, you'd be home by now. So I'll spare you the gory details and get right down to business. Evan Carr dropped any and all charges against you. Apparently, you have a guardian angel watching over you, because his team was ready to go to war. So count that as a victory—your home is safe.

However, things may look completely different if you don't get your ass back here soon. Diane and Riku came up with this crazy idea to completely transform Oasis into a hedonism-style couples resort. And considering that you've got folks trying to visit this place like it's Disneyland for perverts, I think it's a solid plan. Laura and Brad have agreed to come on board full-time, teaching tantric yoga among *other* things. They've even talked to Candi and Jewel about a strip aerobics-type class and a more intimate striptease course for couples. They are all happy to help, Justice. They care about you . . . we all do.

Obviously, Erin was not invited back to the
property. Last I heard, she dropped out of med school
and is one snort away from being a cokcd-out call
girl. Unlucky for her and her bullshit little blackmail
stunt, once the footage was released from, you know,
that day . . . her audiotape was worthless. So not
only is she a lying whore, she's a broke, jobless, lying
whore.

I don't know if you're reading these, or if you're
even somewhere that has Wi-Fi, but just know that
we're rooting for you. Nobody blames you for what
you did to Evan; that little shit deserved it. And now
that everyone knows that you're Winston Carr II's
abandoned son, the whole world sympathizes with you
and understands why you reacted the way you did.

They stole everything from you, Justice. Don't let
them take away everything that you've accomplished
as well.

Okay, until next time. Maybe you'll actually reply
and let me know that you're not dead in some ditch
in Rio. Like I said before, we're all here for you. If
you want to leave Justice Drake behind, I totally
understand. But don't leave us behind. Don't desert
the people who love you, okay?

Heidi

—Delete—

THE E-MAIL IS one of many I've read and discarded, stowing them all in that numb place inside me that isn't allowed to feel or grieve. It's better that way, for me, for everyone.

Heidi is right—I don't keep up with current events. I don't even watch television. Sometimes I pass a newsstand at an airport, and a familiar face looks back at me from the pages of a tabloid, but even that occurs less and less. According to the chatter among the local youth, I've gathered that a young Hollywood starlet is pregnant and she isn't sure which Franco brother is the father. Ouch. Considering she's barely legal, my money's on Big Franco.

I'm sitting in a coffee shop in Amsterdam, enjoying a cup of herbal tea—you know . . . the fun kind—listening to the sounds of the city. It's busy here, alive. Yet there's something so relaxing and mellow about this place. Maybe it's the pot talking. Maybe my mind is finally distracted enough to feel something other than anger and regret. I even almost smile. Almost.

The barista grins at me, and I nod back. She's beautiful, exotic with dark hair and features, yet her eyes are hauntingly light. A couple months ago, my gaze might have lingered on her just a little bit longer. Maybe I'd have given her a small smile back. Just enough to show her that she had my attention, and could keep it, for a night.

The shop is empty, so she switches the television from a soccer match to what sounds like a sitcom.

"Is this okay?" she asks me in heavily accented English.

I nod without looking at the screen and give her a forced

grin. She takes it as an invitation and comes to stand at my little table.

"This is my favorite," she says, smiling toward the TV. "And I'm glad they play the reruns in English. It helped me learn."

I finally pull my attention away from the tiny bits of herb floating in my teacup and glance at the television. And the moment my eyes fall on the screen, I feel like I've been dumped into a dark, endless pool of ice-cold water. Just when I think someone has shown me mercy and thrown me a life preserver, I realize that it's weighted, and I sink straight to the bottom.

I can't escape this.

I can't escape her.

No matter where I go, she's there. Even when she's a million miles away.

Quirky Phoebe is comforting Ross, telling him to hang in there because no matter what, Rachel is his lobster. And once lobsters meet and fall in love, they mate for life. They always find each other. And sooner or later, Rachel and Ross will be together.

For the next half hour, I watch as pathetic Ross uses that reasoning with Rachel, trying to make her see that he's the only one for her. He fails miserably, of course, and Rachel dismisses him in favor of more appealing prospects. Prospects like the Evan Carrs of the world. Because girls like Rachel don't go for guys like Ross. No one wants the runner-up.

The gang is sitting around Monica's living room watching

an old VHS tape of high school prom. Rachel is distraught after being stood up by her date, Chip. In the background sits lonely Ross—silent and unseen. His parents persuade him to take Rachel to the prom, and after some pressure, he agrees. And I see it—the light in Ross's eyes. The very moment he is filled with hope and dreams and blind foolishness.

All of which is crushed into a speck of dust when Rachel runs past him and out the door . . . with Chip.

No one ever knew just how deeply Ross felt for her. He never told anyone. He isolated himself in his pain and rejection because he thought he wasn't good enough. He knew he was the *less than*.

Adult Rachel sees him—finally *sees* him. And she understands. Ross was made for her. She was made for him. And no amount of time or distance or circumstance can change that.

The two lock lips, and a giddy Phoebe repeats her heartfelt declaration from earlier. *"See . . . he's her lobster."*

As the episode ends, I get it. I finally get what Ally meant that day. And without rhyme or reason, I laugh.

Like, *really* laugh.

I laugh so hard that I'm doubled over, holding my side. The barista backs away slowly, startled by my sudden burst of hysterics. She probably thinks I'm high as a kite, and maybe I am. I don't even care. It feels good just to release . . . *something*.

"Damn you, Phoebe Buffay," I say out loud, shaking my head with a stupid grin on my face. "Damn you."

Realization

Dear Ally,

~~I know you're wondering where I've been and what~~
~~I've been doing. Or maybe you're not. Maybe you~~
~~never want to hear from me again. And I guess . . .~~
~~that's understandable. But still . . .~~
~~I have to make this better. I have to make you~~
~~see that I never intended to hurt you. I just don't~~
~~know how.~~
~~I know Evan has probably made you believe that I~~
~~used you to get to him, but that could not be further~~
~~from the truth.~~
~~I don't give a fuck about Evan.~~
~~This isn't about him.~~

~~Ally, yes I knew who you were from the start, but that's not what drew me to you. You were kind, and gentle, and . . . no.~~

~~Honestly?~~

~~Ally, you were unexpectedly goofy, corny, clumsy as hell, and whenever I was with you, I couldn't keep the dumb smile off my face. That's what drew me to you. That's what made me realize that my attraction to you was so much more than morbid curiosity. And once I accepted that realization, I knew that I had to be with you. There was no other way to get around it.~~

~~Everything changed when you walked into my life. I changed. The things I thought I wanted, the person I thought I was . . . none of it made sense anymore. But you did. You made sense for me.~~

~~I liked the way you made me feel when we were together. I liked ME when we were together.~~

~~I don't know what I can say to make you believe that you were right. You're my lobster too. And no matter what we go through, or who you're married to, or the distance between us, we'll find each other again. We have to.~~

I'm sorry.

Conclusion

Abu Dhabi

$\mathcal{I}$ had been contemplating going home for weeks. But every time I thought about returning, I was left with the same bitter realization—I didn't have a home anymore.

Oasis is still mine, yet it's been tainted by paparazzi and tourists hoping to get a peek at Justice Drake. It's no longer the refuge I found after being banished from the city as soon as I graduated high school. I used to blame my mother for taking the money in exchange for her silence, but then I realized that she did what she had to do to survive. Going against the Carrs would have been suicide, and I don't mean that figuratively. If they truly wanted us to disappear, there's no doubt in my mind we'd have been struck down by some convenient "accident." And even as a young Polish immigrant, with big dreams in the big city, she knew the kind of clout the Carrs held. So they bought our silence, and I learned the power of the almighty dollar. You could buy happiness, buy love, and buy your freedom. And me? I bought a new life.

So here I am, trading one oasis for another, still trying to figure out what's next, and exactly who I was before people even knew that Justice Drake existed.

I feel like him—I *am* him. But I'm also Sean Michael Dovak, the kid who was named after two movie stars. The kid who once slightly resembled Winston Carr II and his son Evan.

In an attempt to separate myself from that stigma, I did everything I could do *not* to look like them. I cut my hair shorter, bulked up—the Carr men had naturally slender frames—and spent every moment I could outdoors, deepening the color of my inherited, tanned skin. Luckily, my mother's strong European features erased most of the remaining traces of Carr genetics as I grew older. Yet every so often, someone who had seen Evan and me as children would squint their eyes and tilt their head to the side with curiosity. And Mrs. Carr, the devil's surrogate herself, did not appreciate the speculation.

Being Sean Michael always held a negative connotation. So I became Justice Drake. And there was no shame in that.

The apartment I'm renting is about a third the size of the mansion at Oasis, but it suits me. Grandiosity has never been my thing, and I fell in love with the clean, modern design of the space the moment I saw it. And since I really had no immediate plans to return to Arizona, I thought, *What the hell?* What better place to start over than an entirely different country?

That was about a month ago, and my little slice of Abu Dhabi still doesn't feel like home. And part of me thinks that maybe it never will.

I make my way down from the luxury high-rise and out into the morning sunlight, taking in the scents of car exhaust, spiced foods, and incense. I bypass the nearby souks and tourist areas and head down to a local café by the beach. Luckily, it's early, and I nab my favorite table outside right away. One of the waiters recognizes me and hurries over to bring me a cup of coffee.

"Fresh fruit today, sir?" he asks, remembering my usual order.

"Yes, please." I nod.

He bows with a knowing look and heads back into the restaurant to retrieve my usual platter of melon, grapefruit, mango, and pear.

"Humph. Figures you would order something healthy. Question: If you could only eat fruit or chicken and waffles for the rest of your life, which one would you choose?"

I freeze, nearly dropping the steaming cup of coffee just as it touches my lips. I set it down as carefully as I can manage and turn toward the voice. Toward the woman draped all in black, from the hijab covering her head to the long, silken abaya touching her sandaled feet.

And I'm home.

Home in those eyes that aren't quite blue and not quite green. Eyes that are too wild and too bright to possibly be real. A single ringlet of fiery hair breaks free and falls into those animated eyes. She tries to blow it away, causing her niqab to billow, and she laughs. She laughs, and it sounds like the sweetest music ever composed would sound to someone who has suffered for years in deafening silence.

I don't know what to say.

I just laugh too.

Fresh from vacationing in St. Tropez, the new It Couple looked fresh and very much in love as they enjoyed the sounds of Pharrell and Arcade Fire at the Coachella music festival in California this weekend. The pair held hands and even snuck a few kisses between lip-syncing their favorite songs. Allison even showed off some of her more audacious dance moves while doting boyfriend, Justice, laughed along.

"Allison has never looked happier," an attendee remarked. "We've never gotten to see this side of her. It's like she's a real person just like the rest of us, and can finally be herself!"

This is just a week after her divorce from ex Evan Carr was finalized. It was also revealed months ago that Carr is actually Drake's half-brother, the product of an affair by his father, Winston Carr, II, 30 years ago. Drake was also the center of a media frenzy surrounding his unconventional program at his property, Oasis. Since then, countless celebrity wives have come forward to speak up on his behalf.

"He saved my marriage," commented Lacey Rose, wife of legendary rocker, Skylar Rose. "I had lost the confidence that my husband had fallen in *love with when I was younger. I thought that since I was a mom and a wife, I couldn't be sexy. Jus-tice Drake changed that. He showed us all that we could be honest about our sexuality and please our husbands, yet feel good about ourselves while doing it."*

Since then, Justice has revamped his program and is focusing on a more couple-friendly curriculum.

"He realizes that it takes two in a relationship," a source close to the allusive "sex doctor" told us. "He was putting all the responsibility on the wives to fix their marriages, when it was the men that were destroying them. Now he sees things differently . . . now that he has Ally."

And coming soon from
New York Times bestselling author
S.L. Jennings,

TRYST

Heidi DuCane is a tough-as-nails publicist with a passion for success and her husband Tucker. While they're polar opposites, what they do have in common is a fierce love and commitment to each other. But their relationship—in and out of the bedroom—will be put to the ultimate test.

Rock superstar Ransom Reed is every woman's fantasy, including Heidi's. While Tucker is the perfect lover—generous, attentive, and gentle—she needs much more. She needs the mind-blowing ecstasy Ransom offers.

When she meets Ransom, she shares a wild night with him where Heidi gets to play—and Tucker watches, and enjoys, the pleasure Ransom gives Heidi. Though Tucker was a willing participant, Heidi still can't help reeling with guilt.

Tucker isn't blind to the fact that Heidi has unconventional needs which he can't satisfy. He loves his wife and will do anything to please her. But as Tucker and Heidi soon realize, it's not just the sex that is enticing. Heidi felt something within her awaken, and she felt so deliciously sated and loved by both men. Tucker felt it too, and he finds it impossible not to want that feeling again. Ransom and Tucker satisfy a need within Heidi. And now that she's had them, she can never go back to the way things were before.

Summer 2015